SENTINEL

Until You, Book Two

Karrie Roman

A NineStar Press Publication

Published by NineStar Press
P.O. Box 91792,
Albuquerque, New Mexico, 87199 USA.
www.ninestarpress.com

Sentinel

Printed in the USA
First Edition
September, 2018

Print ISBN: 978-1-949340-72-3

Also available in eBook, ISBN: 978-1-949340-69-3

Never allowing anyone too close, Ethan Stone has lived a solitary life since he was disowned by his family when he discovered their darkest secret. He spends his days as a quiet sentinel, protecting others to make up for the ones he didn't. Love, friendship, and family have no place in his world.

Ben Cronin is a warrior, haunted by a past he excelled at, which almost robbed him of his humanity. He became a professional bodyguard to save lives rather than take them. And he has loved his stoic colleague, Ethan Stone, from the day they met.

When Ethan's sister suddenly comes back into his life in desperate need of his help, Ethan doesn't hesitate to do whatever he needs to do. To his surprise, Ben—the man who makes him want things he shouldn't—is right there beside him, risking everything to help him and finally coaxing Ethan's feelings back to life.

A desperate race to find his missing nieces leads Ethan to a place he never thought he'd be and takes Ben exactly where he wanted to be—in a life filled with love and desire. But how long can they keep it when evil stalks their every step?

To the fabulous staff at NineStar Press for their patience, understanding and hard work. You are an awesome bunch. Thank you for bringing my dreams to life.

Prologue

"LAST QUESTION."

"What now for you, Ryan?"

"Um…the short answer is I really don't know. I'm going to take some time with Lucas while the show is on hiatus and think about what's next for me. I hope people will understand why I've chosen to step away from the spotlight and will be gracious enough to give me the space I need to work out where to go from here. But for right this minute, Lucas and I are getting on a plane to locations unknown and we're going to relax and enjoy being us."

The press conference was a compromise between the very intrusive media and Lucas and Ryan. They wanted some peace, some space to recover from the events of the last couple of months, and now that their show, Witches' Hammer, had wrapped up for a break, and Lucas had been given a clean bill of health, they were taking some time for themselves. Nobody deserved it more after what they'd been through.

Ethan watched, ever vigilant, as they stepped down from the podium and walked hand in hand toward the waiting car. His gaze rested on their joined hands for a second or two too long, but it was hard to look away from something that he desired for himself so very much. Not that he wanted either Lucas or Ryan. They were both great men and smoking fucking hot, but they weren't for him. What he wanted was what they had—intimacy and love.

After years of self-imposed isolation from anything resembling a close relationship, Ethan wanted more.

Once his two charges were settled in the car, Ethan climbed into the passenger seat and gave the nod to Max. The big car roared to life and Max deftly drove them toward the airport and their waiting plane.

His former bosses, Patricia and Roger Krispin, had let Ethan go from their security agency when he called to resign, as he'd breached their no-skeletons-in-the-closet rule, but Lucas and Ryan had hired him as their personal bodyguard and had kept the Krispin's professional teams as backup whenever needed. Ethan would be traveling to Australia with them, and Harry and Christina would meet them there for extra security, if needed.

"Looking forward to the Aussie girls in their bikinis, Ethan?" Ryan asked from the back seat.

"I'm more of a man in...what do you Aussies call them...boardies type of guy."

"Oh, shit...sorry. Well, there's plenty of them too. Maybe we can find a hot lifeguard for you while we're there." He didn't need to turn to know Lucas and Ryan would be giggling to themselves, no doubt planning some kind of setup for him. He loved working for these two men and often wondered at his good fortune, especially after the shit had hit the fan following the revelation of who he was.

For almost four weeks, Ryan and Lucas had dominated the front pages and headlined the news. When the media had discovered that Ethan Lockard had come out of the woodwork and was somehow embroiled in the *Lovers* saga, the scrutiny had begun to border on the ridiculous. Ethan had offered to resign and had given serious thought to running again. It would be harder to pick a new identity and hide this time, but he'd manage. He was so tired of running and so fucking tired of being lonely.

Eight years ago, he'd lost his entire family, and though he hadn't allowed any of them to get too close, the men and women he'd worked with over the last few years had become a family of sorts. He wasn't going to let his brother take another family away from him this time.

"Okay, jet's fueled and ready. Wheels up as soon as you arrive." Paulina's voice sounded in his ear.

"Copy. We're about ten minutes out. All clear," he replied. Despite the press coverage and the revelations that had been made about him, nobody from Krispins had seemed to care. They'd all accepted his apology for lying to them and admitted they'd have probably done the same if they were in his shoes.

The only person he hadn't seen or spoken to since his true identity had been discovered was Ben. He hadn't been back to see Ben since that day at the hospital when he'd been exposed. Ben's brother, Cameron, had called to let him know the doctors had successfully woken him and called a few more times with updates, but Ethan had refused when Cameron had told him Ben had been asking for him to visit. He was such a fucking coward, but he knew he couldn't bear to see disappointment in Ben's eyes. What if Ben hated him for lying and keeping his past quiet? Ethan could stand anybody else's hatred—but not Ben's.

The private jet was waiting on the tarmac as promised, and Max drove them virtually to the open door. Ethan scanned the area as the car pulled up. He expected no trouble, and thankfully, he found none. Once satisfied, he stepped out and moved around the front of the car so he could open the back door nearest to the plane. Lucas stepped out, closely followed by Ryan, their hands immediately re-entwined as soon as they were both clear of the car. Ethan felt that pang of envy bite into him again at the intimacy the two men shared. God, he wanted it.

It wasn't the first private jet he'd been on, but it was one of the nicest. Lucas and Ryan were already seated on the sofa that ran along one side of the cabin by the time he boarded. Ethan took the single seat across from them. He'd seen the bedroom toward the back of the plane as he'd entered the jet and wondered, with a sly grin on his face, how long it'd take before Lucas and Ryan made use of that.

"How are you with flying, Ethan?" Lucas asked as he continued to settle himself in and clip his seat belt.

"No problem with it. I can't say I've done a huge amount, but I don't mind it. Once the captain turns the seat belt sign off, I'll pop this chair back, shut my eyes, and keep them closed until we touch down." Ethan didn't miss the look the two men opposite him shared, no doubt delighted they would, more or less, have the jet to themselves.

The engines had been idling since they'd boarded, and Ethan both felt and heard them roar to life now.

"All passengers, please ensure your seat belts are engaged and prepare for takeoff," came a disembodied voice over the PA. The jet eased forward, slowly rolling toward the runway. It turned easily—nothing like the clunky turns of much larger passenger planes—before coming to a brief stop.

As the engines rumbled louder and louder and he was pushed back into his seat as the jet surged forward, increasing its speed to get it off the ground, Ethan had a sudden, inexplicable urge to run to the door and jump from the moving craft. He knew deep in his gut he was leaving something—or someone—behind.

He was sure he had everything he needed, and anything he'd forgotten he'd be able to buy in Australia, but he couldn't escape that feeling of loss. Then, as he looked over the lights of the city below, he thought about pale-blue eyes that were usually dancing with laughter or mischief but had instead been filled with pain and determination the last time he'd seen them open, and he knew in his heart what he'd left behind—or rather who.

Chapter One

ETHAN

"Have you heard anything more, Ethan?"

They were at thirty-seven thousand feet so Ethan should be fast asleep by now. He suspected he wouldn't be getting much in the coming days, but no matter how many times he closed his eyes and tried to drift off, he remained steadfastly awake.

"No. I've tried the number she gave me, but it keeps going to voicemail." Ethan turned to Ryan, who was standing at the door to the little bedroom on the private jet taking them back to the US much sooner than planned. It seemed like only yesterday they'd sat in these same seats heading toward a well-deserved break in Australia. "I'm sorry, again. You and Lucas could have stayed. Harry and Christina were there."

"We know, but we owe you so much, if you need to get back to help your sister, then we're coming with. Whatever we can do to help, we're there." They'd been holidaying in Australia for a few weeks when his sister's call had come the day before. Ethan had offered to leave alone, but both Ryan and Lucas had packed up their picnic lunch on the pristinely white beach in the Great Barrier Reef and then moved heaven and earth to get them back to the mainland and out of the country.

"Thank you, Ryan. I wish she'd have told me more. It's the not knowing that's so fucking hard."

"How long since you've heard from her?"

"Eight years." Ethan hadn't seen or heard from his sister since his brother's trial. She'd idolized Ethan—before everything went to shit.

Ethan had been thirty-two when he'd sent his younger brother to prison and lost his family all at the same time. The last memory he had of Maggie was her being dragged from the courtroom by his parents, with tears streaming down her face, once the guilty verdict had been read. He hadn't shown up for sentencing—his parents had made it abundantly clear that he was no longer part of their family and wouldn't be welcome.

Ryan shifted uncomfortably and Ethan could tell he wanted to ask more, but Ryan was never one to pry.

"She used to call me Thor. Maggie was into mythology even before these Marvel movies came along. She used to tell the kids at school that her biggest brother was Thor, and if they messed with her, I'd mess with them. I'm sixteen years older than her, but we were close. I'm not much of a hero to her anymore."

"Oh, I don't know. Who did she call when she got into trouble? Seems she still thinks of you as her hero."

Ethan nodded, trying to believe Ryan's words but falling short. He was nobody's hero.

"Try to sleep, Ethan. We've still got another eight hours before we get to LA to refuel and then another couple of hours to get to Casper."

"Thanks, Ryan. Thanks again for organizing the plane and everything else. I appreciate it."

Ryan nodded and turned back toward the bedroom. He stopped short of entering and then looked over his shoulder at Ethan. "I know what it's like to have no family. To have no one but yourself to rely on. But you're not alone now, Ethan. Whatever we can do...okay?"

Ethan swallowed past the knot in his throat and only nodded his head, not trusting his voice to come out steady. Ryan walked into the bedroom, and Ethan went back to the frustrating agony of trying to fall asleep when it just wouldn't come.

IT WAS A little over thirty-four hours since he'd gotten the desperate call for help from his sister, and Ethan felt dead on his feet. They'd landed in Casper forty minutes ago, and now he, Lucas, and Ryan were left standing with their luggage outside a large gray shed waiting for their helicopter to arrive. His ex-employers, the Krispins, had organized their travel plans and had promised a chopper waiting for them to take them on to Cody, where Maggie was living. Some kind of FAA issue had forbidden them from landing the jet directly at Cody airport, but the two to three hour drive time should have been considerably reduced, if the chopper had been here on time.

"Hey, I spoke to that head guy again and he said it's five minutes out. We should hear the sound any minute. Flight time should be under an hour, depending on wind. Not much longer now," Lucas advised him before he turned from Ethan and once again grabbed his boyfriend's hand, the two speaking quietly to each other as they waited.

Within moments, Ethan heard the *chop chop* of the arriving helicopter's rotors. He looked toward the noise and could make out a dark-colored helicopter approaching from the north. As it came in to land on the helipad, Ethan could see a large gold star, almost like a sheriff's badge, on the underside and red-and-white stripes on the rotors. The craft itself was dark-blue with "rescue" emblazoned in large, white letters on the side. It was a rescue chopper?

One of the ground crew who'd come out to wave the pilot in called them forward once the chopper was safely down, opening the door to the cabin for them. The three each picked up their bags and ran forward, head down on instinct, toward the waiting helicopter.

There was a single seat behind the cockpit and two seats directly behind that. The stretcher lining the other side confirmed that it was indeed a rescue helicopter. Ethan jumped into the single seat and gave a wave to the watching pilot before clipping his seat belt. In seconds, they were airborne.

Liftoff was completely unlike taking off in a plane. The helicopter rose vertically, tilted its nose down, and suddenly they were racing back the way the chopper had come. The ground crew had given them each a helmet, and through it, Ethan could hear the pilot talking, he assumed, to the tower. It was a whole lot of jargon that made no sense to Ethan, but all he cared about was that he was getting closer and closer to his sister.

He wanted to ask the pilot how long until they arrived in Cody, once he'd stopped speaking to the tower, but he had no idea how to make himself heard through the helmet. He hadn't glanced toward Ryan and Lucas but suspected they would have been enjoying the flight. Given different circumstances, he would have too.

The view below was magnificent once they'd passed the urban areas, nothing but green trees and lakes. They were just coming into winter, so though it would still be cold, there was no snow around. He wondered how his sister had ended up in this part of the country. It was a far cry from where she'd grown up in New Orleans.

"Jesus Christ, I wish I'd have known it was you." The pilot's voice uttered in his ear, and Ethan wondered if he was a *Samdom* fan. He knew the Krispins would have booked them under aliases, but he also knew Ryan and Lucas were the most famous celebrity couple in the world at the moment, and a couple of fake names wouldn't keep them from being recognized by anyone who took even a passing glance at the news.

Ethan turned his gaze to gauge the reaction from the two stars, but they were both peering out the window, Lucas pointing out something he'd spotted to Ryan, and they both seemed blissfully unaware of the pilot's comments.

"They can't hear me, Ethan. I'm talking to you. What the fuck are *you* doing here?"

Even if he knew how to answer through the helmet, he couldn't have because he had no fucking idea who this guy was or what his problem was. He knew he'd garnered plenty of attention in the press lately, too, thanks to the attack on Lucas and his role in the events.

The possibility that this man may have known or been related to one of his brother's victims slammed into him, and despite being the one who'd put a stop to his brother's murder spree, he knew it would be difficult for a victim's friend or loved one to be confronted with the brother of their killer.

"Just talk. Your mic will pick you up, and I'll be able to hear you. Tell me what the fuck you're doing here."

"I...ah...my sister lives in Cody and she called me for help. I'm not sure what's wrong, but I'm only here to help her, not cause trouble." He had no way of knowing if he'd been heard, and as the silence stretched on he began to doubt that he had.

Finally, the pilot responded, "I thought you had nothing to do with your family?"

"I haven't, not for eight years, but Maggie called me and I had to come."

"Maggie Godfrey? Is that your sister?"

The fact that he didn't know if that was her name hit him like a sledgehammer. He had no fucking idea if his sister was now Maggie Godfrey. If so, she'd either changed her name to hide her family history, as well, or she'd married.

"I don't know. I'm not sure what name she goes by now." Who the fuck was this guy?

"And those two. Why did they come?"

"They're friends and they came to help if they can." There was no way Ethan was telling this guy who they were. Chances were he already knew, but he hadn't indicated that, so Ethan was keeping quiet. The pilot fell silent once again and Ethan let it lay. He really didn't want to get into an argument with him, but once they landed he'd talk to him. If Maggie was hiding her identity, he didn't want to ruin it for her. Maybe he could talk this guy into keeping who he was under wraps. Though it was a strong bet he wasn't the only one in town who watched the news.

Another half hour passed in silence before Ethan heard the pilot's voice again. The jargon was back so he must have been speaking to the tower wherever they were landing. He could see dwellings below, dotted randomly throughout the landscape. It was so green and rural compared to what he was used to.

"We're coming in to Cody. There's a rental car waiting for you guys. Should be another ten minutes and you'll be on your way."

Twenty minutes, maybe half an hour at most, and he'd be standing in front of his sister again. He remembered her as a kid, a teenager. She was an adult now and he'd missed it all; he had no idea what kind of woman she'd turned out to be. She'd always been sweet, kind-hearted. Had she lost that to the bitterness of being a Lockard? Surely, her childhood—her innocence—had been pounded out of her with the fall of the judge's gavel. One brother in jail for murder, the other a pariah because he'd put him there.

The vertical drop of the helicopter was as off-putting as the takeoff. After flying solely in planes, it felt wrong—not scary—just wrong. Another person opened the door for them once they were on the ground while the chopper was powering down. He turned to look back at the pilot once he was out of the craft and saw he was removing his helmet, so hopefully, he'd be out soon. As eager as he was to get to Maggie, before they left he had to speak to this guy to ask for his discretion, for Maggie's sake, if not his.

Ryan and Lucas had their bags and wandered toward the only building in sight, but Ethan stayed where he was at the side of the helicopter, waiting. The door to the cockpit finally opened, and Ethan watched as the pilot ducked to step out.

When the pilot moved away from the door, he stopped in front of Ethan and stood at his full height—he was a big man. Ethan was shocked when he got his first proper view of the man who seemed to dislike him so much.

"Cameron? Fucking hell."

"Yeah, fucking hell," Cameron replied and moved to walk away from him. Ethan considered grabbing his arm to stop him, but given the anger he'd felt dripping from the big man, he wasn't at all sure he wouldn't end up with a fist to his face for his trouble.

Nevertheless, he followed Cameron toward the building where Lucas and Ryan were waiting because he was determined to get him to promise to keep Maggie's secret if that's what she wanted. "Cameron, wait. Please."

Cameron stopped and Ethan watched his back as he drew in deep breaths, his fists clenching before he turned to face him. "Please? Funny that. I seem to remember my brother asking me over and over again to *please* get you to come to see him in the hospital. I also remember me asking you over and over to *please* visit him. So, you know what, Ethan? I'm going to show you the same consideration you showed us and walk the fuck away from you—now, before I fucking do something I might one day regret."

Jesus, Cameron was fucking pissed, and Ethan couldn't blame him. He could only imagine how furious Ben must be. He should never have run like he did; he was a fucking coward and he deserved their anger. He watched as Cameron continued walking toward the building.

Back when his actions had sent his brother to jail and broken up his family, Ethan had never been ashamed of himself because he'd always known he'd done the right thing. This time, though, he was ashamed. He should have gone to see Ben in the hospital—even if it had only been to say goodbye and even if that would have hurt like fucking hell.

Ethan was aware he was standing on the helipad, alone, probably looking like a fish out of water as he tried to parse the situation. He bent to pick up his bag and follow Cameron toward the building, but when he saw Cameron stop and quickly flick a look back to him over his shoulder, Ethan didn't miss the distress on his face. Cameron began hurriedly walking forward now, and Ethan tried to see what had bothered him. He knew Ryan and Lucas were in front of him, but they were blocked by Cameron's big body and Ethan hoped he wasn't going to have words with them. They'd both gone to see Ben since he'd woken from his coma. They'd said their goodbyes, and as far as Ethan knew, they'd left on very friendly terms.

It was quiet now that the helicopter had completely powered down, and even from this distance, Ethan could hear quiet chatting coming from Ryan and Lucas. He also had no trouble hearing when Cameron suddenly called out in their direction. "No, fuck, what are you doing here? Let's go. Now."

Was he talking to Ryan and Lucas? Surely, he'd known it was them, and why was he so upset to see them?

"Is he really here?" A new voice floated to him, and Ethan's heart fluttered as his stomach dropped. As if to confirm what Ethan already knew, Ben appeared from behind his brother's body, his gaze already locked onto Ethan. Fuck, he looked good. And yet, at the same time, he looked wrong.

At the sound of Ben's voice, Ethan stopped walking and was left standing stationary while his world flipped on its end again. Ben marched past Cameron, avoiding the arm that flung out to try to stop him. He stalked toward Ethan until they were standing inches apart.

This close, Ethan could see the usual lightness in Ben's eyes had dimmed and the smile he always wore had morphed into a frown. It was wrong. His light caramel hair was longer and far curlier than usual. His body looked even tighter than it had—more buff—if that was possible, because Ben had always been damn fit. In spite of the fog of sadness that hung around him, Ben was the hottest fucking thing Ethan had ever seen.

There was at least four inches difference in height between them, so for Ben to reach up and grab the collar of his shirt, he had to go up on tiptoes. And, when he smacked his lips onto Ethan's, he had to drag him down into the kiss.

It wasn't a passionate kiss—it was an angry kiss. It was a "Fuck, I missed you, but I'm so fucking angry with you" kiss. It was their first kiss.

Before Ethan could even think about moving his lips against Ben's to soften the onslaught, Ben pulled back. He released Ethan's collar and Ethan couldn't help wondering what came next. He had his answer when Ben cocked his arm back and unleashed the most brutal right hook Ethan had ever been the unhappy recipient of—and he couldn't say it was undeserved.

Chapter Two

BEN

"Welcome to Wyoming, asshole," Ben spat at Ethan's kneeling form. Blood was dripping from between Ethan's fingers where he was clutching at his nose. Ben didn't think he'd broken it, but goddamn, it had felt fucking good.

Ethan peered up at him from behind his cupped hands, and Ben had to force himself not to lean down and comfort him. He'd promised himself that punch weeks ago when Ethan failed to come back to see him at the hospital, but the kiss had come out of the blue. *Damn it.*

When Ben had regained consciousness in the hospital, all he'd wanted was Ethan. He'd been told that he'd survived the effects of the fire, but Ben needed to see for himself. His last memory had been of them taking an unconscious Ethan away from him in the back of an ambulance. Fuck. Fuck! Ben had been in love with Ethan for years, and he hadn't ever expected anything from him, but dammit, he'd needed to see for himself Ethan was fine, and he'd fucking denied Ben that opportunity.

The most painful part was that Ethan hadn't cared enough to check on him, hadn't fucking bothered to come and say goodbye before he'd jetted off to a country thousands of miles away. Ethan couldn't have been clearer, if he'd had it written in skywriting, that he didn't give a fuck about him. It hurt. It hurt far more than Craig Evers's bullets had. He'd recovered from those, but he hadn't recovered from Ethan.

"Ben, Jesus. Come on, let's go," Cameron's voice was hesitant, nervous. He was probably wondering if there was more violence to come from him. Cameron had been by his side since the shooting, so he knew the damage that had been done. He knew the pain he was in. He turned to his brother to assure him he was done and spotted the horrified faces of Lucas and Ryan peering out from behind his brother.

Fuck Ethan. Fuck him straight to hell. He hadn't wanted to do that in front of those two men. He'd lost control. After two exhausting years of rigidly controlling his feelings around Ethan, he was done. He had nothing left to fight with.

"I'm sorry, guys. I'm sorry, that was…"

"Exactly what he deserved," Lucas suggested to him with a raised eyebrow.

"Lucas!" Ryan turned his horrified expression on his boyfriend.

"What? You heard Cameron back there. He didn't even say goodbye to Ben, never went to see him once he woke up. What's up with that?"

"It's not our business, babe." Ryan was pulling at Lucas's arm now, dragging him from the awkward scene.

"Ben, I'm gonna take these two over to the car. I'll wait for you there. Okay?"

"Thanks, Cam. I won't be long." He turned back to Ethan, who was standing again, with his head slightly tilted back and his fingers pinching his nose. "Ethan, I…um—"

"Don't. I deserved that. It was shitty of me not to come to see you." Ethan's voice was muffled behind his hands and probably the blood trickling down the back of his throat. Ben had taken enough blows to know exactly how it felt.

Where did they go from here? If he was sensible, he'd say goodbye, get in the car with Cameron and forget that Ethan Stone—or was it Lockard now—was in town. Ben was many things but, clearly, sensible wasn't one of them as he reached out to Ethan, circling his hand around his elbow to guide him.

"Come on. Let's get you cleaned up." He began moving them forward, doing his best to ignore the tingles where his fingers were touching Ethan. "So, Ryan tells me you're here to help your sister. What's going on?"

Ethan bowed his head a little. Ben could tell the big man was hurting—and not just from the hit to his nose. "No clue. She called two days ago and said she needed help. Here I am."

Fucking goddamn it. This was why he'd fallen so hard for Ethan. How many people would fly back from Australia at a moment's notice to help a sister who had written them off years ago? "Where are you staying?"

"The Best Western, I think. Patricia booked it for us."

"No, you're not. You'll all stay at Cameron's. His place is huge. Plenty of room and less chance of the whole town finding out that *Lovers* is here."

"Ben, thank you, but I really don't think Cameron is gonna want me there."

"Oh, hell no, he's not." He grinned imagining his brother's reaction. "But he'll get over it." Would Ben though? What the hell was he thinking? So much for pretending Ethan wasn't in town.

They remained silent for the last bit of the walk to the car where Lucas was waiting with a wet cloth and a bag of ice. "Here, big guy." He thrust the items at Ethan who grabbed at them and began gently dabbing at his nose with the cloth.

"Ah, Cam, I've um...invited them to stay at your place, less chance of any of them being recognized." Ben could tell by the expression on Cameron's face he was not in the least bit happy about his invitation. He loved that his brother was looking out for him, but this was the right thing to do.

"Jesus, Ben, I'm not happy about that. I mean if it was just these two...no problem, but I don't really want that ass—"

"Cam, please. I know you're angry, I haven't forgiven the fucker, either, but he needs our help."

Cameron flicked his glance between him and Ethan, his lips curling in anger whenever his gaze landed on Ethan. "Jesus, why here? I mean it's a big fucking country so why did his sister have to wind up here?" But finally, Cameron nodded his assent. "All right, but one step outta line, Ethan, and I'll take you down."

Ben laughed and patted his brother's chest. "All right, big brother, take it down a notch, okay?"

"Let's go," Cameron grumbled.

Ryan, Lucas, and Ethan followed behind in their rental car and reached Cameron's place within ten minutes. It was a large house on a couple of acres on the outskirts of town. Cameron had bought it a few years ago when he got the job as rescue pilot for the sheriff's department. His zone covered Yellowstone National Park, Shoshone National Forest, and across into Grand Teton National Park on occasion. It was fucking gorgeous out here. Cameron had done well for himself.

Ben watched as Ryan and Lucas got out of the big Tahoe they'd rented. They'd left the engine running and had grabbed some of the bags out already. Ryan was reaching for the last one as he and Cameron approached.

"Ethan wants to head straight over to his sister's. So we'll get his bag in and get settled while he's gone. He thinks it's best if he goes alone, since he doesn't know what to expect and doesn't want to freak her out by turning up with us," Lucas explained.

Ben walked around to the passenger door, opened it, and climbed in. "Let's go."

"I think it would be best if I went alone," Ethan tried.

"Yeah, I heard all that. Let's go. I don't care if I sit and wait outside, but I'm coming. Like you said, Ethan, you don't know what to expect, so I'm gonna be there if you need me." He clipped his seat belt and looked straight out the front window, but he could feel Ethan staring at him.

After a few moments, Ethan put the car in gear and pulled away from Cameron's house. "Okay. You're right, I guess. Maybe I should have someone there."

Ben snorted. "I'm always right, Ethan. How many more times do I have to tell you that?"

"I know, I know. I somehow keep forgetting about your greatness."

"Yeah, well maybe it's time you stopped forgetting." Ben couldn't keep the hint of bitterness completely out of his words but threw in a laugh to, hopefully, disguise it from Ethan.

Ben realized Ethan must have already entered his sister's address in the GPS when that electronic voice started spitting out directions. Nowhere in Cody was too far from anywhere else so in only minutes they were sitting outside of a bleak-looking little house fairly close to what would be the center of town. The yard was a little overgrown but not too bad—it looked as though whoever lived there cared but was perhaps too busy to maintain it scrupulously.

"You ready, Ethan?" Ben asked after they'd sat in the stationary car for a few minutes with Ethan just staring at the little house.

Ethan turned to him, sighed, and let Ben see how nervous he was. "I don't know. I haven't seen her in so long. What if she still hates me? What if I can't help her, and I let her down again?"

Ben didn't hesitate to put a comforting hand on Ethan's thigh, feeling the muscle bunching under his fingers. "I know you would walk through hell for her...for anyone. How could that possibly be a disappointment? You won't let her down."

Ethan shook his head as though weighing Ben's words and Ben could tell he'd found them wanting. "I let you down," Ethan whispered.

What could Ben say to that? Ethan had let him down, but what he couldn't figure out was why. It was out of character for Ethan to have taken off like he did. Ben knew that if nothing else they had been friends, and Ethan cared about him—he'd seen the look of fear in Ethan's eyes when he'd been shot.

"Come on, man. Let's go see your sister." Ben opened his door and stepped out of the car, hoping Ethan would follow his lead.

They strode together up the short path. When they reached the front door, Ethan pressed the buzzer beside it. They could hear the sound echoing through the house and they waited. After several minutes they exchanged a look, and Ethan reached to press the buzzer again just as the door opened.

Ben hadn't imagined what Ethan's sister would look like, so he couldn't say how close he'd been in his predictions, but when he saw the haggard-looking young woman before him, he was horrified.

She was a little shorter than him and far, far too skinny. Ink-black circles beneath her eyes contrasted vividly with the sickly pallor of her skin. She wore a beanie on her head, and Ben assumed if he were to pull it off, there'd be nothing but scalp beneath it. Ben had watched cancer ravage and eventually steal his mother from him, and he knew he was standing face-to-face with that same killer once more.

"Ethan?" Her voice was tiny and unsure, but Ben could see a spark in her eyes—hope or happiness, maybe?

"Maggie? Oh, god, Maggie," Ethan replied, carefully taking his sister into his arms. She was so tiny it seemed as though Ethan's body had consumed her. Ethan didn't hold her for long, and Ben wondered if that was because he was terrified he might break her—he certainly would have been.

"It's so good to see you, Ethan. Come in, please."

They followed her slow-moving frame into a dimly lit room with little in the way of furniture aside from two sofas facing each other. A small table was set up beside one of the sofas, with a tissue box, a half-empty glass of water, and several pill bottles. Ben could tell from the pillows and blankets scattered over it that the sofa was being used as a bed. Maggie practically fell onto it and pulled one of the covers over her legs.

Ben sat on the opposite sofa, and Ethan moved to sit beside his sister, gently taking her hand in one of his. "Maggie, this is Ben. He and I used to work together. His brother lives here in Cody, and I ran into— Jesus, Maggie. I'm so sorry. What...which one is it?"

"Pancreatic. Nothing more they can do. I've got...maybe six months." Ben watched a tear slip down her cheek. He couldn't look at Ethan because he didn't know what he'd do if there were tears falling from his eyes. Maybe she'd called him here to ask his forgiveness before...

"No. No... There must be something. I've got... I've got some money, friends with more money, maybe there's a treatment..."

Maggie shook her head. "Even if I had more money than Bill Gates, Ethan, there's nothing more they can do."

Ethan untangled his fingers from Maggie's, stood, and started pacing around the small room. Feeling helpless was a terrible thing, and when a loved one had cancer, Ben knew from experience that feeling helpless was a constant state of being.

"I'm so sorry, Maggie," Ben interjected when it became clear Ethan was lost in his grief. "What can we do to help? What can Ethan do?"

Ethan stopped and turned to his sister once Ben's question was out. Maggie looked back and forth between the two men, and her gaze finally came to rest on his.

"I'm sorry, I think you've misunderstood. I didn't ask Ethan for help for me. It's nothing to do with my cancer." She turned her gaze to her brother, and Ben watched her visibly straighten her spine. "Ethan, I asked you to come here because they've... They've kidnapped my babies."

Chapter Three

ETHAN

He couldn't have heard right. *Kidnapped her babies*. Maggie had babies? Maggie was dying and someone had taken her kids? What the hell was happening here?

"I'm sorry, what?" Ethan sat next to his sister, and this time she reached out and took his large hand in her much smaller, much frailer one.

"So much has happened since...since New Orleans. Um...where do I start? I guess back then." She stopped to reach for her glass and take a sip of water. "Can I offer either of you anything?"

Ben jumped up from his seat on the opposite couch. "How about I make us all a cup of coffee or maybe tea while you two start talking?" he offered, and Ethan thanked god again that Ben had insisted on coming. Despite not being able to touch him as he wanted, simply knowing Ben was there had given him strength when that door had opened and he'd seen his sister standing before him so clearly unwell and suffering.

"Thank you. The kitchen's through there. There's...not much, but you should be able to hunt around for enough to make some tea. I'll take mine black, no sugar. Thank you."

"Same," Ethan absentmindedly declared. He didn't really drink tea, and if he did, he had it white with plenty of sugar, but right then it didn't matter at all. Ben headed in the direction of the kitchen, and Ethan turned his full attention back to Maggie.

"Okay, so...um. After the trial, Mom and Dad...well, they didn't handle it well. They blamed you for everything. They wouldn't let me see you or call you or anything. They wiped you from the family as though you never existed. No photos, no mention of you, nothing of yours left in the house. The only way I had of rebelling was to refuse to visit Stewart. Every week they went, as though he hadn't killed all those girls—some of them younger than I was then."

Wiped from the family as though he'd never been. Jesus. He'd suspected they'd gone that far but to hear it confirmed? That hurt.

"When I was eighteen, I left—couldn't take their shit anymore. I had no idea where you were or how to even begin trying to find you. Anyway, after a couple of weeks living on a friend's couch, I met this guy...and, yes, you can guess where the story goes. I was young and so desperate for love I never saw the bad in him. Not until it was too late." Maggie took another sip of her water and coughed a little. She may not want any help with her cancer, but at the very least, he was going to get her out of this dump and get her proper care.

"Peter was... He was part of a cult, a sort of survivalist, religious cult. I didn't see it as a cult back then; all I saw was this group of people who would love me and look after me and not put me in second place behind a murderer. I...enthusiastically joined up. Peter was close to the leader. His name is Arnold Piper, and he believes he's God's spokesman on earth. They move around a lot. They live in a tent city, I guess, so they can move whenever Arnold, or god, deem it necessary. Now that I'm out, I can see it's your garden-variety cult where the head guys marry a half-dozen or so women each and have a hundred kids with them so they can repopulate the earth with their 'goodness.' It's not that big yet, thank god, but the numbers are growing. I was such a fool, Ethan. I didn't even care at the start when the brides were getting younger and younger."

Maggie swallowed and her tiny body was suddenly wracked with violent coughing. Ethan felt utterly useless when the only help he could offer was a reassuring hand on her shoulder. Ben came into the room with a couple of mugs of tea, handing one to Ethan and putting Maggie's on the little table at her side. Then he moved around the back of the couch and began rubbing Maggie's back. In moments, the coughing eased. Ethan flicked a glance at Ben, who gave him a small smile in return.

"Thank you," Maggie murmured before taking a sip of tea. "Anyway, after nearly two years of being married to Peter, I started to get uncomfortable about what was going on. At the same time, Peter was getting angrier and angrier with me because I hadn't gotten pregnant yet. One day Arnold.... God, I watched Arnold marry a fourteen-year-old girl, and she looked terrified. I knew then it was all so wrong and I wanted to get out. About the same time, I began to suspect I had finally gotten pregnant. I spoke to Peter and told him I wanted out... I was terrified of his reaction, but he was actually happy, because as it turns out, he thought I was useless to him since I hadn't given him any children as god and Arnold demanded."

"So, you didn't tell him you thought you may be pregnant?" Ben asked. He was back on the other sofa now with his cup of tea in his hands.

"No. No way. If I had, I'm pretty sure they wouldn't have let me go. I came here to Cody and confirmed that I was pregnant...twin girls." Maggie sobbed and Ethan's heart clenched at the pain radiating from his sister. He put his arm around her narrow shoulders and pulled her to his chest as she softly wept. Her body felt so small against him, and Ethan felt sick at the thought of the life he'd abandoned his sister to. She'd never hated him, never turned her back on him, but he'd deserted her.

Maggie cried herself dry and then pulled away from him. She looked up and he did his best to give her a reassuring smile.

"They turned two about six months ago. Maya and Riley."

"Beautiful names, Maggie," Ben said into the silence that followed.

"You named one after me?" Ethan choked out.

"Yes, after you Ethan Reilly Lockard, or rather Stone now."

"Tell us what happened," Ethan encouraged once he had himself under control again.

"Well, the pregnancy went along fine. I got a job cleaning at one of the local hotels, and the owner there was really lovely. She let me stay in a little apartment over her garage, no charge, and she helped me out when I had to stop working to have the girls. Once they came along, I was able to go back to work because she let me work my hours around them. She'd watch the girls for me while I cleaned the rooms, and a local schoolgirl would babysit whenever she couldn't do it. Everything was going great for a little over a year, and that's when I couldn't put it off any longer. I had to go to the doctor. I was so tired all the time, so sick, and I had such bad back pain. He sent me for a few tests, and then he gave me the news about the cancer. He said I had about eighteen months. Two days was all it took to go from feeling a little poorly to be given a death sentence. It all happened so fast. I didn't even cry when he told me. My head was spinning."

"Did you have any treatment, Maggie?"

"A little. I started on chemo, but it made me so sick, Ethan, and the doctors said it wouldn't cure me, only drag out the suffering, really. I couldn't afford anything, anyway, once the insurance ran out."

"What about Mom and Dad?"

"I haven't spoken to them since I left. Not after what they did to you."

Ethan would grovel and plead with Lucas and Ryan if he had to, and he didn't care if he had to work for them for nothing for the rest of his life, but he was getting Maggie to the best damn specialists available. There was no room for pride when a loved one's life was on the line.

"Elsie, she's my boss, put me up here and she comes around when she can to help me out. She's been so good to me, but she's elderly herself and she hasn't been well lately. She doesn't even know... I haven't told her about the girls."

Ben sat farther forward in his seat. "When were they taken?"

"Five days ago. Peter... About a week ago, Peter turned up. It was a particularly bad day, and I didn't have the energy to keep him out. He found the girls and he knew straight away they were his. I could see in his eyes that he wanted them. He stayed here and told me how happy he was and how we could be a family again, that Arnold would welcome me back now that I had provided the children god demanded. I didn't have a chance of stopping him—I knew that. I was even prepared to go with him so I could do whatever I had to do to protect them at the commune, but it all changed again when he found out my diagnosis. When I woke up the next morning, they were gone. All three of them. He didn't even take their clothes or any of their toys. Poor Maya hasn't even got Cuddles and Riley... She can't sleep without her little blanket."

Ethan held her again, helpless, as her tears flowed freely. How had this happened to his sweet baby sister? Nobody deserved what was happening to Maggie, but least of all her. "I'm sorry, Ethan, that I've dragged you into this. I didn't know who else to turn to."

"Why didn't you go to the cops?" Ben asked.

"Arnold is... He's a mad man. He always told us that he was above the law and man's laws didn't apply to him. Peter told me once that Arnold never had to worry about people leaving and going to the cops, because they knew at the first hint of the law coming for him, he was going to, and I'm quoting here, 'implement the Jonestown protocol.'"

Ethan's stomach bottomed out. He didn't know the details, but he knew enough to know that hundreds of people had died during the Jonestown incident, most by their own hand at the say-so of their leader, Jim Jones.

"I couldn't risk it. I couldn't risk sending the cops and having that nutjob kill my girls and everyone else. I don't trust that Peter would be able to say no to him. I think he'd do it... I think he'd kill my babies." Maggie stood; it was slow and labored and Ethan's heart throbbed again. "I'm gonna use the bathroom. Excuse me."

As he watched her walk away from him, Ethan had the crazy thought that he never wanted her out of his sight again. All those years apart—wasted—lost. And now that they'd found each other again, there was so little time left to them.

Once she'd left the room, Ben stood and walked over to where he was sitting. Kneeling, he put his hands on Ethan's thighs, slowly sliding them back and forth.

"Ethan, how're you doing?"

"I...I'm not okay." He shook his head. There was so much he wanted to say, so much he wanted to talk over with

Ben because he knew he'd need this man if he had any hope of getting through this. He couldn't get anything out though. He'd been hit with blow after blow since he'd walked through that front door, and nothing was making sense to him.

Ben stood and grabbed his hands, yanking him up, pulling him into a hug. Ethan knew he was the physically bigger man, but in that embrace he felt engulfed by Ben, wrapped up and so very safe. He knew that feeling would be fleeting, but he was going to enjoy it for as long as he could.

"I'm here, okay? I'm not going anywhere. We'll get those babies back, Ethan. Your nieces... You're an uncle," Ben whispered into his ear.

While listening to the horror of his sister's life story, the fact that he was an uncle had been completely lost on him. "I'm an uncle," he murmured. He wanted to stand there forever, wrapped up in the warmth and strength of Ben's body, basking in the news of his baby nieces. But he had work to do. He had to rescue them. He wouldn't let anything happen to them. Was it even possible to love people you'd never met? Because he'd never met Maya and Riley but he already knew he'd lay down his life for them in a heartbeat.

Ben released him and they both sat again. Ethan kept his gaze on Ben as he settled on the sofa. For the two years they'd worked together, Ethan had always known Ben to be reliable, and deadly, if needed. He couldn't have asked for anyone better to be here with him now. His face throbbed where Ben had hit him earlier as if to remind him of the skill the younger man possessed. It also reminded him of that fucking kiss that he didn't want to dwell on yet. He was so fucked.

"How do you wanna play this?" Ben asked.

"I'm not sure, yet. We've gotta get some more intel from Maggie. See if she knows where they're camped, numbers, weapons. This can't turn into another Waco, especially not with kids involved."

"Look, what say we round Maggie up, get her back to Cameron's, and get this thing started."

"You think Cameron'll be okay with another guest?"

"She's not staying here, Ethan. Cam's got a couple of days off, and Lucas and Ryan are there to help. They can watch her while we go in and get the girls."

Ethan had already decided that Lucas and Ryan would be staying behind when they went wherever the hell they had to go to rescue his nieces. As generous as their offer to come to help had been, they had no experience with this sort of thing, and he was pretty sure neither of them had expected *this* sort of help to be needed.

"Ben, you don't have—"

"If you finish that fucking sentence, I'm gonna give you a matching black eye to go with that nose. I'm going with you. Whatever it takes, I'm in."

Chapter Four

BEN

"Maggie?"

"Hello, Cameron." The short trip from her place to Cameron's seemed to have exhausted Maggie, who leaned heavily on her brother as they made their way from the car to the open front door where Cameron was waiting.

Ben had a small bag filled with Maggie's scant belongings and medications. He'd arrange for the rest of her stuff and her daughters' clothes and toys to be picked up at some point. Right now, he simply wanted to get her settled inside so she'd be able to rest. Ben could hardly believe the tale he'd heard from her, and he could only imagine the anguish Ethan must be feeling.

Cameron continued watching Maggie and Ethan as they made their way through the door, Ben close on their heels. Ben spared a glance at his brother as he passed him and murmured, "I'll explain soon."

Ethan and Maggie had stopped just inside the door, neither knowing the house at all. "This way," Ben called to them and began leading them down the hallway toward the bedrooms. He'd put Maggie in his room as it had a bathroom attached so she'd have a bit of privacy. Ryan and Lucas would have been put in the next largest room, and he had no doubt Cameron would have Ethan's things in the smallest, dingiest room. That left Ben with the sofa, not that he cared;

he could sleep anywhere—something that had come in handy over the years.

There was no time to change the bedding, so Ben pulled the covers up and helped Maggie to lie down once they were in the room. Ethan covered her with the blanket that had been at the end of the bed. Ben was pretty confident she'd been asleep before her head had even hit the pillow. He left her bag in the corner of the room and walked to the door. Looking back, he saw Ethan standing over his sister, unmoving—a silent sentinel.

At almost forty, Ethan was nine years older than Ben, but that was just a number as far as Ben was concerned. Ethan was the most beautiful and amazing man Ben had ever met. He clearly remembered the first time he'd laid eyes on him in the Krispin's office. He'd been newly hired by Patricia and she'd called Ethan in to take him under his wing, so to speak. Ben was not a shy man in any way, but he'd found himself tongue-tied when he'd come face-to-face with six-foot-four of hotness.

Ethan's dark brown hair had grayed a little at the temples, and he'd started wearing a hint of a beard since that day, but he still took Ben's breath away every single damn time he laid eyes on him. How no one had ever picked up on Ben's feelings was a mystery—maybe he was a better fucking actor than the two stars currently in the house.

"Ethan," he whispered, trying hard not to wake Maggie. Ethan heard him though and turned his head. "I'll be right outside, okay?"

Ethan nodded and Ben just caught the whispered "thank you" as he turned back to his sister. He knew Cameron would be waiting for some answers, and as angry as his brother was with Ethan, Ben knew he was a good guy who would never turn away people who needed help.

Ben found Cameron sitting with Ryan and Lucas on the outdoor lounge set on the deck. There was a gorgeous view from the back of Cameron's house that Ben had spent many hours enjoying since he'd arrived here to recuperate after the shooting. Ben could be quiet when he needed to be, and none of the men on the deck had noticed his approach. He leaned against the wall, listening to both Lucas and Ryan telling Cameron how wonderful Ethan was. They knew what Ethan had done, or rather hadn't done, after the shooting, but he didn't think they knew why it had hurt so fucking much. Cameron knew everything; he'd confessed to his brother that he was in love with Ethan and had been for years. He wished now he had never told him; he hated that Cameron thought less of Ethan because of it.

"He sure is one of the good guys," he interrupted as Ryan was trying to sell Ethan's positive traits to Cameron. And it was true. Ethan was a decent guy, but he had flaws—like every other person on the planet.

"How are they?" Lucas asked as he joined them on one of the sofas.

"Maggie's asleep. Ethan's...watching over her."

Cameron sat forward in his seat and asked, "What's going on, Ben? What kind of trouble is Maggie in?"

If they were going to help Maggie, and if there was any hope of getting Ethan's nieces back, there couldn't be any secrets, so Ben told them all as much as he knew.

It was Ryan who rather succinctly summed up the situation. "Oh, fuck, that's awful." It was more than awful; it was fucking tragic, and the fact that there were at least two innocent little girls in harm's way made Ben's blood boil.

"So, what do we do?" Lucas added.

"*We* do nothing." Ethan's soft voice came from behind them. He sounded so fucking weary that Ben knew it wasn't just the long trip from Australia exhausting him. Ethan would be suffering. There'd be misplaced guilt riding his ass as much as the fear and worry for his sister and her girls.

Both Lucas and Ryan looked as though they were getting ready to argue, but Ethan continued without giving them the chance. "No. I mean it. You two are not getting involved. This could be dangerous. If this guy's serious about wiping everyone out, then I don't think he's going to care much about killing anybody who might try to stop him."

Ben could see Ryan and Lucas exchanging glances and wondered if he and Ethan were gonna have a fight on their hands to get them to see reason. Their intentions to help Ethan were honorable, but the execution could be deadly if they got in over their heads.

"You're right, Ethan. Lucas and I have no business charging into something like this, but we want to help you. There has to be something we can do."

A flush crept up Ethan's neck; Ben knew how hard it must be for him to ask for anything. He also knew Ethan would do anything for someone he cared about. "Actually there is something. I um…I've got some money saved, but it won't be enough. Maggie needs treatment, care. I was hoping maybe I could borrow against my future wages so I can get her the help she needs…"

It was plain on his face how much that request had cost Ethan, but he'd done it. Ben suspected Lucas and Ryan would easily hand over the money, and he wondered how that would sit with Ethan.

"God, Ethan, you can have the money—"

"No, Lucas, I can't accept that. We can work out some kind of payment plan or—"

"You damn well can accept that. You're family, Ethan, and we—"

"Lucas…" Ethan shook his head. "It's too much. I can pay it back."

Goddamn stubborn bastard. Even though Ben couldn't deny he was enjoying watching Ethan go toe to toe with somebody who appeared to be every bit as stubborn as he was, this little contest was getting them nowhere. "Hey, mules," he interrupted as the "yes you can, no I can't" debate raged, "Maybe we can have this argument some other time. Jesus, you two are the most pigheaded assholes I've come across; no wonder that fire didn't get either of you."

While Ryan and Cameron laughed at Ben's words, Lucas and Ethan looked suitably chastised. Ben hoped they'd be able to get on with planning more important things than who was footing the bill. "Too soon to joke?" Ben asked with a smirk.

Cameron cleared his throat and said, "So, I'm guessing you're not going to go to the cops. What are you thinking of doing then?"

Ben glanced at Ethan, quickly deciding he should be the one to tell his brother because he knew he wasn't going to be happy about it. "Ethan and I are going to go in and get them. Just the two of us. If we do it right, we can be in and out before they even realize we've been there."

Ben had been expecting some opposition to the idea, but he hadn't expected all three men to stand up and start arguing with him. Ryan and Lucas were saying something about having a death wish and being crazy, but Cameron stood towering over him, a look of fear on his face.

"That's not who you are anymore, Ben. Don't do this…please." He hoped Ethan was too busy with Ryan and Lucas to overhear this exchange between him and Cameron.

"I have to do it, Cameron. It won't be like before. I swear. They're babies and it's…it's for Ethan." He moved closer to his brother. "I won't let him down, and I won't let him be hurt—by anything." He looked up at Cameron, hoping like hell he understood.

Cameron had been in love once before and he'd been savaged by it, but he would understand that need to do whatever you had to do for the person you loved. He'd know why he had to be there for Ethan, why he'd have to open up that deadly side of himself again.

"Does he know?" Cameron flicked his gaze to Ethan, who was mercifully still trying to calm Ryan and Lucas.

"No."

"Then you need to tell him, Ben. He needs to know what he's asking of you. Promise me you'll tell him."

It wasn't a conversation he was looking forward to; he hated even thinking about that dark time in his past, but he knew Cameron was right. This would be entirely different to working as a bodyguard, and Ethan needed to know what might be unleashed.

"I'll tell him. Just...let me do it in my own time, okay? I never wanted him to know about that side of me."

"I know. I know how hard it is, Ben, but it's not your fault. You've come so far... You got out, even though they tried to keep you in. You're a good person. Don't you forget that, little brother."

Ben wasn't so sure Cameron was right about that, but he had worked hard on being better since he'd gotten away from the shit storm he'd been embroiled in, and he had to hope that counted for something.

With things somewhat sorted out with his brother, Ben turned his full attention to the ongoing battle Ethan was currently engaging in with Ryan and Lucas. It looked as though they were double-teaming Ethan—and not in the good way. Part of him wanted to jump in and defend Ethan but another smaller part was enjoying watching him squirm.

"Ryan, nobody said anything about going in guns blazing. It'll be—"

"I mean, what's it gonna be? Like two against two hundred or something? Those cult folks are... They're fanatical and there's no reasoning with that. What if they catch you in there? There'll be no talking your way out. You're hot and charming and all, but that's not going to get you anywhere with these people."

Ryan was getting redder in the face as he spoke, and Ben watched as Lucas rubbed circles into his back. "Okay, baby. Breathe. I think we've got our point across."

"Look. I appreciate your concerns. I do, but Ben and I are going to plan this out meticulously. We're going to be very careful and safe. All of us are going to get out of there."

"Don't promise us that, Ethan. You can't possibly know what might happen." Cameron interjected.

"I know, Cameron. I know." Ethan closed his eyes and shook his head a little. "If I thought for a second that I could do this on my own, I'd leave Ben behind, but I can't get out with two toddlers by myself."

Ben had heard more than enough. He appreciated all the concern, but strip the situation to the bone and what it came down to was that two little girls were in danger, and if Ben knew anything about the men in this room, it was that none of them would be able to live with themselves if they didn't do everything they could to help them.

"Okay. Here it is in a nutshell. Ethan and I will be going in to get the girls. Ryan and Lucas you're gonna be getting Maggie into the best damn care facility you can manage, and Cameron, we're gonna need you to do some flyovers tomorrow. See if you can find the camp and maybe get us some intel on it." Ben may be the smallest man in the room, but if there was one thing his first boyfriend had taught him, it was that size didn't matter—it was all in how you used what you had.

"Actually, I may already have an idea of where the camp is," Cameron began. "We noticed a large camp setting up a few days ago over in Shoshone. Actually, the sheriff asked us to keep an eye on it because we weren't sure what was going on there."

"That'd be great if it's them. It'll mean it's a new campsite, and they might not know the terrain well; might not have had time to set up a proper perimeter. That'll work in our favor." There was the barest hint of optimism in Ethan's voice that was reassuring to hear.

"Maybe you can take us out there tomorrow, Cam, so we can take a look around. But right now, I'm gonna fix us some dinner, and after that, you and I need to have a talk, Ethan." He held the other man's gaze for a few moments before turning his back and walking inside, heading for Cameron's well-appointed kitchen.

Ben looked at the two steaks he'd taken out to defrost this morning and knew they wouldn't be enough—not now that he'd be feeding five big men and one very sick lady. He thought maybe soup would be good for Maggie, and that was easily taken care of. He got a few more steaks out to defrost before he started working on the potatoes. He wasn't a gourmet chef by any stretch, but in the months after he'd left the service, Ben had discovered how much cooking relaxed him. It had been a lifesaver during that difficult time.

As awful as it was to think about his past, Ben knew having to tell Ethan all the sordid details was going to completely suck. He also knew that Cameron was right— Ethan did need to know and not only for this mission. Ben wanted Ethan—for keeps—so if there was going to be any chance of something happening between them, Ethan needed to know exactly who he'd be getting.

Chapter Five

ETHAN

"No more, Ethan. Thank you."

Ethan's gaze traveled over his sister's pathetically thin frame, and he wanted to force the rest of the soup down her throat. Maybe if he was able to fatten her up a bit, she'd have more strength to fight.

She'd been lying awake when he came in with her dinner a short while ago, so he'd helped her sit up and eat as much as she could manage—which wasn't much at all.

"The medication makes me sick. I'd like to eat more, but I can't stomach it," Maggie explained.

"I am so sorry, Maggie. I should have been there for you."

"It's not your fault—none of it. I'd have still gotten the cancer whether or not you were around, and I can't wish for things to have been different, because if they were, I might not have my girls." Tears pooled in her eyes, but she continued on with the strength of love in her voice, "They are so beautiful, Ethan. They look exactly alike, but there's a tell. I'll let you see if you can figure it out when you meet them."

Maggie sighed, her gaze far off, hopefully in happier memories. "Riley's quiet and thoughtful, like you, but Maya's got this wild streak, and I have a feeling she's gonna be a handful when she's a teenager."

Ethan swallowed past the lump in his throat as he watched his baby sister trying to pull herself together at the thought that she wouldn't be around when her daughters were teens. He was thinking the same fucking thing, and the thought gutted him.

"I've um... I've asked so much of you already, but I need to ask you one more thing. When I'm gone—"

"Maggie—"

"Please, Ethan, hear me out. When I'm gone, I want you to raise the girls. Mom and Dad don't know about them, and I don't want them anywhere near. Promise me you'll take Maya and Riley. Raise them to be as good as you are, Thor. Please." She gave a slight smile at the childhood nickname, but it was this that made the tears Ethan had held in so tightly finally fall.

Ethan wiped at his eyes and then ran the back of his fingers gently down Maggie's cheek. "Of course," he choked out. He cleared his throat before continuing. "Whatever you need, Mags. It's done. Okay. Please try...try not to worry. I'm here. All right?"

"I stopped worrying the second I saw you, Ethan. I know you're gonna do everything you can for me and the girls, so how can I possibly worry anymore? You always were the best of us."

Jesus, he'd been through some shit in his life, but Ethan had never felt so emotionally spent as he did right then. "I love you, Mags. I never stopped loving you... I just wish—"

"No regrets. Not now." Maggie's tiny hand patted his thigh, and the effort looked like it exhausted her, though he'd hardly felt her touch. "I love you too..."

Ethan watched her eyes slip shut as she fell back asleep. He didn't know how long he sat with her before he decided he'd best go and get the talk with Ben over with. He didn't have a clue what Ben needed to say to him, other than maybe an explanation for the kiss earlier. He honestly hadn't had much time to even think about it, but it was there in the back of his mind, scratching away at him so he couldn't forget it.

It certainly hadn't been the kind of first kiss he'd imagined them sharing, but those kisses had all been ridiculously romantic fantasy kisses that only ever happened in movies. In all honesty, he'd never thought he'd actually get the chance to kiss Ben and now...well...now he wanted more. He wanted to taste him properly, hold him tightly against his own body and spend hours exploring that sinful fucking mouth—for starters.

Images of kissing Ben the right way chased him to the man's side. He found him out on the deck again laid out on one of the deck lounges with a beer in hand, the only light coming from a lamp just inside the door and the bright, almost full moon. Ethan dragged one of the single chairs closer and sat beside him. He allowed himself a moment to let his gaze trail down the length of Ben's perfect body and felt a twitch in his semi-hard cock. Ben was fucking gorgeous.

"See something you like?" Ben's question exploded through the silence, and Ethan didn't have a fucking clue how to answer. "Relax, Ethan. I don't bite...much." He laughed and sat up, swinging his legs off the lounge so he faced Ethan.

The moonlight hit his light hair, turning it an almost white color and his pale-blue eyes glowed almost silver. He looked like a mythical creature from some other realm sent here to seduce the mortals with his beauty. Ethan turned his chair a little so he was sitting more face-on to him. He couldn't fucking look away.

Ben unexpectedly reached out, grabbed his hand and started playing gently with his fingers. Ethan held his breath at the intimacy of the action. Ben was always a little touchy-feely with others but never before with him. It wasn't a sexy touch, but it was the hottest fucking thing Ethan had ever felt.

"Ethan."

The sound of his name whispered from Ben's lips made his dick even fucking harder. It was ridiculous how turned on he was, and Ben had done absolutely nothing sexual to him at all. "You...ah you said you needed to talk to me..."

Ben nodded and drew in a deep breath. It was clear to Ethan this was not going to be a happy talk. "You know my background is the army, right?"

"Yeah. I don't know details though..."

"I joined as soon as I was old enough. Mom had recently died; we lost her to bowel cancer, and I was so fucking angry—it was a long and painful death. Anyway, when I joined, they quickly discovered I had a talent. I was an excellent shot. The short story is that I was moved to sniper training before my first deployment. I excelled at it." Ben huffed out a grunt and reached for the beer on the ground near their feet. He took a long swallow, and Ethan watched, fascinated at the way his throat worked. He itched to nip at the long column of skin with his teeth.

"When I got over there, I...I was still so angry, Ethan, and I enjoyed it. All of it: the constant fear, walking so close to death, the adrenaline...even the killing. I'd take risks and I'd always be first to pull the trigger. What I didn't know was that while the army higher-ups were getting concerned about me maybe enjoying it all too much, someone else was watching me. When I came home from my first deployment, I was approached by a man who said he wanted to hire me to do what I so obviously loved. He was from one of the letter agencies and said he could get me out of the army early. As I was a sniper, I'm sure you can imagine what he wanted to hire me for." Ben had his head bowed, playing with Ethan's fingers while he talked, but at last he looked up at Ethan. Ethan could see a dozen emotions churning behind his sad eyes but fear shone brightest. He was waiting for Ethan to judge him—to hate him.

Whichever agency it was, and clearly Ben couldn't tell him, had hired Ben to be an assassin. Ethan wanted so badly to dismiss it as no big deal, but he needed to hear the entire story—Ben needed him to hear it. In his gut, he knew Ben was a good man, and he didn't care about his past. But if he didn't learn the whole story, he'd always wonder, always have a niggle somewhere in the back of his mind that maybe there was something more he should know about Ben.

"I signed up. I was so fucking happy to do it. They were bad guys—the ones they sent me after. They *were* bad guys, Ethan. I promise you. I always insisted on a full brief of my targets. I would never hurt someone innocent. I hope you can believe that." Ben squeezed the fingers he'd never stopped playing with, and Ethan squeezed back, producing a hint of a smile on Ben's handsome face.

"So, anyway, time passed, and I was working for *them* now and enjoying it. But eventually I realized I couldn't look at myself in the mirror some days. I started to hate the guy who was looking back. My argument that they were bad guys began to wear thin and the anger about Mom was fading. Even I could see I had turned into a scary guy. I can't go into details, but it wasn't easy getting out. Once they have a valuable asset..."

"Ben, if you're worried I might think less of you because of this, then don't. I know the kind of man you are now, and I know even back then you'd never have hurt someone who didn't deserve it," Ethan reassured.

"But I enjoyed it, Ethan, and that's why I had to stop. I never wanted you to know about that side of me, but I needed to tell you because if we get out there and it comes down to it, I'll be that man again, Ethan. It took me a long time to lock that part of me away, but if it'll save you or the twins, I need you to know I'll do *whatever* I have to."

Ethan was never good with words, so all he could think of doing was holding Ben. He knelt between his spread thighs and pulled Ben to him. He came willingly, burrowing his head into Ethan's chest and letting himself be surrounded by Ethan's embrace. "Thank you. I know I'm asking too much of you, but thank you," Ethan whispered into his hair.

When they eventually pulled away and resumed their seats, Ben picked up right where he'd left off playing with Ethan's fingers. And Ethan felt the heat of his touch radiating throughout his body once more. He felt his cock filling again, ludicrously excited by such a simple touch from this man.

"Can I ask you something?"

"Sure."

"Is that why you became a bodyguard?"

Ben tilted his head and smiled. "How perceptive of you, Mr. Stone. You're right. I saw it as recompense for what I'd done. Instead, I started protecting others from people like me. I hoped it might assuage the guilt, but now I know my past is something I have to live with."

The few men Ethan had dated in his life had all invariably, at some point in the relationship, left him due to his "stunted emotional growth" and "repressed personality." He'd never been able to give them affection or intimacy, so he was shocked when he pulled Ben's hand to his mouth and gently kissed each knuckle. He was further shocked when he reached out with his other hand and slid it around to cup the back of Ben's neck, his thumb sliding back and forth over the smooth skin of his cheek.

"Ben, if this might be too much for you, I can call in Max or Harry or any of the others. I'm sure they'd help. I never want to do anything again that might hurt you—"

"No. I need to be there for you. Please. I can handle it. Promise."

Ethan stared into Ben's eyes, assessing and gauging everything he found in them until he was satisfied. He nodded and Ben let out the breath he'd been holding. He wondered if their talk was done now, and if so, what happened next? Clearly, there was something going on between them, but the timing was appalling.

"Why'd you leave me? Why didn't you come back to see me at the hospital?"

Fuck. Okay. So, it wasn't over. The least he could do was repay Ben's honesty with his own.

"I was scared. I couldn't stand the thought of you hating me for who I really was."

"Jesus, Ethan, what was to hate? You turned your brother in because he was killing women." Ben shook his head and mumbled, "So much time wasted."

"I'd been lying to you all. Not even Patricia and Roger knew."

"And with damn good reason." Ben reached up and cupped Ethan's neck with one hand, favoring him with a small smile. "Phew. I don't know about you, but I'm done with all this deep shit for one night. Tell me something about you I don't know, Ethan. Something easy, simple...happy."

"Like what?"

"I don't know. Like...what's your favorite band? Your favorite ice cream flavor? What do you like doing when you're not at work with your panties in a twist?"

Ethan chuckled. Ever since they'd known each other, Ben had accused him of being uptight, with good reason, yet Ben could usually always coax at least a smile out of him, if not a good belly laugh.

"Okay. Favorite band is Creedence Clearwater Revival. Ice cream flavor is boring old chocolate, and when I'm not at work, I like to read. Also my favorite color is pale blue, and I like dancing in the moonlight, and long strolls along the beach." Ethan laughed, hoping Ben would enjoy his attempt at humor.

Ben did laugh, but then turned serious eyes upon him. "I love Creedence. My favorite color changes every day. I hate ice cream and reading, but I love dancing and the beach, so I'm gonna hold you to those, Ethan Stone, and when this is over, you are going to twirl me in the moonlight while we're walking along the beach. Got it?"

The way Ben was looking at him, Ethan would have agreed to anything. The fact that Ben was virtually telling him when this was over he wanted more than friendship had him nodding vigorously in agreement. He wasn't fucking stupid enough to say no to that. "Yeah. I got it."

Ben's smile was brilliant as he nodded. "Good. Now, bed for you. You look exhausted, and we need to be rested for what's to come." Ben rose and held his hand out for Ethan to take, which he did willingly. He stood next to Ben, fascinated again by their height difference. All of Ethan's other lovers had been around his own size, so this was new… and fucking hot, as far as he was concerned. Ben also looked particularly young tonight, and he wondered if the age difference should be a consideration. But fuck, it was only a number, and Ben was an adult. He wouldn't insult him by treating him like a child who didn't understand the choices he was making. If Ben wanted Ethan, then he could have him. He knew he wanted Ben. He wanted every bit of him.

Chapter Six

BEN

Cameron's garage looked like an REI store had come to die in it. Every possible piece of equipment they could need had to be in there.

"Where do we start?" Ryan asked from beside him, where he was similarly surveying the mass of equipment laid out in a very organized manner. It was all here: tents, sleeping bags, boots, backpacks, flashlights, climbing gear, anything and everything they could possibly need.

While Cameron was preparing the chopper and Ethan and Lucas were attending to Maggie, Ben and Ryan had been tasked with sorting through Cameron's camping equipment and deciding what, if anything, they would need to buy. From the looks of things, it would be a very short shopping list.

"Jesus, I don't even know. Who knew Cam was a hoarder? Or maybe he's got some sort of camping kink." Ben winked at Ryan, who returned his wink with laughter. Ben and Ryan had gotten along from the moment they'd met. As Ben would say, they shared a similar joyful enthusiasm for life. Lucas had once said that watching them interact was like watching two little boys planning what mischief they'd get up to next. But on a more serious note, Ben genuinely liked both Ryan and Lucas and couldn't have been happier about the contentment so visibly imprinted on both their faces.

Ben turned to Ryan and clasped him on the arm. "It's so good to see you. You look fucking happy, Ryan."

"I am. Never happier. I mean, it was rough there for a while, and we still have to face the press when we get back, but he's worth it, Ben. He is so fucking worth it."

Ben could understand the sentiment. He'd walk through fire for Ethan, and even as he burned, he'd still be thinking he was worth it. "I didn't see much of the media bullshit, but Cam told me you've quit Hollywood. What's next for you?"

Ryan had begun suffering from panic attacks, particularly in large crowds and he'd come to the decision that the Hollywood lifestyle was not for him. Ryan had the world at his feet, but he'd chosen to walk away.

"No fucking idea. It was too much, you know. You saw the panic attacks, the price Luke and I have both paid for fame and it was too high. I've got plenty of money to tide me over, and Luke's said he'll support me with whatever I decide, so I guess I'll have to wait for inspiration to hit."

Ben suspected Ryan was one of those people who excelled at everything they put their minds to.

"How about you? Are you going back to being a bodyguard eventually?"

Was he? He hadn't really thought too much about the future while he'd been recuperating. He'd spent most of his days wavering between a healthy anger at Ethan and not-so-healthy plans for either vengeance or seducing him back to his side. "I really don't know, to be honest. My job's there for me if I want it, but I get kinda restless after a while, so it may be time to look at something new. But right now, I'm gonna focus on getting those little girls back."

"I can't believe what's happened to poor Maggie, and I can't understand why people would follow someone like that Piper guy."

"Lots of lonely people out there, Ryan. Lot of people looking for something, someone to help them get through, make them feel like they belong somewhere. If people feel like they don't fit or they're unloved, it makes them vulnerable, especially to predators like Arnold Piper. Here, help me with this, would ya?" Ben started digging through the equipment and passing suitable items to Ryan to be put to the side for him and Ethan to take with them.

"You'll be careful out there, hey? Watch each other's backs?"

"I'll bring Ethan back...and the girls," Ben vowed.

Ryan's hand squeezed Ben's shoulder, and Ben looked up into his eyes. "Bring yourself back too, Ben. Like Lucas said, you're family now, and we don't want to lose you."

"We'll all make it home. I'm not that easy to get rid of."

It took them another hour, but by the time they'd finished, all that Ben had on his shopping list was a couple of hiking carriers that could hold the girls when they carted them through the wilderness.

When he and Ryan walked back into the house, they found Ethan and Cameron peering over a giant map laid out on the dining room table.

"Hey. Did you find something?" Ben asked.

"I'm showing Ethan the area where that camp is. I can't get the chopper till this afternoon, so we'll do our flyover then," Cameron answered.

Ethan's gaze was still fixed on the map when he spoke. "I'm checking out the terrain, looking for other possible sites for the camp, in case the area Cameron's thinking of isn't it. Did you guys get the gear sorted?"

"All we need are the carriers for the girls. What're you thinking, Ethan? Fly in, fly out?"

"I'm thinking hike in, fly out. We can't risk alerting them that we're coming. Who knows how jumpy Piper is? So, if we trek in, there's less chance of them spotting us. Once we've got the girls, we'll head to a prearranged extraction point and fly out, hopefully before anyone at the camp can raise the alarm."

"Look, ah... I'm being devil's advocate here, but what about the people left behind? What if this Piper character decides to wipe out the camp once he notices the girls are gone?" Cameron shifted uncomfortably and kept his gaze down as he spoke, but Ben knew he'd raised a very valid concern. It was something he'd thought about a lot last night. He had a plan in mind, but it wasn't something he was willing to share quite yet.

Ben could tell from the tensing of Ethan's body that he'd thought about the possibility of Arnold Piper enacting the Jonestown plan too. "I don't know what else to do." Ethan's voice sounded so broken...so lost.

"This is the right thing, Ethan, and we're gonna do everything we can to make sure that doesn't happen." He wasn't sure if his words would reassure Ethan, but he couldn't tell him yet what he planned to do to make sure nobody died out there. In fact, if he could somehow manage it, Ethan would never have to know.

"Yeah, yeah, okay." Ethan nodded and held Ben's gaze, searching. Whatever he was looking for he must have found, because he smiled and bent back down to the map. "So, if this is the camp, Cameron, where can you land nearby to pick us up?"

As they continued poring over the map and making tentative plans, while they waited to get up in the helicopter, Ben's mind was stuck on his own secret agenda. All he knew for certain about the coming days was that Arnold Piper may not be walking away from this.

BEN'S PHONE RANG at the most inopportune time. The tension between Ethan and Cameron was thicker than ever as they waited at the heliport for their clearance. Somehow, while they'd been discussing plans for this op, Ethan and Cameron had butted heads again. Ben wasn't fucking stupid; he knew most of the contention between them had been about him, though, they'd ridiculously tried to conceal that.

Reluctantly, he stepped away from them to answer his call. It was Ryan, who'd been sent out with the task of getting the rigs for the carriers together. Apparently, his written instructions hadn't been clear enough, and he bombarded Ben with a plethora of questions. While he was answering those questions, Ben kept one eye on Ethan and Cameron. He rolled his eyes as he watched them circle each other like two alpha predators getting ready to go in for the kill. When the posturing stopped and the hand gestures began, Ben hurried to get Ryan off the line.

"Ryan, I gotta go. Do the best you can and it'll be fine. Okay?"

"Yeah, but—" Ben hung up before Ryan could suck him back in to his uncertainty. Ryan knew what was needed, and he'd get it done; he might doubt himself, but Ben didn't.

Once the call ended, he turned his entire focus to the two very big men in front of him. Ben clearly heard what they were saying, and he didn't know whether to laugh his ass off or slap them both.

"I'm just saying, Ethan, that he's my baby brother, and if you hurt him—"

"I don't plan on hurting him, Cameron. I care about him."

"Really? Cause it sure didn't seem like it a few weeks ago. He's more sensitive than you might think, and you need to treat him—"

"Oh, for fuck's sake," Ben broke in. He'd heard enough. Cameron might be bigger than him, and ten minutes older, but that didn't make him his keeper. "Cam, I can't believe you're actually doing the 'what are your intentions' talk. I appreciate your concern. I really do, but Ethan's apologized and explained why he did what he did. I'm not a dainty little flower you have to protect."

"No, but you are my brother, and I *just* nearly lost you and it was...awful, so you're gonna have to forgive me if I get a little overprotective right now."

Normally, he and Cameron shied away from the feels, but he knew his shooting had hit Cameron hard. They'd lost both parents, and they were all they had left, so yes, Ben could give him some leeway—but not too much.

"Bring it in, Cam." He stretched out his arms waiting for his brother to step into the gap before closing them around his much bigger body. "Thank you, but I promise you, Cameron... I promise you Ethan is a good guy." He felt Cameron nod and hoped that was one issue they could put to bed.

"Cameron," Ethan's deep voice broke in, and Ben was almost tempted to face-palm, worried that Ethan might say something to ruin the moment. He released his brother, and they both turned to face Ethan. "I know I hurt Ben, and I know that hurt you, and I'm so sorry for that. But you have to know that I would never...never intentionally hurt him. I care very much about him."

Ben's heart throbbed a little faster at Ethan's words. It wasn't a declaration of love, but Ben knew it was way too early for that for Ethan. For himself, he'd sing it at the top of his voice right now if he didn't think it'd send Ethan running screaming away from him. But Ben had been in love with Ethan almost from the moment they'd met, and he suspected whatever feelings Ethan may be harboring for Ben were only now slowly creeping up on him. And knowing Ethan, they were probably scaring the fuck out of him.

Cameron was silent for a moment, sizing Ethan up before answering, "I'm trusting you with him again, Ethan. Don't fuck it up." They shook hands before Cameron went to check on the status of their helicopter.

"I can't believe he did that, Ethan. I'm sorry," Ben offered once Cameron was out of sight.

"Don't be. I deserved it, but I meant what I said, Ben. I won't ever intentionally hurt you."

"I know. I trust you, Ethan, and I hope you trust me, otherwise it's not going to work out there."

"With my life, Ben, and what's more—with my niece's lives."

It felt like a hugging moment, but Ben wasn't exactly sure their relationship was there yet. The moment was turning into an uncomfortable silence while they stared at each other, so Ben took a chance and grabbed Ethan, pulling him in tight for an embrace. Risks were something he could definitely do.

It wasn't until he heard the clearing of a throat that he reluctantly pulled away from the warmth of Ethan's body. He was so big and so solid. There was nothing soft about his body—it felt so fucking good to be wrapped up in it. But he was glad his brother was interrupting them because his thoughts were turning carnal and now wasn't the time or place.

"Okay, we've got clearance to go, so let's get this done before we lose the light."

They followed Cameron to the waiting chopper, and Ben motioned for Ethan to take the seat alongside Cameron. He sat in the back and placed his helmet on. They'd all be able to communicate via the earpieces in the helmets.

Cameron had them in the air in minutes. Ben loved flying with him, especially over such gorgeous countryside, but this wasn't a sightseeing flight; he needed to keep his eyes open and his wits about him.

In the front, Cameron was pointing things out to Ethan, landmarks, open spaces for landing, dangerous spots. Ben knew Ethan would be absorbing it all, doing everything possible to ensure the safety of all those who'd be involved in this operation.

"Okay, off to the right there, you should be able to see the camp coming into view. They've tried to keep much of it in the tree line for cover, I'd assume, but some of the bigger tents have had to be erected in the clearing."

Ben moved to the opposite window to get a better view of the camp. It was set out as Cameron had described but may have grown bigger than he'd been expecting.

As though reading his mind, Cameron continued, "It's gotten bigger. Way more tents. Look at the people. They kinda look like they're running for cover."

Ben watched the people on the ground. He'd estimate maybe a hundred were in sight, and it did appear as if they were trying to hide, though they were trying to be very nonchalant about it. Those on the ground clearly didn't want them to know how many were down there, and if maybe a hundred were visible, then Ben suspected the true number was probably at least double that. It was a big camp, and if he wasn't mistaken, it was an armed camp. Several of the men he could see—the ones who weren't trying to get under cover—seemed to be holding guns—big ones. It was potentially a warning to them—a warning that they were armed, and they weren't at all concerned that whoever was in the helicopter buzzing over them now knew it.

Chapter Seven

ETHAN

"Okay, so if what we saw today was the camp, what's our best way in?" Ethan wouldn't say he was excited, because the situation he'd found himself in was fraught with danger, but it felt good that they were making progress. He and Ben were fairly certain they'd flown over Arnold Piper's cult camp today, but Cameron had promised that he'd do a grid search starting tomorrow on the off chance that what they'd seen had nothing to do with Piper and Ethan's nieces.

"Well, if we stick to a twenty-mile exclusion zone so we won't be spotted, then there are probably three areas I could drop you. Here, here, and here." Cameron pointed to the map. They'd circled the area where they'd found the camp, and Ethan marked the three potential drop-off zones with a cross. They wanted to be far enough away to go in undetected but not so far that it would take days to walk to the camp. Piper was an unknown quantity, and Ethan had no idea how reckless the man really was.

"With what we'll be carrying, we can assume a flat hike of twenty miles would take us maybe eight to ten hours. But there is no flat route in so we need to add at least an hour for every thousand feet elevation. It's not gonna be a one-day hike, Ethan," Ben added.

"You're right, but I don't think we can risk getting dropped off any closer. Maggie said the camp had a military feel to it, which probably means they'll have scouts staggered out a fair way to watch for anyone approaching. Maybe if we go in here at Hawk's Rest, we've got a couple of big peaks between there and the campsite to offer some cover. What do you think, Cameron?"

Despite their rocky relationship, Ethan liked Cameron Cronin. He was a good man who obviously cared a great deal about Ben, which gave him bonus points as far as Ethan was concerned. He also had the added benefit of knowing this area very well.

While Ben had been in his coma after the shooting, before Ethan had fucked things up, he and Cameron had spent a lot of time together, waiting and talking. He knew Cameron had worked these ranges for years, though he'd always assumed he lived nearer to Jackson, where the search and rescue base was located. He guessed the commute was nothing when you had a helicopter virtually at your disposal.

The map area they were looking at was so vast that Ethan couldn't imagine how long it might have taken them, if ever, to find the camp if it hadn't been spotted and noted a few days earlier. He liked to think of it as providence and an excellent sign of impending success. Failure couldn't be an option.

Cameron was still studying the map with an unshakeable intensity, but he finally looked up, shifting his gaze between him and Ben. "Yeah, I agree. I think Hawk's Rest is your best way in. It's got the peaks to give you coverage, but the terrain isn't as rough as the other two possible entry points. Once you get past Thorofare Plateau, it's a straight shot to the camp."

It was Ben's turn to peer at the map. Both he and Cameron remained silent as Ben considered the terrain, knowing that he had the most experience with this kind of operation. Ben reached for a sharpie and began making little crosses on the map and then explained. "If there is someone running this thing with a military background like Maggie thinks, then I'm guessing there's going to be lookouts here and here if we take this route. It should be easy enough for us to disable at least one of them, thereby rendering them ineffective. How much time that will buy us will depend on what kind of checks and balances they have in place. If one of their outposts doesn't call in, that should raise an alarm. If they're smart, they'll have them checking in every half hour to forty minutes, given that's the approximate walk time from the outpost to camp."

Ben bent his head back down and continued making marks on the map. Ethan could have listened to him all day. He'd always known that behind the laid-back, fun-loving exterior there lurked a whip-smart and dangerous man, but hearing him talk like this—planning this operation—was turning him the fuck on.

"What kind of guards we might encounter at the camp is anyone's guess, so we'll have to go in slow and watch the campsite for a few hours to see how their watch has been set up. Darkness is going to be our friend, but the biggest problem I foresee is working out which tent the girls are in, unless we get very fucking lucky and we happen to see them while we're observing the camp."

Ethan was openly staring at Ben now, enthralled by the confident way he'd taken control and the absolute certainty in his tone that they'd be able to do this. His assertiveness and surety were a heady combination Ethan's dick was noticeably approving.

"Ethan?"

"Huh?"

"You okay? I've been calling your name, but I think from the glazed look on your face that your dick might have been running the show for a while there." Ben smirked and winked, oblivious to Ethan's mortification that he'd been called out in front of Cameron, who'd...Cameron who'd gone, he realized as he scanned the room. "Yeah, Cam left. I think he may have been a little uncomfortable with the way you were undressing his baby brother with your eyes."

Ethan couldn't help the rush of laughter that shot out of him. Contrary to his usual reserved nature, he reached out and pulled Ben to him, wrapping his big arms around him and gazing down into pale-blue eyes that blazed with desire. "Christ, you're gonna be fun to fuck," he murmured before slamming his lips down onto Ben's slightly parted ones. Ben's were warm and so fucking soft as they moved against his own, the heat and friction coming from their kiss setting his body alight with fiery need.

This was what he'd fantasized about sharing with Ben.

"Oh, you've got no idea," Ben mumbled as they pulled away to take a breath. And then he pressed his body even tighter against Ethan's—almost like he was trying to climb inside the bigger man. Ben's lips pressed against his once more, wantonly moving against Ethan's as Ethan submitted to the pleasure.

Jesus, he could have kissed Ben for hours, but he was uncomfortably aware that he was in the dining room of somebody else's home where several people could walk in at any time. He'd love to get Ben somewhere private, where they could really go to town. Ben pulled back, but he never turned away from Ethan's gaze, and he never released the grip he had on Ethan's shirt as he dragged him forward. In a few steps, they'd reached the table, where Ben lithely jumped up, spread his legs, and pulled Ethan into the space between his thighs.

Ethan tangled one of his hands in the hair at the back of Ben's head, snagging him forward to taste those perfect fucking lips again, while his other hand found the small of Ben's back, forcing his pelvis closer so it pressed against Ethan's cock. Ethan could feel how hard Ben was, even through the thick denim of his jeans, but before he could make a grab for Ben's cock, Ben had wrapped his legs around Ethan's hips. Throaty moans from both men were slipping from between their joined lips, and Ben seemed incapable of stopping the constant writhing of his body. Even when Ethan pulled him tighter, Ben's body refused to remain still.

With little choice, Ethan cupped his hands under Ben's ass, carrying him away from the table that he'd all but wiggled off. Though Ben was smaller than Ethan, he was still a big man and he certainly wasn't light. Ethan made a beeline for the nearest wall, slamming Ben's back against it for added support. He'd never literally picked someone up during sex, but it now may be his new favorite thing. The hypnotic wriggling movements of Ben's body had ensnared his own, and he moved against Ben, searching for the friction they needed.

"Fuck, Ethan. I knew it'd be like this with you. I'm gonna fucking come in my pants like a schoolboy," Ben hissed before biting into Ethan's earlobe.

Ben was going to fucking kill him, but he couldn't help thinking what an awesome way to go. Ethan knew he was seconds away from coming. Ben's constant movements, his filthy words, and the way he was curling his fucking tongue around Ethan's ear was too much.

Ben squeezed his hand between their bodies and seemed to struggle to get both of their pants open and down. He only needed enough room to pull their cocks free, but it apparently wasn't fucking easy.

Anything could be achieved with a little determination, and Ben seemed resolved to prove it and make him come. When he finally had both in his hand, Ethan groaned at the feel of their hard dicks rubbing against each other, the contact eased by the combined precome dribbling all over. Ben's hand encircled both as he pulled and tugged, adding extra friction.

Suddenly, Ben jolted against him with a long drawn-out moan. Ben coming was all he needed to tip him over the edge, and he wallowed in the sticky evidence of their shared passion.

Ethan never wanted to put Ben down. He kept his hand cupped under that perfect ass as he languidly kissed Ben through the trailing moments of their pleasure until they were both wrung out and spent. Even then, when neither had anything left to give, Ethan didn't release his hold on Ben—it felt too fucking perfect.

"When this is over and we've gotten your nieces safely back to their mother, we're gonna find a bed, Ethan, and we're not gonna leave it for two fucking days—" Ben pulled back and glanced down Ethan's body, taking his time as he went. "—Make that four fucking days. Now, put me down, and go get yourself cleaned up, you nasty boy."

Ethan's cock gave a valiant little twitch at Ben's words and the carnal look in his eyes, but after his orgasm had wrung everything he had out of him, Ethan knew there'd be nothing doing—for a while anyway. He gently eased Ben to his feet but kept him close to give a last sweet, lingering kiss before he zipped up and turned to head for a shower and to sit with his sister while she ate.

Cameron's dining room opened on one end to a large living area and at the other end connected to the kitchen by a smaller door. He walked through this door and found himself face-to-face with Ryan and Lucas. He could tell by their wide eyes, poorly concealed giggles, and the fact that neither of them would look him directly in the eye they'd probably heard what had gone on in the other room.

"Ryan. Lucas."

"Ethan," they responded together. Ethan kept his head held high as he fled from them in as dignified a manner as he could muster. He didn't miss the laughter that followed him out of the kitchen, nor did he miss Ben's "You two are assholes" comment.

By the time he'd finished his shower, Ben had heated up a delicious smelling stew for his sister. He hoped she'd manage more than a few mouthfuls tonight, but after only half the bowl had been emptied, Maggie pleaded with him to take it away.

Ethan hurt as he watched Maggie move her tiny frame around, trying to find a comfortable position. Even if there was nothing that could be done for her, he'd feel better when she was in a proper facility getting the care she needed.

Once she was settled, Maggie reached for his hand, and he linked their fingers together, careful of his greater strength.

"Do you remember my fifteenth birthday party, Ethan?" Maggie's voice was so soft Ethan had to strain to hear her.

"How could I forget it?" He chuckled.

Maggie smiled a little, a wistful look passing over her features. "I had six friends over and every one of them fell for you. God, they spent the entire party asking me questions about you and doing whatever they could to get you to notice them."

Ethan huffed. "Yeah, I remember. Especially that one girl...what was her name? The one who paraded around all day in that ridiculously short skirt and kept trying to get me to pick her up to show how strong I was... Cassie, Kaylee—"

"Corrine."

"That's it."

Maggie squeezed his fingers, but the pressure was negligible. "You were so good with them. You never once made them feel stupid or pathetic for crushing on someone so much older, but at the same time, you made sure they knew nothing was going to happen. You are such a good man, Ethan." When her eyes fluttered shut, Ethan wondered if she'd drift off to sleep, so he sat quietly, his thumb stroking over Maggie's fingers where they were linked with his. He'd do anything to swap places with her.

"I don't know if you knew, but Stewart was there that day too—briefly," she whispered.

Ethan startled when she continued. He hadn't known about Stewart being there that day. It was right around the time he'd started to seriously suspect his brother was responsible for the murders that had been plaguing the area for a few years.

"He'd popped in to get something from Dad, and he came out to wish me happy birthday. Ethan, I was terrified of him that day. He looked at me and my friends, and there was such a look of... I can only describe it as evil on his face. I didn't understand until he was arrested, but, Ethan, I think... I really believe if you hadn't stopped him, I'd have ended up one of his victims."

Ethan closed his eyes against the flood of memories and fears from that time. He had no idea Maggie had ever been afraid of Stewart. Once Stewart had moved out, she hadn't really had much to do with him. Neither had he, when he thought about it. Stewart had always been a prick, but it had still come as a shock that he was as depraved as he was. Only their parents refused to see Stewart for the monster he was.

"Then I'm even more grateful that I stopped him." He bent and pressed a kiss to her forehead. Turning in his brother had cost him everything, but he'd do it again in a heartbeat; he just wished he'd done it sooner.

"I'm so happy you're here. So happy," Maggie murmured before closing her eyes.

Ethan stayed by her side for a few more hours as she fitfully slept. He'd have stayed there all night, but he needed a good night's sleep for what was to come. As he stood and turned to leave the room, he found Lucas leaning against the open door.

"Go and get some sleep, Ethan. I'll sit with her."

"Thank you. For everything, Lucas."

Lucas flashed one of his movie star smiles, which had made him so famous and loved around the world, but unlike some of the ones he'd seen grace his lips, Ethan knew this smile was real. "Anytime. You know that."

Ethan clapped him on the shoulder as he walked past and headed to his room. Noticing Ben curled up on the sofa as he passed, he headed over to the sleeping man. Crouching beside him, he gently shook his shoulder, but he should have known better.

Ben sat bolt upright, wide awake, with a knife pressed to Ethan's neck, before Ethan could even take a breath. "Ethan?"

"Yeah, it's me." He swallowed, trying to keep as still as possible in case he spooked Ben even further.

"Shit. Sorry, man."

When Ethan felt the cool of the knife pull away from his neck, he finally let out the breath he'd been holding. "Ben, come with me. You can't sleep out here." He held his hand out and watched Ben shift his gaze between his eyes and his offered hand before he reached out and took it.

Neither spoke as Ethan led Ben into his room. Ben wiggled himself under the covers while Ethan stripped down to the boxers he'd sleep in. Once he was under the covers, Ben twisted and squirmed around some more until he was lying with his head on Ethan's chest and his body cuddled into Ethan's like a koala on a tree branch.

In minutes, Ben was softly snoring. Ethan lay there inhaling Ben's cinnamon scent while carding his fingers through the silky curls of Ben's hair. It was hard to sleep when he didn't know if this would be the only time he'd get to enjoy the feel of Ben curled up against him like this.

Chapter Eight

BEN

Under different circumstances, Ben would have been having the time of his life. He was out hiking in some truly beautiful scenery, walking beside the man he'd loved for two years, the man he wanted above all others. Cameron had dropped them at Hawk's Rest a few hours ago, and he and Ethan had been walking side by side from that moment. It had been too long since he'd been able to get into the outdoors like this.

Ben could feel the tension radiating from Ethan. He knew saying goodbye to Maggie this morning had been hard for him, but with any luck, he'd be back with her tomorrow or the day after at the latest.

"It's beautiful here," he ventured, hoping to distract Ethan from where Ben suspected his thoughts were headed.

"Yeah it is. Did you grow up around here?" Ethan asked.

"No. We grew up in Vegas, but both Mom and Dad were big outdoorsy people, so we spent a lot of time camping and hiking when I was growing up."

"Vegas, huh? That must have been an interesting childhood."

Ben had loved his childhood, loved his family. They'd been close. His parents' relationship was one of those very rare ones that had not only lasted for many years but had never lost the passion—until his mother became ill. He'd lost count of how many times he and Cameron had come home from school to his parents' locked bedroom door. It was seeing that lasting love and passion that drove Ben not to settle for anything less until he'd found the one. Corny as it might be, he knew Ethan was the one for him—had known it practically at first sight.

"It's a one-of-a-kind town, but I have nothing but fond memories until...until we lost Mom and everything went to shit."

"I'm sorry, Ben."

"Thank you. After that, Cameron, Dad, and I kinda splintered apart. For some, tragedy pulls them closer, but for us, it was the opposite. I think we were all hurting so much we couldn't bear to see each other's pain. So, we all kind of ran away from each other. Cam went to flight school, and I went into the army."

"What about your dad? Where did he end up?"

It's hard to lose someone you love to a vile and senseless disease like cancer, but at least his mother had played no part in her own fate, and they'd had time to say their goodbyes. Ben's father was another matter altogether.

"Ah...we lost him a few years after Mom. He got drunk before getting into his boat. It took a few days before his body washed up with the tide."

"Jesus, Ben."

"Yeah. It always gets me how life can turn on a dime. Happy families one minute, and then in the blink of an eye it's all gone." Ben never liked to get bogged down in the past—at least not that part of it, but at the same time, he loved that he and Ethan were talking like this. He wanted closeness with Ethan—intimacy. It was something he'd never had with past lovers, and he'd really never wanted it, because he hadn't been in love with them. "Hey, how 'bout a quick break for lunch? I'm fine, but your old bones have gotta be starting to ache a little." He smirked and only narrowly dodged the swat Ethan aimed at his ass.

They found a little cluster of boulders not much farther along the little stream they'd been following. After setting their packs down, they each found one of the rocks to sit against and ripped into one of their Mountain House ration packs. Compared to the MREs he was used to from his military days, Ben was pleasantly surprised. The meal was no restaurant-quality gourmet fare, but it was edible and had a palatable enough taste.

When done, Ben leaned back against the rock and closed his eyes, allowing the warmth of the sun and the cool, crisp air to imbue his body with calm. This was why he loved the outdoors.

"Ben? You okay?"

As a trained sniper, Ben had developed the habit of remaining unnaturally still for extended periods of time when needed. It was off-putting for most people to see. "I'm good. Just resting."

"You didn't move for...well, for the longest time. It hardly even seemed as though you were breathing."

Ben opened one eye and peered at Ethan, observing his concerned expression. "Ex-sniper," he said by way of explanation. "I'm like a conundrum—half the time I'm wiggling about like a worm on a hook, and the other half I'm like a statue. You'll get used to it." At least, Ben hoped he would. Last night had been a good start. You couldn't fake that kind of desire. Ethan was no actor, so Ben had to believe that, while he may not be in love with Ben yet, Ethan definitely wanted him, and he could work with that.

"We can do this, can't we?" Ethan's tone was hesitant, nervous. Ben couldn't blame him. Ethan's background was in law enforcement, but Ben assumed it had rarely involved storming a compound with military-like precision.

Ben shifted to face Ethan; he climbed onto his lap, kneeled on either side of Ethan's massive body, and took hold of his hands. He stared unflinchingly into Ethan's dark-blue eyes, waiting until he saw them soften. "We will do this, Ethan. I promise we are gonna walk out of that camp with those little girls, and then we're gonna get them home to their momma." He leaned over and sealed his vow with a soft kiss that Ethan yielded to immediately. Where last night's kisses had been a raging sea of passion, this one was all tranquil tenderness.

When they reluctantly broke apart, Ben rested his forehead against Ethan's as his breathing calmed and the warmth of their affection lulled him into drowsiness that could have easily sent him to sleep. "Show me their picture again, Ethan."

Ethan moved beneath him as he reached for the photo Maggie had given him of the girls. Ben had already seen it; the two of them sitting on Santa's lap, one with a huge smile on her cherub face and the other with her face scrunched up, tears coursing down her cheeks. They were adorable, but then, their uncle was smoking fucking hot, so good genes must run in that family.

Ethan held the photo in one large hand so they could both see it. Ben watched as Ethan gently traced the images of his two nieces with the tips of his fingers. "I can't wait to meet them, Ben. It's unbelievable how much I love them already."

"They're gonna adore you too. Did you ever want kids of your own?"

"Never really thought about it, actually. I think I always thought it'd never be on the table for me, but now...once Maggie...when we lose Maggie, she wants me to raise the girls, so I guess whether or not I want them is moot because I'm gonna have two of them to raise way too soon anyway."

"Maggie's a great lady, Ethan. It's awful what she's been through—still going through."

Ethan hung his head and his shoulders slumped. "Yeah. If I could trade places with her..."

"I know you would. I know." Ben searched out Ethan's full lips again. The kiss remained sweet and yet almost fierce with its tenderness. "You about ready to get on the move again? Another few hours and we should find somewhere to make camp for the night. Tomorrow should only be a quick few hours to reach the commune, and then we can scope things out and hit it tomorrow night."

Ethan nodded. "Thank you. For doing this, for being here with me. It means a lot."

"I've got your back, Ethan. Always."

After another few hours, the sun began to fall low on the horizon and the chill of the coming night started seeping into their bones. Ben wanted their camp assembled before darkness fully hit them. As he rounded a curve in the stream they'd been following, he came across a natural hot spring and a clearing in the tree line. It would be perfect.

"Okay, this looks good. Let's get this tent up and then how about you and I make use of that hot spring right there?" He nodded his head toward the steam and waggled his eyebrows.

Ethan's returning grin was nothing short of lecherous. "Can't think of a better way to clean off."

"Christ, we're gonna have to work on that dirty talk of yours." He laughed before pressing a kiss to Ethan's soft, warm lips. "Let's do this, huh?"

It took ten minutes for them to get their camp set up and only a fraction of that was erecting the actual tent. The new pop-up tent Cameron supplied them with was a marvel. The fucker even had built-in LED lighting.

Ben was cautious of making any assumptions where Ethan was concerned, so he left him to arrange the bedding. If Ben had his way, they'd be cozying up inside only one of the sleeping bags.

While Ethan was busy with the interior, Ben got a campfire going. He missed this shit. So many fond memories of he and Cameron and their parents sitting around a campfire assailed him as he worked. Ben promised himself that if he got even a sniff of a future with Ethan and his nieces, he was going to make sure camping would be a part of it too.

Once the fire blazed, the hypnotic dance of the flames drew Ben in so he startled when Ethan crouched behind him and wrapped him in his arms. He pressed a kiss to Ben's temple and murmured in his ear, "I'm ready to get all dirty with you in the hot springs, babe."

Ben groaned in reply and did his best not to face-palm at Ethan's cheesy line. The man was trying, and Ben supported that.

"Shit, that was bad, wasn't it?"

"Baby steps, Ethan. Baby steps." Ben stood and quickly divested himself of every stitch of clothing he wore. It was cold now that the sun was all but beyond the horizon so this part of their romp had to be done as quickly as possible. Once they were in the heat of the spring, Ben could take as much time as he wanted with Ethan.

The warmth of the water instantly drove the cold from Ben's body. It was like stepping into a soothing hot bath. He looked around, trying to find somewhere to sit that wasn't going to scrape his ass too badly. Once he was settled, he turned to Ethan, expecting to find him at least partially undressed. Instead, he was standing stock-still, his gaze boring into Ben's very fucking soul.

"Christ, you're fucking gorgeous," Ethan practically groaned the words. "Every fucking inch of you."

"I'm gonna blow you so hard for that," Ben replied, crooking his fingers at Ethan in a come-hither gesture. Ethan wasted no more time getting his gear off. He was in the water with Ben almost before he could blink. Rather than going straight for Ben, though, Ethan stayed on the opposite side of the hot springs, wearing nothing but a smug grin. *Oh, two could play at this game.*

Ben slunk farther back against the edge of the spring and lifted his arms so his elbows rested on the rocks surrounding the water. He kept his gaze fixed firmly on Ethan's and let all the heat and desire he felt bleed into his pale-blue eyes. The water level was just below his navel, and Ben let one of his hands drift down to gently tug on each nipple. He gave a satisfied smirk as he watched Ethan's gaze follow his hand and a soft moan slip from his lips. Poor Ethan had no fucking idea who he was dealing with here. There was a vast repertoire of seduction tactics for Ben to choose from because he'd wanted Ethan for years, and there wasn't a single fantasy or erotic thought he hadn't already had.

Ben was fascinated by the struggle so plainly visible on Ethan's gorgeous face. He knew how difficult it must be for Ethan not to reach out and grab him, because he was having the same damn fight. It was simply a matter of who'd give in first. He thought he had this one in the bag—until Ethan's tongue slipped out from between his parted lips and slowly licked along the plump bottom edge.

As if that wasn't torment enough, Ethan's hand trailed down his own torso before Ben lost sight of it under the warm waters. It didn't take a genius to figure out where it had gone when a low moan escaped from Ethan and his eyes rolled. Ethan shifted his big body, and suddenly Ben could see, in brilliant glory, the way Ethan was handling his own cock as the shaft peeked out of the water and his thumb played across the tip. Ben was no damn saint—this was too fucking much.

With one last smirk, he launched himself across the spring and climbed onto Ethan's lap. "Well played, Ethan, but it's my turn now." Ben slammed their lips together with little finesse and no tenderness—it was more of a clash of teeth than a kiss. This would bruise, but Ethan didn't back down an inch. *Christ, Ethan could fucking kiss.* He gave every bit as good as what Ben gave him and Ben soon found himself holding on as they writhed around in the water together.

Reluctantly, Ben pulled away from the kiss as he began the slow slide of his lips down Ethan's amazing torso. It was fucking artwork, if you asked him, and Ben was constantly distracted by the hard plains and dips, the coarse brown hair that covered Ethan's chest thinning out into a fucking perfect trail straight to his prize.

It was awkward and difficult for Ben to get his mouth around Ethan's cock while it was bobbing in the water but nothing was going to stop him. He reached down and cupped his hands around Ethan's ass cheeks, encouraging him to lift a little so his dick was sitting farther out of the water. *Perfect. Fucking perfect.*

Ben licked a trail up the shaft and glided his tongue around the head and was rewarded with a carnal groan from Ethan. "Fuck my mouth, Ethan. Hard...please." The request was easy enough to make, the begging wasn't, but Ben needed this. He needed it a little on the rougher side, and he fucking hoped that didn't spook Ethan. He held Ethan's gaze for a brief moment before turning his attention back to the hard cock in his hands.

Taking a breath, Ben opened his mouth, relaxed his throat, and swallowed every fucking inch of Ethan. He was a big man, and everything was in proportion, so it wasn't easy, but Ben didn't stop until his nose brushed wet, wiry hair, and then he swallowed. Ethan's cock jumped a little in his mouth, and his fingers fisted in his hair. Ethan held him steady and tight and began to really move. His hips punched forward and back—just as rough as Ben needed.

Under the water, Ben had one hand holding himself steady on a rock and the other furiously working his own hard cock. Tears were forming in his eyes as he looked up at Ethan from beneath his lashes, and for a brief moment he saw hesitancy in Ethan's navy eyes. For this to work, Ethan had to trust him; he had to know that Ben would call a halt if it was too much. Whatever Ethan had seen reflected back in Ben's eyes had worked because his pace picked up as he rammed his cock down Ben's throat. *Fucking perfect.*

"I'm gonna come, Ben. Ah...Jesus, fuck." Ethan's cock throbbed in his mouth as he came, and Ben did his best to catch every drop offered.

Seconds later, Ben's mind shattered as he came too. As pleasure flooded through him, everything became pure sensation and mindless movement. A small trickle of come escaped from the corner of Ben's mouth, but he would clean that as soon as he could think clearly again.

Chapter Nine

ETHAN

It had dropped well into the low-twenties overnight, but Ethan felt nothing except warmth as he spent the night curled around Ben's body, both of them tucked inside a down sleeping bag. He allowed his nose to trail through the soft curls of Ben's fair hair as he slowly came awake. Beneath the leftover trace of their campfire smoke, which had permeated through his curls, Ethan could still smell Ben's natural scent. Cinnamon mixed with Ben's male muskiness, making Ethan's pulse throb a little quicker.

Doing his best not to wake Ben, Ethan pressed a kiss to the top of his head and began gently maneuvering his body away from Ben's. His arms got only a couple of inches away from the warm body they were holding when Ben suddenly stretched out and pulled Ethan's arms tighter around his body.

"Not yet," Ben whispered.

With a contented little sigh, Ethan coiled himself back around Ben and pressed a flurry of gentle kisses to his nape. "Just a few more minutes," he allowed.

"Ethan, if I asked you something, would you answer me?"

That itself was a hard question to answer. There was so much in Ethan's past that he never talked about—never even wanted to think about. But this was Ben, and he had already given so much to Ethan. Besides, if Ethan really wanted the intimacy he so envied between Lucas and Ryan, then he had to be prepared to flay himself open for Ben. "I'll do my best." It was the most honest answer he was able to give.

"How'd you know about Stewart?"

Ethan suspected that would be the question, knowing Ben would ask at some point. Ben may have read all about his family's sordid mess online, but the finer points had been kept from the media. Very few people knew the truth about how Ethan had come to suspect his brother, and he preferred it that way.

As always, when he thought about those events from almost nine years ago, Ethan felt the familiar boulder of guilt fall heavily upon his shoulders. Some days it felt as though he were holding an entire world of guilt up, desperately trying to keep it from crushing him to the ground beneath his feet.

Ethan dragged in a breath and cinched his arms tighter around Ben as if that would somehow help him bear the load. "Stewart and I were never close. He was two years older and he was...cruel. All through my childhood, he took every chance he got to torment me in some way. Whenever I spoke to my parents, they invariably told me to harden up, be more of a man. I quickly learned to shut my mouth and keep my distance.

"Stewart moved out when I was in my late-teens, and I really didn't see much of him after that, but he'd occasionally insinuate himself into my life in some way— never a good way. We were both cops but at different stations, yet he still managed to cause trouble for me— stupid shit, like outing me and starting ridiculous rumors that I had crushes on various colleagues. It's better, but there's still that undercurrent of homophobic bullshit in the macho world of the police force. The stupid thing is that even with all that, and knowing his nature, I still couldn't believe he'd done it... I hesitated to report him, and it cost...it cost a girl her life."

"Oh, Ethan. I didn't know. I'm so sorry."

Ethan shook his head, determined to get his story out. "He taunted me...the killer. He started leaving me messages at the scenes. Even sent Polaroids of his victims to my home. Nobody could work out why me. I wasn't even a lead on his case. I'd attended a few of the scenes, and I was on the task force, but I was a nobody on the case."

Ben began shifting in his arms, and Ethan suspected he was going to turn around to face him, but Ethan couldn't do this with Ben watching him; he couldn't bear to see the flinch of disgust he knew would come. Even if Ben did somehow understand Ethan's actions, there would always be that brief moment of revulsion and disappointment when Ethan explained how he'd let an innocent seventeen-year-old girl die terribly at the hands of his brother.

"Please, Ben, stay where you are." Ben didn't argue and stopped turning over, moving instead to curl back into Ethan's arms. "Elizabeth Lanewood was the second-last girl to die. She should have been the last. Stewart was trying to get caught... I think he really wanted it all to end, but I couldn't, or maybe wouldn't, accept it was him, even when he presented me with such obvious evidence." Ethan shook his head, disgusted with himself all over again, just as he was every single time he thought about it.

"About a month after we found Elizabeth's body, he sent me a Polaroid. In it, she was tied up like all the other girls had been, except there was a difference, but it was insignificant—except to me. When Stewart was particularly cruel to me when we were little, he'd tie my hands and feet and beat the holy hell out of me. He'd always tie the rope in a bow; he said it was to make a little fag boy like me look pretty. In the Polaroid, Elizabeth's ropes were tied in bows, and her initials, EL, were the same as mine. I saw it, Ben. I knew deep down what it meant, but I couldn't believe... He'd always been an asshole, sure, but a killer? I couldn't wrap my head around it. For days, I tried to convince myself to report it, but by the time I'd found the guts, his need to kill had won again, and seventeen-year-old Jaymee Price died because of my weakness."

"Jesus, Ethan. Have you been carrying this around with you all this time?"

"I could have saved her. I could have. Half of the officers on the task force hated me for not saying anything sooner, and the other half hated me for saying anything at all. You know that old brothers-in-blue logic. I couldn't win, and my parents...well, they still believe Stewart is innocent and I set him up. I fucked up. I fucked up, and a girl died because of it, Ben."

Whether he wanted it or not, Ethan felt Ben turn in his arms and grab his cheeks, forcing him to hold eye contact. "None of it was your fault. None of it. A rope tied in a bow...the same initials as one of the victims? Come on, man. That's pretty thin. They're lucky you thought of it at all. You did your best. You trust your family. I bet you've seen plenty of people thoroughly shocked that it was their loved one who did it."

"But I was a cop. I should have known better."

"Ethan, the only one who should be feeling guilt about any of this is Stewart. And don't get me started on your parents."

Ethan wanted so badly to believe him and maybe one day he could throw off the shackles of guilt, but not just yet.

"You're from New Orleans, right?" Ben asked.

"Yeah."

"What happened to the accent?"

Ethan had the famous Cajun accent at one point, but when he'd taken off, changed his name, and found a new life, he'd shed the accent when he'd discarded his last name. "I got rid of it. Tried to talk with as little accent as possible. I was in hiding, so losing the accent was part of my disguise."

Ben smiled sadly and pressed his lips softly to his. What could he possibly say about the shit show that had been his life?

After a quick breakfast and a few minutes packing up their campsite, they were on their way at a pace that should see them reaching the commune around lunchtime. That would give them several hours of daylight to observe the comings and goings and find a safe way in and out. They'd done the hard part of the trek the day before; today should be mostly heading back downhill.

Ethan had never felt so raw or exposed to another person, but in a weird sort of way he felt so much better for having shared his past with Ben. There was a lightness to him as though that planet-sized guilt he'd been holding up for so long was now the size of a small moon. It was a start.

They spent much of the morning trekking in either silence or in low voices of lighthearted conversation, a welcome change from the heaviness of the morning. After a few hours, Ben suddenly stopped stock-still before him. He held up one hand with a closed fist, and though Ethan had never been in the military, he recognized it for what it was— a command for him to stop and remain still. It took a few moments for Ethan to hear what had clearly alerted Ben— soft voices coming from a little way ahead of them. It could be sentries, or it could be nothing—a couple of random hikers crossing their path—but if they were spotted and the cult warned, this was all for nothing.

Whoever they were; they were coming closer.

Ben gestured for Ethan to follow him and the finger to his lips indicated for Ethan to do so silently, not that he needed the hint. He followed Ben into the thicker tree line where they both very carefully removed their packs and waited.

In minutes, three people approached and were almost at the spot where he and Ben had left the trail. One was a young man, possibly no more than twenty. He was a little above average height but he could have used a few pounds as he was far too thin. His feet dragged as he shuffled along, and Ethan thought he was about five minutes away from collapse. With him were two girls, obviously sisters, though one looked year or two younger and the other no more than fifteen, maybe even younger. Neither was quite as thin as the young man, but they looked every bit as exhausted. Ethan tried to concentrate on what they were saying.

"Zach, maybe we should rest. It won't do us any good for you to collapse in a heap," the older girl suggested.

"Not yet, Phia. We're not far enough away. I can manage."

"What if they catch us, Phia? I don't wanna marry him. Please."

"Don't worry, Mary. They won't catch us. They probably don't even know we've gone yet. Come on." It was Zach who answered the younger girl, and Ethan could see the fear on all of their faces in spite of Zach's confident words.

From beside him, Ethan could feel Ben turn and lean his head closer so that his lips were right at Ethan's ear. "I'm gonna go out and talk to them. I'm betting they're from the cult and are trying to get out. We may be able to help each other." The words were barely whispered, but Ethan heard them and agreed. He nodded his head and followed as Ben cautiously slipped out from the trees they'd sought shelter in.

All three young people startled immediately at their approach, the youngest girl doing her best, but not quite managing, to completely stifle a scream. Zach immediately moved to place himself in front of the girls, and though he was the oldest, Phia, refused to move from his side.

For a tense, awkward moment nobody spoke. Standing there eyeing each other was getting them nowhere, so Ethan put his hands out in front of him, palms up—the universal "I'm not going to hurt you" gesture. "It's all right. It's okay. We won't hurt you," he said. He watched as Phia and Zach glanced briefly at each other before turning their untrusting gaze back to him. "Are you three okay? Can we help you?"

"We're fine. We don't need any help," Zach answered, his manner fiery, despite his obvious exhaustion.

"Look," Ben spoke for the first time. "Did you guys come from the commune, from Arnold Piper's camp?"

Another look was exchanged between the older two, and this time it was laced with terror. "No. I don't even know who that is." The lie was as plain in Zach's voice as it was on his guileless face.

"We can help you. Help you get away. We're here to try to get two little girls out. Maya and Riley. They're Ethan's nieces," Ben said as he gestured to Ethan. "We can help you."

"Two little girls?" Phia clarified. "How old?"

"Two and a half. They're twins," Ethan answered.

"There's twin girls at the camp, arrived last week, but we were told their names are Rebecca and Miriam." It was the younger girl, Mary, who spoke.

Ethan rooted around in his pocket and pulled out the photo Maggie had given him. "Is this them?"

All three of the young people looked at the photo and all three silently nodded their heads. Mary broke the silence this time. "They're your nieces?"

"Yes. Their mom is very sick and she asked me to come and get them. She doesn't want... She needs them with her." Ethan wasn't sure yet how much these three disliked Piper and whatever was going on in the cult. For all he knew, they may be fleeing for a very personal and insular reason, but still believed in what Piper was doing, so he decided it was best not to say anything that may get their backs up.

"He said their mother was dead," Mary whispered.

"Can you help us?" Ben asked.

Ethan could already see Zach's head shaking, and for a brief moment, he thought they weren't going to help them, but then Zach turned his large green eyes to him. Ethan could see tears pooling, and he could feel the tremble in Zach's body when he reached out and grabbed onto Ethan's forearms. "You have to get them out. You have to get them out now." Zach desperately warned. Ethan could see he was shaking violently now. Was it with anger, fear, or a bit of both? "Listen, please, you must listen. My father's insane. He's going to... I think he plans for everyone at the camp to die by the end of the week."

From the gasps and near collapse of the two girls, Ethan suspected this was news to them also. Phia recovered first, turning fierce anger to Zach. "What are you talking about? Why didn't you tell us? We could have gotten more out."

"No, we couldn't have, Phia. You know the rest still believe every single thing he says. You're only leaving because... You only wanted to get out because of Mary."

"But the children, Zach...the babies," she pleaded.

"I know. I know," Zach said through gritted teeth while still keeping a death grip on Ethan's arms. "I was gonna report it as soon as we got out and hope someone would be able to go in and save them. We couldn't... How could we bring them out with us? Which ones would we have chosen to save and which would we have left behind?"

Both Phia and Mary quietly sobbed at Zach's words. Zach released Ethan and did his best to hold them both in his scrawny arms—a heavy burden for such a young man.

"How many kids are in the camp?" Ben asked.

"About twenty, from newborns to those around Mary's age. I left because...Master Piper was going to marry Mary tomorrow, and she was so scared. She's only fourteen. I was seventeen when I was married to Jonah a few months ago," Phia said with conviction, as if being married off at seventeen was so much better. "We've left them behind... twenty children and babies."

"Listen to me," Ben's voice took on an authoritative tone, and Ethan couldn't help the shiver that raced through his body at the sound of it. "Ethan and I can help. But we'll need you to help us too. We need a map of the camp, information on guards, weapons, anything at all. Can you do that?"

"I can." Zach's voice resonated with a strength his body seemed to be sorely lacking. "Arnold Piper is my father, but he believed I was weak, pathetic, so he never gave me much thought. He usually forgot I was around. He never kept his secrets from me like he did with everyone else. I was no threat to him. I have whatever information you need to know about that camp. I can help you."

"Ben, I think we should call in the authorities. This is too big for just the two of us."

Ethan watched as Ben thought over his suggestion. No matter how good they were, and Ethan knew Ben's skills were unsurpassed, they needed more manpower. "Agreed. But let's hold off...at least until we've seen the camp and hopefully gotten the girls out. Once we've done that and have more intel, then we make the call. Please. Trust me on this," he pleaded, though, Ethan didn't know why Ben thought he'd have to beg him. He'd have trusted Ben with his life.

"Deal. We go in, get the girls, gather information, and then call in the cavalry." Ben's answering smile took his breath away with both its beauty and obvious joy at the trust Ethan had given him. He was surprised how this thing had blown up so big and so quickly, but Ethan knew he couldn't have had a better man by his side now that it had.

Chapter Ten

BEN

After much discussion and arguing back and forth, they agreed to set up camp for Phia and Mary in a small clearing off the main trail along the edge of the stream. The girls were left there with sufficient supplies to see them through several days and a sat phone they had agreed to use to call Cameron if he, Ethan, and Zach were not back at the camp by seven the next morning. Ethan had to teach the girls how to use the phone; they'd never even seen one, never mind used one.

Zach was forced to eat a substantial meal before they set off. Ben suspected that as the "pathetic and weak" son of Arnold Piper, Zach had been more or less neglected. He hadn't missed the almost-faded yellowing on the left side of Zach's face, nor did he miss the unnatural angle of several of the young man's fingers. So, he had to assume that when Zach wasn't being neglected, he was being abused. It was yet another bone Ben had to pick with Arnold Piper.

Zach had told them how he and Phia had grown up together and how, despite the shunning Zach endured from the rest of the commune on the word of his father, Phia had maintained a secret friendship with him. So, it was natural she turned to Zach when the need to get her sister away from the camp had become urgent.

Ben had known it for years, but he couldn't help marveling again at what a fucked-up world humans had made for themselves. Power and money. That's what it usually came down to. Lucas's brother had tried to kill him for money, and Zach's father had brutalized him for power. If he lived to a hundred, Ben would never understand people, and he wasn't entirely sure he wanted to.

"The first lookout is about five minutes that way," Zach advised. He and the two girls had slipped past the lookouts when they'd fled, but Ben wanted to disable the closest one to the camp they'd set up so it was one less thing to worry about on their way out. Zach had told him that the guard only changed every couple of days, and there wasn't a change due for another twenty-four hours at least. No regular check-in was required by the sentries, so Ben could safely incapacitate the guard without fear of discovery. Perhaps this Piper clown wasn't as smart as he thought.

"Stay here," Ben ordered, but despite meaning it for both men, he could sense Ethan on his tail as he slipped away closer to the watch post. "I meant you, too, Ethan."

"I know you did but I'm not letting you do this alone." Ethan's tone brooked no argument so Ben merely shrugged and continued on his way.

The watch post consisted of one small tent manned by two young men. They couldn't have been much older than Zach, and they looked placid, not at all threatening. Looks could be deceiving though, so Ben and Ethan still approached from behind with caution.

As it turned out, it was incredibly effortless to have them both tied and gagged before they even seemed to register the presence of Ethan and Ben. Ethan had been stealthy and efficient as he'd dealt with his man, and Ben was ridiculously turned on as he watched him work.

"Okay, now, we move to the other post?" Ethan asked as he shuffled the young man he'd bound over to sit beside the one Ben had dealt with.

"I think we can probably leave it. There's a few miles between each. That should be a large enough area to work with. Good job, by the way." He winked and smiled a little at the blush that crept across Ethan's face. He leaned in and pressed a kiss to Ethan's cold and wind-roughened lips. A soft gasp came from behind them and they turned to find Zach watching at the entry flap of the tent; his eye's boggled and his lips parted in a little oval shape of shock. He offered a stuttered apology and slunk away, back into the tree line.

Did no one follow his fucking orders?

Ben knew exactly what many of these religious cults thought of homosexuality and wondered if they'd just lost their guide. Ethan started to move forward to go after him, but Ben reached out and held him back by the forearm. "I'll go," he said. Of the two, Ben was definitely the less physically threatening, so he figured that might help Zach feel a little more comfortable if a fear of homosexuals had been drilled into him.

Surprisingly, Zach had only retreated a few meters into the trees, so Ben found him easily. His face was flushed, and he was breathing heavily as he rested against one of the larger trunks.

"You okay, Zach?"

Zach was maybe six foot, possibly even a little taller, if he carried himself without the hunch to his shoulders, but he had slid a fair way down the trunk so his enormous green eyes had to peek up at him from beneath his sandy brown hair. "I never... I didn't think such a thing was possible," he managed to splutter.

"Two men kissing?" Ben asked, somewhat confused. He'd expected derision and disgust, but Zach seemed to be completely ignorant of homosexuality actually existing.

"Yeah...I mean it's a man and a woman." Zach shook his head. "Are there other men who kiss?"

Christ, talk about your sheltered upbringing. "Yeah, Zach. There's all kinds of sexuality: gays, lesbians, asexual, bisexual... Look, it's a long list. You've never heard about any of that? Ya know, two guys together, two girls..."

If possible, Zach's eyes boggled even larger. "No. My father never taught us anything like that. It was always a man and a woman together, well, a man with several women, really. We had very little contact with the outside world. Some of the people who joined us would tell us bits and pieces about what it was like...how sinful the world was, but there was never any mention—" Zach's sudden flurry of tears caught Ben off guard. He'd never been much of a crier and never knew how to handle people around him who were doing it.

He stood quietly until Zach's tears seemed to dry up. Zach sniffled and wiped at his nose before turning to look at Ben. "I never knew...I always thought there was something terribly, terribly wrong with me..." Tears formed again in his wide eyes but refused to fall.

Well, that seemed to explain Zach's reaction.

"Zach, there's nothing wrong with you at all. It's completely natural...whoever you might be attracted to." Jesus, this wasn't the time or the place—and he wasn't the person to deal with someone's coming out or sexual awakening or whatever you wanted to call it. "Come on. Let's go be heroes, and I promise when this is over we'll have a good, long chat about...stuff."

As Zach rose, Ben noticed he stood a little taller, maybe even a little prouder. Fuck others for making people feel bad about who they were—that was something else about people he'd never understand.

Ethan was hovering over one of the captured men at the watch post when he and Zach walked back into the clearing and headed for the tent. For a brief moment Ben thought perhaps there'd been trouble until he realized that Ethan was helping the man drink from a water bottle. Ethan flicked a quick glance at them as they approached before going back to his task.

"Thought I'd better give them something to drink now; they could be tied up here for a while," Ethan explained.

Ben didn't have the heart to remind Ethan that they'd have no way of getting themselves to any kind of toilet once they were gone, but he supposed it was a better option than becoming dehydrated. With any luck, this would all be over by morning anyway.

"Everything okay?" Ethan side-eyed Zach as he asked the question of Ben.

"I think it's gonna be," Ben answered and again pressed a kiss to Ethan's waiting lips. There was no gasp this time, but he definitely heard Zach's breath hitch. "Okay. So, how far, Zach?" he turned to address the young man and just caught the tail end of a blush flittering over his features.

"It took us about an hour, maybe, to reach the watch post from the camp."

"Excellent. Once we get there, we're going to observe for a while. But anything you can tell us on the way that may help…"

"I'll be able to point out the tent the girls are in, the tent that's my father's, where the guns are…all of that." Zach's help would be invaluable and save a hell of a lot of time.

They should be able to get the twins out with little trouble. Ben's private plans hadn't changed, and in fact, were even more urgent after what Zach had told them.

A full-on FBI incursion was bound to lead to some, maybe even many deaths, but if Ben could pull off his plan—well, there might still be deaths—a death—but at least no innocents should be among them.

AS BEN WATCHED the people of the commune go about their daily business, he thought about how so many of them seemed to have that same hunch to their posture that Zach had and the same placid, almost docile, equanimity of the guards at the watch post. They were not quite zombie-like, but most of them would definitely not put up any kind of fight, especially the women. A handful of men seemed to move about the camp with purpose—and with weapons.

Ben saw at least eight men carrying Ruger 10/22 rifles, and he suspected a few more had handguns concealed on their body, judging from a few ill-placed bulges he'd spotted. He felt the reassurance of his own weapon strapped along the length of his back and hoped he'd only have to use it once. As far as he'd been able to detect, the women were unarmed, as were most of the younger men. There was no discernable patrolling of the camp's border, which lined up to what Zach had told them about "border protection of the camp being everyone's responsibility."

Ethan was kneeling in the undergrowth beside him, and Ben could see his body straining forward as though it was a constant battle for him to keep himself from charging blindly into the camp and grabbing his baby nieces. Ben could certainly understand the inclination toward action. There was a madman in charge here, and at any moment, he could call for the deaths of every person in the camp. They were so close it must be maddening for Ethan to be so near and yet have to hold himself back.

Suddenly, Ethan collapsed a little onto his knees, and Ben heard the softest little puff of "Oh, Jesus" fall from his lips. When Ben turned his gaze in the direction Ethan was staring, he saw what had disturbed him. Walking hand in hand with a young girl of maybe fifteen were Maya and Riley. They both had golden hair swept up in pigtails and cherubic faces that should have been coated with unconstrained joy, but instead, both little girls seemed listless and entirely disinterested in the world around them. For a moment, Ben considered they may have been drugged. They moved as though they were merely going through the motions, and though Ben had no experience with young children, even he could see that it was a terribly unnatural state for a couple of two-year-olds.

Guessing how Ethan must be feeling at the sight, Ben reached out and grabbed his nearest hand, bringing it to his lips and pressing several kisses to Ethan's knuckles before giving it a gentle squeeze. It was meant as a gesture of comfort but also as an anchor to keep Ethan from charging into the clearing.

When Ethan turned to look at him, Ben offered a slight smile before flicking his head backward to signal for them to retreat to the spot where they had left Zach. Ben got there first and immediately turned and opened his arms wide. Ethan walked straight into them, and that right there was everything he'd ever dreamed of having with Ethan.

Ben held him until he'd calmed, and they eventually pulled away from each other. "Are you all right?"

Ethan nodded. "What have they done to my nieces?"

"Don't know. Zach?" Ben called to the young man who'd stood silently since their return. "Do they drug the kids? You know, like give them anything to make them...calm?" Calm wasn't a fitting enough descriptor, but Ben couldn't bring himself to utter words like trance, daze, shock. The ramifications of something other than drugs causing that kind of abnormal behavior was not something he wanted to think about.

"I don't... I'm not really sure. The kids are always quiet, but they're not allowed to be anything but. Women and children are supposed to be quiet...um, do as they're told, I guess. If they drug them, I'm not sure what they might use. I'm sorry."

"Don't be. You've been a great help, Zach." Ethan turned his attention back to Ben and asked, "What's our next move?"

Ben sat cross-legged on the ground and pulled out the roughly drawn map of the camp that Zach had sketched for them. "Zach, what's the night routine? Do people settle down early? Are there extra patrols? Anything like that?"

Both Ethan and Zach joined him on the ground and peered over the diagram. Ben could see the tent where the twins slept clearly marked. It was, unfortunately, right in the center of the camp. They'd need to be exceptionally quiet going in. As much as he hated to even think it, it might actually be a good thing that the girls appeared so docile—maybe they'd be quiet enough during the extraction not to raise the alarm.

"Okay." Zach's too-thin arm moved over the map, his finger pointing a circle around the edge of the camp. "So, at night, two men walk the perimeter here, in opposite directions so they pass each other once every circuit. Another three men usually walk a kind of zigzag pattern across the interior, and they usually pass each other at different intervals too. Most people are in their tents just after dark."

Ben nodded. It was a satisfactory enough guard detail, but there were gaping holes—ones he and Ethan could easily exploit to get the twins out. The biggest risk as far as he was concerned was still going to be one or both of the girls making a fuss.

Beside him, Ethan practically vibrated with tension, and Ben would have done anything to alleviate the strain he had to be under. "Okay, so, we wait an hour after dark, head back to the camp and watch a couple of circuits. Once we're in the camp, there's not a lot of cover, so we're gonna have to try to get to the girls' tent in one go, otherwise we risk one of the inner guards spotting us. Zach, who'll be in the tent with the girls?"

"Um, besides them, I think there's two other kids in there as well as their mother—" Zach winced and flicked a startled and pained glance and Ethan. "I'm sorry, I mean obviously not your nieces' mother, but the other children's."

Ben watched pain fall over Ethan's features at the reminder of Maggie and what she was enduring. He loved Ethan with his entire heart, but he suspected the love between a parent and a child was a completely different kind of love, and he couldn't even begin to imagine the pain Maggie must be enduring being separated from her girls.

"Okay, Ethan, we're gonna get in that tent, and I'm sorry, but the mother will have to be neutralized first—she's our biggest risk. With luck, we won't wake the other kids, but the twins will definitely wake when we grab them. I, um...I have to know you'll be able to um—" Ben squirmed and shuffled around where he sat, hating to even have to say what was coming next, but it had to be said. "We may need to subdue the girls, Ethan, and I have to know you'll be able to do it."

Ethan was silent for so long Ben couldn't even find the courage to look up at him. "I understand, Ben. I can do it, promise." Finally Ben looked at Ethan. His face was pale and drawn, his body crumpled in on itself. Ben recognized the fear and nerves that would be wreaking the havoc he could plainly see hounding Ethan's body.

With any luck, this time tomorrow they'd all be home safely and be enjoying the reunion between mother and daughters—and watching Ethan squirm as he dealt with two toddlers who'd just hit the terrible twos.

Chapter Eleven

ETHAN

It was the eleventh time they'd watched the same men pass each other as they did their circuit of the camp. Ethan wondered if they'd watched long enough or if Ben would keep them waiting and watching even longer. They were well hidden, but the cold of the night was starting to ache in his bones, regardless of the cold-weather gear he was bundled in.

Despite his own career in law enforcement, Ethan was content to defer to Ben. Coming from a military background for one thing, Ben had more experience with this kind of mission. But Ethan also knew his emotional attachment to his sister and her daughters was compromising his ability to think clearly. He'd have loved nothing more than to walk into that camp with guns blazing, even though he knew what a disaster that would likely be. There were people in this camp who'd hurt his sister, and would one day hurt his nieces, if he did nothing to stop them, but there were also innocents, and he didn't want them hurt if he could avoid it.

From the corner of his eye, he caught Ben's hand signal for retreat. As quietly as he could, Ethan maneuvered himself backward, only turning when they were a safe distance from the edge of camp. Behind him, Ben moved with an absolute silence that only someone with his training could manage.

"Okay, Ethan, I think we're ready. When the two outer guards cross we have two minutes, no more, to make our way to the tent where the girls are before the inner guards crisscross the area. Once we're at the tent, we need to get to the eastern side for our entry point. There should be no one in that area for a good five minutes. That should be plenty of time to get in and out again. We'll have to sit tight with the girls while the guards cross on the opposite side, and then we'll have another minute, maximum, to get completely out of camp before the outer guards pass again."

It sounded close, only minutes here and there, but Ethan knew that in situations like this minutes felt like hours. The trouble would come from the unexpected: one of the guards stopping to tie a shoelace, an unforeseen change of guards, one of the other cult members suddenly needing to use a toilet. Anything could happen, and they'd need to be ready for it.

"Ethan? You gonna be okay to do this?"

As scared as he was, the terror of leaving the girls behind was far worse. He couldn't lose them—or Ben. "Yeah. I can do this."

They were standing in a press of trees, the only light coming from the three-quarter moon. Ethan grunted when Ben's body hit his, forcing his back to slam into the tree behind him. Ben's kiss was hard and punishing and messy, and Ethan felt every bit of emotion bleeding from Ben into him through the kiss. Ben's body wriggled in his arms, his hands grabbing and pulling at Ethan as though he was trying to either climb Ethan's body or split him open and crawl inside. Ethan gave it all back to Ben in equal measure. He knew it for what it was. It was a goodbye kiss, in case something went horribly wrong.

In the quiet of the night, all Ethan could hear was the occasional click of their teeth and the heavy breaths from him and Ben, escaping whenever there was a tiny gap between their lips. Ben pulled away and Ethan chased after him, unwilling to let the kiss die. Never had he felt such desperation and desire twirling through the air between them, preventing Ethan from allowing Ben to escape. He could have stayed like this forever; all he needed was Ben.

All too soon, the present came battering back, and he reluctantly released the fierce grip he'd had on Ben. Ethan's body struggled between near collapse from the ferociousness of the kiss and igniting into an unstoppable flame of passion. His primordial brain ached to reach out and grab Ben again, pull him closer, taste every fucking inch of him, but his more practical brain fought and won. They had work to do.

Ethan stepped farther away from Ben, who stood before him panting hard, eyes wide and unmoving from Ethan's, a sly grin slowly forming on his kiss-swollen lips.

"Jesus Christ, Ethan, when this is over..." Ben let his words trail off, but Ethan knew exactly where his thoughts were heading.

"When this is over, Ben, I'm gonna have you every fucking way I can think of."

The sly grin transformed into a beaming smile. "Now, we're getting somewhere with the dirty talk." Ben leaned forward again, but this kiss was sweet and sensual, whereas the previous one had been unbridled passion. Ben felt so good against Ethan's body and in his arms.

Finally, they managed to extract themselves, and Ethan could see in Ben's features that he was all lethal sniper once again. "Okay. Let's get this done."

Ethan followed behind Ben as they worked their way back to the campsite. It took only a few minutes of waiting before the guards bypassed each other just meters in front of where they were hiding, and Ethan straightened as soon as Ben started to move. He trod as silently and as quickly as he could, hardly daring to breathe in case he was heard. He held his nerve as soon as they breached the open space of the campground, only relaxing once they'd made it to the eastern side of the tent that contained his tiny nieces.

Ben stood at his side watching, his quiet sentinel, as he flicked open his knife to cut through the material of the tent. They were cheap tents, so the material cut easily. He'd made a gash of little more than two feet when he felt Ben's hand drop to his shoulder—signaling him to stop. Ethan turned his head to peer up at Ben, whose gaze was fixed on a point somewhere to his right. Ethan could hear the crunch of booted feet obviously unconcerned with being caught. He froze. The sound was coming from behind him, from whatever point Ben was staring at. He carefully swiveled and caught a glimpse of a man walking out from between the tents, his back to them. Ethan had no idea what to expect when Ben suddenly struck, his reflexes lightning fast.

The man was taller and considerably bulkier than him, but Ben hadn't hesitated to step up behind him, their bodies almost touching. He snaked one arm around the man's neck, and the other around the man's torso. It almost looked like it was a lover's embrace if he didn't know the true motives behind it. It all happened so fast the man didn't try to strike back. Ben lowered him gently to the ground, and then fished around in his pockets, bringing out a few zip ties. In less than thirty seconds, Ben had the man incapacitated, bound, and gagged. He flicked his eyes up meeting Ethan's searching gaze with uncertainty. Surely, he had to know

Ethan would never judge him for helping with this. Ethan smiled and nodded, the best he could do to quietly reassure him.

Ben gestured to the man's feet and Ethan hurried to help him lift the body. They were making more noise than was ideal, but in situations like these, Ethan knew they had to roll with it and do the best they could. They quickly placed the unconscious body as close to a nearby sheltered tree as they were able, and Ben wasted no time wrapping the body around the trunk and zip tying his linked hands to his linked feet. He wouldn't be going anywhere when he woke.

Ethan returned to the tent, working even faster as time crept on and the risk of discovery became greater. The slash he'd made in the tent was big enough now to allow them entry, and Ethan carefully poked his head inside.

It was dark, but he was able to make out several figures lying huddled together. From their size, he knew they were children, at least four of them. There was another larger figure lying closest to the flap of the tent on the other side of the clustered children. Ethan's heart thundered in his chest, and he took a moment to take a deep breath and do his best to find some calm.

As carefully as he could, Ethan crept inside the tent. He immediately moved to the side to allow Ben entry. They looked at each other, and even in the darkness, Ethan could read the expression on Ben's face. Untangling Maya and Riley from the knotted group of children without waking the others wouldn't be easy. The very last thing Ethan had wanted to do was restrain or frighten the children in any way, but that scenario seemed more and more likely.

Ethan pulled out his flashlight and set the beam to low. In the darkness of the wilderness, even the low setting on his flashlight might be too much, but he had to be able to clearly identify Maya and Riley. He held the light down so it would be less noticeable from the outside of the tent. He trailed the beam over the sleeping bodies of the children, desperately hoping the light was low enough not to wake them.

In the tangle of limbs, Ethan could make out two tiny bodies with their arms wrapped around each other, entwined together as they had probably once been in the womb. Desperate for comfort and safety in the wake of being stolen from their mother, they were clinging to each other even in sleep. Ethan's heart clenched and then swelled like a balloon at the sight, and for just a moment, he wondered if it might burst.

From behind him, he heard the muffled sounds of Ben dealing with the adult who'd been sleeping only moments ago, blissfully unaware of their presence. She wouldn't be hurt, Ethan trusted Ben with that, but she wouldn't be going anywhere for a while, nor would she be alerting anyone else to their presence. He turned briefly and watched as Ben spoke quietly to the woman he'd just finished trussing up. Ethan could see her wide eyes watching Ben's every move. He could tell she was scared, certainly, but not terrified.

Ben moved to his side, and without a word exchanged between them, Ethan pointed the beam of his light again over the sleeping forms of Maya and Riley. It'd be awkward picking them up, especially given that Ethan couldn't stand upright in the tent and Ben could barely manage it.

Carefully stepping around the children, Ethan crouched beside his nieces. They were identical, so he had no idea if it was Maya or Riley that he gently curled his arms around and pulled to his chest. She stirred and wriggled and Ethan softly shushed her, hoping that the fog of sleep would hold tight to her and she wouldn't awaken terrified in a strange man's arms.

As soon as he had her safely cradled against him, he crawled away as best he could on his knees, making room for Ben to similarly grab the other little girl. In seconds, Ben was beside him. Ethan looked down to the child in Ben's arms and found wide eyes staring back at him. Ben had one of his hands hovering over the child's mouth, ready to stifle any sound she may make. She looked alarmed but not terrified so Ethan thought maybe she was used to strange people being around her after the last few days here at the camp.

Moving as carefully as possible so he didn't wake the girl in his arms, Ethan poked his head through the gap in the tent. If their timing was right, they had maybe two minutes to get out and back into the relative safety of the trees.

No one was in sight. They'd have to move now. Ethan turned and nodded once at Ben and quickly flashed a glance at the woman trussed up behind them. She was still, but watching their every move.

Ethan shoved one of his legs through the gap and pushed off so that he stood as soon as his body cleared the tent. He moved as close to a large nearby tree as possible, using it for cover in case somebody wandered by. Again Ben was beside him in moments, and he could hear him gently crooning to the child in his arms. Actually, now that he was closer, Ethan could hear that Ben was singing something about all the pretty little horses and having cake. Jesus, this man had him twisted up in knots.

From their safe distance, they watched as the two guards crossed and waited for a few seconds to pass, before making their move. The inner guards would come by in approximately one minute, so they didn't have much time. When Ben nudged his shoulder, Ethan moved, doing his best not to juggle his niece too much.

It was still all quiet in the camp as Ethan sprinted back toward the cover of trees. He placed his feet as carefully as he could; knowing that a fall now would be disastrous. Once he cleared the tree line, he didn't stop, though, he had to slow his run now that he was back in the trees and his only light the waxing moon. He made his way as quickly as he could to where they'd left Zach. He trusted that Ben was right on his tail, though as always, he couldn't hear the other man. No wonder he'd made such an excellent sniper.

In his arms, the child squirmed, clearly woken by the jostling from his movements, but she made no sound, and as useful as that was right now, it also scared the crap out of Ethan. Both girls should be crying, at the very least, having been woken from sleep by a couple of strange men stealing them in the middle of the night.

After ten minutes, they reached the clearing where Zach waited for them. Ethan could see him pacing as they approached, but a broad grin formed when he turned and saw them.

As soon as he stopped moving, Ethan cuddled the little girl in his arms and murmured softly to her, just nonsense words but occasionally telling her he was taking her back to her mother. Ben was similarly comforting his other niece.

"Holy...you guys did it. I've gotta be honest: I thought maybe you wouldn't make it back."

"Let's save the celebrating for now and get back to Phia and Mary." Ben wasn't even breathing heavily as he spoke. He'd obviously stayed in shape despite his shooting months ago. "Zach, I need you to take the little one for me. I'm gonna drop back—"

"No. We stay together." Ethan sounded desperate and he knew it, but he needed Ben to stay with them. He hated the thought of being separated under these circumstances.

"Ethan, I'll be right behind you, but I need to fall back a bit, in case the camp is alerted and they come after us. I'll be able to give you guys some time." Ethan shook his head. He didn't like this one bit. They should stay together. "Hey, Ethan. Listen to me. I'll be fine. We got out clean; this is just a precaution. Get back to Phia and Mary, call in the cavalry, and I'll be right beside you when that chopper lifts off." Ben threw one of the carriers to Zach who quickly donned it.

Damn it. Ethan hated it, but Ben was right. "You better be."

Ben winked and handed the child off to Zach. She fussed a little and whimpered but soon settled once she was in the rig. Ben walked back over to Ethan and took the child from his arms to allow Ethan to get the other rig on. In a minute he was ready, and Ben handed the little girl back.

Once she was settled, Ben looked down at the little girl. He gently swept the hair away from her face and cupped her cheek, stroking his thumb back and forth before looking up at Ethan. Ethan lowered his face and Ben rewarded him with a sweet, soft kiss, more just a brush of their lips but it spoke volumes. By the time Ethan opened his eyes, Ben was gone, vanished back into the scrub like a ghost.

The last few days since Maggie's call had been like a nightmare all tangled up with utter happiness, and now, having to leave Ben behind... It was fucking hard to do. The small weight in his arms brought him round from those thoughts, though. There were two little toddlers to think about, and he had to get them out. He had to keep them safe.

Gritting his teeth against the pull of going after Ben, Ethan turned and headed in the direction of where they'd left Phia and Mary. It'd be a long trek with their added burdens, but Zach, though skinny, looked fit, and Ethan would carry both girls if it came down to it.

"Come on, Zach. Let's go," Ethan said as he passed the young man still staring back the way Ben had left.

"He's kind of amazing, isn't he?"

"Yeah. Yeah, he is. Ben's...the best," Ethan replied, having no doubt about whom Zach was referring to.

They walked quietly but quickly together, not daring to stop for fear of discovery. The girls slept throughout most of the journey, and Ethan suspected they had definitely been given something. It was unnatural for two-year-olds to be this quiet and subdued. He'd kill those fucking cult nutters if he got the chance.

They were more than halfway back to Phia and Mary when they heard the single shot.

Chapter Twelve

BEN

As soon as Ethan and Zach were safely away, Ben returned to the edge of camp. He pulled his rifle from the halter on his back and prepared to use it. There was only one possible way he could think of to delay Piper's plans for mass suicide in the cult, and that was to sideline him before he gave the order. Ben suspected the second-in-command would follow through on his leader's wishes, but with any luck, he'd want revenge on whoever shot Piper first. It was the best plan he'd been able to come up with.

It was all still quiet in the camp so Ben positioned himself as best he could among the grove of trees. He had a clear line of sight to the tent they'd recently liberated the girls from. Once they were discovered missing, he hoped Piper would be called there, and Ben would get his chance. He settled in to wait.

Thirty minutes passed in the blink of an eye. Ben was used to this: the waiting, the absolute stillness needed to remain undetected, the single-minded focus of his brain on his target area. His body had fallen into that odd state of being on high alert and yet perfectly calm, long ago. All he needed was Arnold fucking Piper to stick his head into the open.

Occasional thoughts of Ethan tried to force their way into his brain, but he resolutely pushed them away. He couldn't afford to fuck up; there were too many lives at stake, not least of which was Ethan's.

The silence was broken by a small cry, almost a whimper, and then Ben could see the entry to the tent where the girls had been kept, jiggling as someone inside fought to open it. The small body of a child maybe four-years-old eventually crept out, and though they were whimpering, they were eerily calm for a frightened child who would have just discovered their mother or caretaker tied up.

Ben tightened his muscles and flexed his fingers as he watched the child toddle toward another tent. The next few minutes were a flurry of activity as a man came out of the tent the child had entered and went to check on the scene the child had obviously reported to him. To his credit, and Ben's relief, the man didn't panic and call out. Instead, he strode purposefully from the tent, the now untied woman in tow, and headed in the direction Ben knew Piper's tent to be in. Men came running, and before he could even see him, Ben heard a man barking out orders. It had to be Piper.

Zach had pointed out the leader to him and Ethan earlier, so Ben had no trouble picking him out when a group of men eventually arrived at the scene of the twins' "abduction." His finger rested a hair's breadth from the trigger, and Ben kept his sight pinned down the barrel of his rifle. He never thought he'd be in this position again, but if the shot was there to be taken, he knew he would.

Piper entered the tent flanked by several other men, all of whom had blocked a clear shot to his target in some way. He could hear their voices drifting across the compound, but despite missing most of the words spoken, Ben could hear anger in the tone.

Even in the cold of the night, Ben could feel a bead of sweat trickle down his forehead and welcomed it. A few years ago, he would have got off the shot without a second thought, with no doubts, no nervous sweating, just a cold hard shot delivered to his target's head. It wasn't so easy now and that was a good thing.

Ethan's gorgeous face flickered across his mind, the faces of the zombie-like little girls stolen from their mother, Maggie's wasted body shaking with tears as she spoke of her stolen children, Mary's panicked face when Phia had told them she was going to be married to Piper. He wasn't usually that man who could take the shot without hesitation anymore, but he could do it this time. For them.

The noise coming from the tent eased off, and Ben watched as man after man came out. Finally, Piper stepped through the flap, and Ben took a steadying breath. At this distance, there was enough light coming from the moon for him to work with. He lined up his shot, aiming at the man's torso and eased out his breath as he gently depressed the trigger. Piper's body flinched and crumpled to the ground before anyone around him had even reacted to the sound of the shot.

Ben resisted the urge to jump up and sprint away. A noisy and inelegant escape would only give away his position sooner, sending men scurrying to tail him. If he edged away as quietly as he could, he'd have more time to put some distance between him and the men in the camp.

After a few moments of watching the growing panic within the camp, Ben began moving as swiftly and quietly as he could. He slid backward until he was farther into the coverage offered by the trees, and then he carefully stood. He stepped cautiously for a hundred or so yards and only then felt confident to run.

After the shot, the noise in the compound had silenced briefly, but from behind him Ben could hear a cacophony of voices, shouting and screaming as panic set into the commune. The sound would provide ample cover for him as he fled through the bushes.

Ethan and Zach shouldn't be far from meeting Phia and Mary, and he knew in the quiet of the night and the echo of the mountains Ethan would have heard the shot. He wished he could have it another way, but if he'd told Ethan of his plans, he would have either tried to stop him or stayed to help, and neither of those options were acceptable.

Ben ran as fast as he could manage in the dark of the night. The moon provided enough light to illuminate the trees, but smaller branches and leaves were lost to the darkness, and he had several scratches on his face already from brushing by them.

Every few hundred yards, he stopped to listen for any sound coming from behind him. So far, he'd heard very little, and certainly not enough for him to be worried about Piper's men being right on his heels. With luck, this would be a clean getaway. Despite his body warming from the exercise, Ben could feel the temperature was dropping, and every so often the moon disappeared behind cloud cover. He suspected a storm was coming and could only hope they'd be safely on Cameron's chopper before it blew in.

Thankfully, Ben had kept up his exercise regime after getting out of the hospital. He was breathing hard already, and if he'd gotten lax after his shooting, he'd be really struggling now. It was only another ten minutes maximum back to where they'd left Phia and Mary if he maintained this pace, and Ben was already feeling drops of rain. He'd seen storms blow in really quick a few times since he'd been staying with Cameron, so he knew there was going to be a downpour and it was going to come soon.

After a few more minutes, Ben noticed a dim light in the distance. He was almost there, and he'd be just in time as the rain was getting heavier. Soon, it wouldn't merely be falling from the sky; it would pour. He passed the last of the trees that sheltered their tent and barreled into Ethan's unmoving bulk. It was like hitting a fucking brick wall, except for the large, strong arms that wrapped him up and pulled him closer.

Ethan's breath ghosted through his hair as he held him close. "Fuck, Ben. I thought maybe I'd lost you," he murmured. Ben felt him press a kiss to the top of his head, and then his body tensed. Ethan's massive hands gripped Ben's arms and pushed him back away from the warmth of his body. "You said you'd be right behind me. I've been going out of my fucking mind. What happened?"

Ben preferred the soft, warm Ethan who'd held him tight and fretted over him, but he knew he'd have to deal with angry, frightened Ethan, who'd want to know exactly where he'd been. "I shot him. Piper...he's wounded—badly, I think. I wanted to slow him down, not kill him. It was the only way I could think of to buy some time both for us and for everyone in the camp. Second-in-command will wanna try to get me before he follows through on Piper's orders—if he follows through at all. Maybe he's not quite so fanatical. The cops or FBI or whoever should be able to get in there first so it won't be a fucking massacre."

Ben chanced a glance at Ethan's face. His expression was cold and stoic, but Ben could see fear coiled tightly behind his eyes. "I'm sorry, Ethan. Maybe I should have told you first, but I just...I couldn't think of another way. Risking one life to save many." Ben stood motionless as Ethan's silence continued, and he waited for his judgment to fall.

"You're right. I know you're right, Ben. I wish you'd have let me in...let me do it." Ethan pulled him closer again, wrapping him up so he was safely cocooned in Ethan's bigger body.

"How're the girls?" Ben asked, his voice muffled against Ethan's chest.

"They're like fucking automatons, but at least they haven't completely freaked out. They're in the tent with Zach, Phia, and Mary; sound asleep when I left them. I tried to call Cameron, but I think the storm's fucking with reception. Ben, I—" Whatever Ethan had been about to say remained a secret when instead of words Ethan used his mouth to kiss the ever-loving fuck out of him. Ben held on and gave back as hard as he could. Fuck, that little nip thing Ethan did right before he pushed his tongue inside Ben's mouth made him hard.

The rain was still coming down and common sense should have them running for cover, but there was nothing logical or practical about fierce desire, and it would win out every time. Their damp bodies slid together as the kiss went on. To an observer, it might have looked as though they were fighting, but the only thing they were fighting was to close the tiny gap between their bodies. Ben couldn't get fucking close enough. His lip stung where their teeth gnashed together, one cutting through the tender flesh of his bottom lip.

"Jesus, Ethan, I wanna fucking eat you alive," Ben panted out when finally, finally, Ethan eased away. He watched, eyes crossing, as Ethan brought his face closer again and licked at Ben's wounded lip.

"Yeah," Ethan managed to puff out before resting his forehead against Ben's. "I was worried about you." Ben felt a shudder tear through Ethan's body, so he gripped him tighter, hoping to reassure him that he was safely back.

"Let's get out of this rain and try Cameron again."

"We're not gonna fit in there. Two-man tent, Ben, and it was way too crowded with only me in there with them. There's no way we'll both get in."

Ben remembered, from when they'd scouted this location earlier, that there was an overhang only about a hundred feet to the east of their position. It would do in a pinch. "Wait here. Give Cameron another try. I'll be right back," he instructed Ethan.

As soon as Ben popped his head in the tent he knew Ethan had been correct, there was no way they'd all fit. "Zach," he whispered.

"Ben?"

"Yeah, it's me. Look we're not gonna fit in here with you so Ethan and I'll wait out the storm about a hundred feet east. We'll be able to keep an eye on things from there, but you call out if you need anything. Okay?"

With little warning, Zach moved and was suddenly way too close for Ben's comfort. He wasn't sure if it was the limited space forcing Zach to get so close or if it was something else...something infinitely more terrifying to Ben—an innocent with a crush. "You're okay? We heard that shot, and I thought maybe my father..." One of Zach's hands reached out, and he pressed shaking fingers to Ben's cheek. "I thought maybe he'd hurt you." Zach's voice cracked a little at the end.

Damn, it was the terrifying option. He'd have to do his best to turn Zach down without breaking his heart. He wasn't the kind of man a naïve young person should be falling for, and besides, if he had his way, he was well and truly spoken for. The fact that he'd wounded Zach's father... He didn't even want to think about that. That was going to be an awful conversation, and even though Ben knew there was absolutely no love lost between them, it was still his father.

"I'm fine, Zach. We won't be far, okay? And as soon as this storm lets up, we'll get that chopper called in and get out of here." Ben glanced around the tent. Maya and Riley were sleeping peacefully, wrapped around each other as they had been when Ben and Ethan rescued them. Mary appeared to be asleep, but he could see Phia's eyes were wide open, staring directly at him. Earlier, he'd had the impression she wasn't at all convinced Arnold Piper and his cult were evil, but there had to be a seed of doubt there, otherwise she'd never have fled with Zach and Mary.

They all had a long road ahead of them, these three, and Ben wondered what kind of support they might expect. How would their mothers react to them once the specter of Arnold Piper was gone? Ben could only hope their youth would work in their favor. He clapped Zach on the shoulder and backed out of the tent.

Ethan was waiting for him, and together they walked the short distance to the overhang.

There wasn't a lot of room under the rock, either, and it didn't look at all comfortable, but Ben had spent nights in far worse places and conditions—and tonight, he'd have Ethan with him, so that was always a good thing as far as he was concerned.

Ethan edged in first, folding and contorting his big body in an effort to squeeze in as far as possible. Once Ethan was somewhat settled, Ben peeked under the overhang, assessing what and where would be the most comfortable spot for him. In the end, it was no contest; there was only one spot he'd choose.

Ben crouched and crawled into the covered area. Once he'd reached Ethan, he knelt and put his hands on Ethan's knees, pulling them apart and opening up a gap to sit in—

his gap, his spot, right where he should be between Ethan's massive legs. Ben had lost count of the number of times they'd met in the gym, only for Ben to have to call it quits early on his workout when the sight of Ethan's calves and thigh muscles bunching and pulling under the strain of exercise had him too hard for comfort or decency in his gym gear.

As he turned and backed into his spot, Ben allowed his hands to drift down Ethan's legs, savoring the power he felt beneath his fingertips. Christ, this fucking man... He leaned back against Ethan's chest and couldn't miss the feel of Ethan's semi-hard dick practically poking him in his lower back. He'd give anything to be able to take advantage of that cock right then.

Both of Ethan's arms wrapped around him from behind and held him tight to his torso. He wasn't going any-fucking-where—not that he wanted to. He felt Ethan's breath tangle in his curls and his lips pressing onto the top of his head. Ben shifted and pulled at Ethan's arms, trying to force him to hold him even tighter.

"Thank god you're okay, Ben. I don't know what... I can't lose you."

"Not going anywhere," Ben murmured in reply.

"I still couldn't get through to Cameron." More kisses peppered the top of his head, and Ben practically melted. "Are you doing okay after...after Piper?"

Was he? He thought so, though, he knew better than anyone the kind of turmoil that could sneak up on a man after shooting someone. He could have taken the kill shot—he had it in his sights, but he wasn't that man anymore, and injuring Piper should be enough to buy them time.

If he wanted real intimacy with Ethan, there would be no better time to open up to him and cross his fingers that it wouldn't send him running, screaming.

Chapter Thirteen

ETHAN

"Ben...?" Ethan tried again after waiting for some kind of reply from the man in his arms.

"I will be all right. At least Cam will be pleased I haven't fallen back into the savagery. I don't feel bad about Piper, but I don't have an itch to rush out and do it again."

Ethan squeezed a little harder and felt one of Ben's hands cover his own. He'd had lovers before, the odd boyfriend even, but never anything like this. This closeness—intimacy—was exactly what he'd been so jealous of when he'd watched Ryan and Lucas together all those weeks. It was fucking perfect—and scary. What if he hurt Ben? He knew he'd never intentionally hurt him, but so much could go wrong and mistakes could be made. He'd as soon cut off his own arm than cause Ben any pain.

"How're we gonna explain this to the authorities? Can we even call it self-defense? And what about down the road? Is this going to catch up to you?" Regrets, self-recriminations, second-guessing—all can happen when average decisions are made. Ben's decision to shoot Piper had been anything but average. Would that decision come back to bite him in the ass?

"It always catches up to you at some point, Ethan. Piper is a monster who was going to kill all those people, his followers. I chose to do what I did, and I can live with that, but if I'd done nothing and all of those people—those kids—died, well, that I couldn't have lived with." Ben wiggled a little in his arms and let out a soft sigh once he'd settled into a comfortable spot.

Ethan knew if they stayed like this his left thigh, which was taking much of Ben's weight, would be aching in no time, but there was no way he was moving. He'd happily endure the discomfort.

"It was a clean shot, but there's a chance he won't make it, especially if the bleeding's bad and they don't get treatment for him," Ben continued. "I've still got some favors I can call in to clean this mess up. I'm not worried about that, Ethan. I'm worried that... I don't want you to think less of me for what I did."

Though he couldn't see Ben clearly in the darkness with his face turned away, Ethan knew his eyes would be shining with vulnerability and fear that Ethan would reject him because of the choice he made. But how could he? "You are a good man, Ben. You've given us and all those people in the cult a chance. How could I think less of you for that?"

"Cameron never understood. He kind of got it, but after he found out what I'd been doing, he looked at me differently. Sometimes I'd catch him watching me, and I knew he was thinking about exactly what I might be capable of. Would I go back to it? He was wondering if I was some kind of deranged killer."

"He still loves you." Ethan knew that for sure. "I saw him at the hospital when you were in the coma. He was frantic...beside himself."

"I know he loves me, but I also know he sees me differently now. I can live with that because I know he won't abandon me. And I'm not psycho, you know. I've been tested and everything." Ethan could hear the smile return to Ben's voice.

Ethan chuckled. "I'm sorry I hurt you when I left with Lucas and Ryan. I abandoned you and you deserved better." He'd apologized before, but it didn't seem enough.

Ben turned his head and tilted it back, asking for a kiss with his actions. Ethan was more than happy to oblige. "I've been in love with you…I think since the day we met. But I never told you; in fact, I did my best to hide it from you. You never knew how important you were to me; how much I needed to see for myself that you were okay. You owed me nothing, Ethan."

In love. Ben was in love with him? Ethan's entire body shook with little jolts of shock, delight, fear. Every fucking emotion was coursing through his body, and he had no clue how to respond. Ben had surprised him many times over the years, but this…

"You don't have to say anything, Ethan. I can feel you freaking out. Maybe one day, when you know one hundred percent in your guts that it's true, you can say it back to me."

"I care about you, Ben—"

"I know you do. And that's enough…for now. I've always been the sharp end of a spear to most people, a weapon, but you always treated me like I was more than just what I could do. When we're done here, and we've got Maggie and the girls settled, I'm going to date you so hard."

Ethan let out another chuckle. He'd always admired Ben's sense of levity and fun, even if he'd had to rein him in many times when they'd been on the job.

"So, tell me… What would a date with Ben Cronin look like?"

Ben shifted his body and began to turn to face Ethan. Ethan grunted when Ben elbowed him in his stomach and hissed in a breath as Ben climbed all over his lap in an effort to get comfortable. Eventually he stilled, his legs straddling

Ethan's and his ass resting on Ethan's thighs. Ben cupped one of Ethan's cheeks in his palm, his other hand resting on Ethan's shoulder. Without real thought, Ethan reached out and twirled Ben's curls through his fingers, absently playing with them as Ben looked away and answered him.

"Well...first, when I come to pick you up, I'll have a big bunch of wild flowers for you because there are usually a lot of pale-blue flowers in those, and you said that's your favorite color. I'd kiss you gently on the lips when I handed the flowers over and watch your sweet ass when you fussed around looking for a vase, which you probably don't have 'cause I don't think anyone's given you flowers before." Ben returned his gaze to Ethan, leaning forward and pressing his lips to his.

"I'd take you to the California Academy of Sciences, and then when you've exhausted your nerdy little heart there, I'd take you to the Golden Gate Fortune Cookie Factory, grab some of those cookies you love so much, and take you to Land's End lookout so we can eat them while the sun's setting—" He pressed another kiss to Ethan's lips, but this one was deeper, lingering, more passionate. It stole Ethan's breath away.

"If we can still keep our hands to ourselves, I'll take you dancing—slow dancing—our bodies pressed hard together as we move. You know that kind of dancing. But I suspect by then we'll need to get somewhere private so our hands can go wherever they damn well please."

Though it seemed impossible, Ben managed to fit himself even closer, his hands moving to slide through Ethan's hair as he tilted his head to take another kiss. It felt as though they were perfectly aligned, foreheads brushing, their noses nestled into each other's cheeks as their lips moved slowly, gently pushing and pulling against each other. They made an unhurried exploration as they sought to get closer, know each other more intimately. Ethan had never shared a kiss quite like it.

If he was embarrassed by his heavy panting when they pulled apart, Ethan tried not to show it. Besides, his hard cock was a dead giveaway of how turned on he was, how hot and needy Ben made him.

"So…" Ben panted. "How about you? What kind of date would you take me on? Because I have to tell you, I kinda like to be spoiled. There'll be no chicken-wings-in-a-bar dates for me, Ethan."

Ethan smiled at Ben's cheekiness. He knew exactly where he'd take Ben; he'd known for months, before he'd even figured out his feelings for Ben ran deeper than mere friendship.

"Well, date number one will be the date to get you on the hook, so I'll ease you into my fabulousness with a trip to the Walt Disney Family Museum because, well, Donald Duck—"

"There's a Walt Disney Museum!?" Ben practically shouted at him. "How did I not know this?"

"Oh, but it gets better. For our second date, I'm going to take you on a VIP tour of the Burlingame Museum of Pez Memorabilia, which includes a visit to the Banned Toy Museum." Ethan smiled, overtly proud of himself for this one.

"No way…no way. Pez Museum? Fuck, there is a whole world out there I knew nothing about. Pez are my favorite. I've got hundreds, but you know that because I've shown you photos, and I have an old set of lawn darts… They've got to be in the banned toy exhibit."

Ethan could have happily watched and listened for hours as Ben's excitement grew, and he babbled about Pez and banned toys and Donald Duck. He was fucking adorable.

"You really listened to me, didn't you? All those times I was going on and on about things—you listened." Ethan could hear disbelief war with conviction as Ben spoke.

"Well, it's kind of hard not to notice someone's Pez obsession..."

"No. Don't downplay it, Ethan. You paid attention to me... You were secretly in luuurve with me," Ben said in a singsong voice.

"Asshole," Ethan swore and then gave a throaty laugh which was cut off by Ben's lips chasing his once more. This kiss was aggressive, demanding—proprietary.

Beyond the relative safety of the overhang, a tempest railed against the earlier calm of the night. The wind whipped around them, blowing right through their tiny shelter. Sheets of rain cascaded down, the squalls forcing sprays under the rocks that covered their heads. The symphony of nature played on, deafening them with its ferocity, but Ethan hardly noticed. Nothing could compete for attention with the man in his arms.

Only a need for air finally broke them apart. Ethan would give his right arm for a bed right now, but he had his priorities. His nieces were sleeping not far away and he had no idea if Piper's men were out here looking for them, in spite of the storm, even though he doubted it. The storm was ferocious enough to deter anyone from stepping out into it. As desperately as he wanted to fuck Ben, now wasn't the time.

"Tell me about your tattoo?" Ethan asked in an effort to take his mind off the craving for the man still sitting in his lap with his forehead pressed to his. Ethan had noticed the tattoo, which was inked onto his left pectoral, right above his heart, but he'd never had the courage to stare long enough to read the words.

Ben pulled back and Ethan caught his gaze. Ben's pale-blue eyes had that eerily silver look again in this lighting, but rather than giving them a cold appearance, they seemed to blaze with heat, like liquid lightning.

"It's a quote from Aristotle, 'What lies in our power to do, lies in our power not to do.' It seemed kind of appropriate when I got out of the assassin game. Kind of like…just because I can, doesn't mean I should." Ben's eyes lowered and he shook his head slightly. "Guess I kinda forgot that today," he whispered.

Ethan didn't hesitate to put his forefinger on Ben's chin and tip his head so they would once again make eye contact. "Hey. You did the right thing, Benjamin Cronin. Don't you forget that." He dipped forward and pressed his lips to Ben's.

"I haven't been called Benjamin since…well, since Mom died." Ben turned again; settling himself back between Ethan's parted thighs. He was a little side-on and lay his head with his cheek pressing into Ethan's muscled chest. He nuzzled a little before eventually stilling. Ethan brought a hand up and played with Ben's damp curls well after soft snores began emanating from the man.

As uncomfortable as he was with a rock wall at his back, sharper rocks under his ass, and Ben's elbow digging into his gut, Ethan wasn't going to move a fucking inch. This, right here, was fucking perfect.

IT WAS STILL dark when Ethan awoke. The silence was almost deafening after the racket of the storm that had hit them during the night. Ethan was in much the same position he'd been in when he'd finally drifted off, but somehow Ben had managed to wind himself even farther around his body.

His face was pressed into Ethan's side, and his legs were wrapped around Ethan's legs as though he were a giant snake coiled around Ethan's lap. He felt, more than heard, Ben mumble something into his side.

"Do you think you could say that again with your face away from my body so I can actually hear you?" he whispered.

Ben twisted and fidgeted and finally came to rest with his face now tilted upward so Ethan could barely make out his features in the dark. "I said, we should get moving. Storm eased up about half an hour ago. Piper's men could already be on their way."

The reminder of Piper's men still out there had Ethan's hackles up, and he was suddenly very desperate to get moving. He'd do whatever he had to in order to keep his nieces safe, and he knew Ben would be right there with him. That was the nightmare scenario he was going to do his best to avoid at all costs.

"We're gonna be fine, Ethan. All of us," Ben stated and then maneuvered his way out from under the overhang.

Though it was still dark, Ethan made out the beginnings of dawn off to the east. There were still storm clouds around, but the height of the tempest had definitely subsided. He joined Ben in stretching his cramped body, enjoying the pull and strain on his tight muscles. He couldn't take his eyes off Ben as he lengthened his limbs one by one and pulled and twisted with a grace that was mesmerizing. He could hardly wait until he was able to properly and thoroughly enjoy every inch of his man.

Without hesitation, Ben walked over once he'd finished stretching and placed a hand on Ethan's neck, giving just a hint of a squeeze. "I know you're not ready to say it yet, but

I am, and I hope that's okay with you. I love you, Ethan, and we're going to get those little pixies of yours out of here. I promise you." Ben stamped his vow with a gentle kiss to Ethan's lips.

"Pixies?"

"Yeah. Did you see them? Fucking adorable, and so tiny. They reminded me of pixies. Easier than calling them the twins or your nieces all the time, and I don't know which is which yet." Ben winked.

"Ben. Ethan. You there?"

"On our way, Zach," Ethan called back in the direction Zach's voice had come from.

Together, they walked the short distance back to the tent. Zach was pacing in front, and Ethan could hear low words being spoken within, accompanied by soft little whimpers. It seemed his girls were awake. Would they be terrified? Had whatever they'd been given to keep them subdued worn off?

The tent flap opened and Phia gracelessly made her way out with one squirming toddler in her arms. Mary quickly followed, the other toddler barely held in her grasp. Both little girls were far more animated than they had been during the escape.

Ben clapped him on the shoulder and leaned in. "I'm gonna try Cam. Be right back."

Ethan took hesitant steps toward his nieces, who had stopped twisting so much in the older girls' arms and were both staring at his approach. It was getting lighter and lighter with each second that passed to welcome the new day. He could make out their faces quite clearly now, and they looked exactly like his decades-old memories of their mother when she'd been their age.

From the moment his sixteen-year-old self had first held Maggie in his arms, he'd adored her. She was a sweet baby but certainly knew how to vocalize any complaints she'd had. He remembered more than a few nights walking the floor with her when he'd gone to his desperate parents to offer to try to settle her because they'd been unable to. He could also remember the soft padding of her tiny feet stalking his every move when she'd been old enough to toddle.

The agony of knowing he was more than likely going to lose her all over again far too soon stabbed at his heart, all but rendering him useless. Only the thought of getting her daughters safely back to her prevented him from curling into a fucking ball and sobbing his heart out in frustration and sorrow.

Ethan walked to each girl and gently trailed his fingers down their cheeks, offering them a smile. He had no fucking idea what else to do. The one Mary held reached out and grabbed at his fingers, squeezing them in her tiny fist and giving him the most adorable little giggle he'd ever heard. His heart, which had been constricting in pain for his sister, suddenly swelled with a love he hadn't felt since his family had walked away from him.

"I still can't get through to Cam." Ben's voice pierced his reverie and dragged him back to their dangerous situation. "Let's get packed and moving anyway." Ben turned and glanced quickly at the five young people who were silently watching him.

Ethan acknowledged Ben with a nod, trying his best not to freak out. The thought of not being able to get through to Cameron and having to walk out with the kids in tow was not at all appealing. The pickup location was higher up, though, so maybe they'd have more luck getting a signal from there.

Chapter Fourteen

BEN

"Okay, Zach, Phia, and Mary, we're going to need you guys to carry the packs. Ethan and I will have the girls in the rigs."

"How far are we going?" Zach asked.

"It's about a two-hour walk to the spot where we're going to be picked up by my brother. We'll make our way there and hope we can get through to Cameron."

"And if we can't?" Phia timidly asked. Ben suspected females speaking up like this hadn't exactly been welcomed in Piper's cult.

Ben exchanged a glance with Ethan. He didn't want to have to walk out of here with this little group, but he knew if it came to it, both he and Ethan could do it. He'd delay that option as long as possible though.

"We keep moving. We've got plenty of supplies, everything we need to be fine for days. People from your... um, your...camp might be following us so we can't stay still."

It didn't take them long to pack up their gear. Mary and Ethan fed and organized the twins while he, Zach, and Phia pulled down the tent and packed the bags with the most essential equipment. He'd debated about leaving anything behind as he had no idea when they'd be able to get through to Cam and how long they might be stranded out here—with more mouths to feed than they'd planned for.

"Ben?"

"Yeah, Zach?"

"That gunshot..."

Ben turned to find Zach's wide eyes fixed on him. Ben was no expert on reading people, but even he could see the question lurking in the young man's gaze. He had a choice. He could lie to Zach; there was no reason he ever had to find out what Ben had done—at least, not when he was standing two feet away from him. Or he could tell him the truth. Zach had been lied to all his life, most especially by his father, from what Ben understood. Maybe it was time for people to stop lying to him.

"It was me," Ben answered simply. "Zach, I... I'm so sorry, but I shot..." Admitting his actions was so much harder than he thought. He'd never had to admit what he'd done to the family of his targets before. If he had, maybe he'd never have lasted so long.

"My father," Zach whispered. They were far enough away from the others that nobody would hear their conversation. Phia, at least, would freak out if she heard, understandably so.

Zach sat on the ground, doing his best to get the collapsed tent back into its cover while they spoke. Ben sat beside him, turning so he could look him in the eyes; he wouldn't shy away from what he'd done.

"I'm sorry. I didn't know how else to stop him."

"He wasn't a good man, but he was my father... Is he dead?"

"He wasn't when I left, but..." He shook his head and reached out a tentative hand to place on Zach's shoulder. He had no idea what the response to his touch would be, but he wasn't really surprised when Zach flinched away from him.

Ben dropped his hand back to his lap. Zach turned his body a little so he no longer looked at Ben.

"I'm sorry, Zach. I know that doesn't mean anything right now, but I am sorry."

Zach stood, picking up the tent as he went. He turned toward where Phia was stuffing items into the backpacks. Before he got more than a few steps away, he looked over his shoulder toward Ben, though his eyes wouldn't meet Ben's own. "You did the right thing. But I...I can't talk to you about it right now."

Ben watched him walk away, his shoulders hunched once more.

"You okay?" Ethan asked quietly. Ben had been so consumed with Zach he hadn't even heard Ethan approach. That was unusual for him, trained as he'd been to always be aware of his surroundings.

"I told him about his dad."

"How'd that go?"

Ben shrugged. "Way better than how it should have gone."

"Zach seems like a pretty switched-on kid to me, Ben. And he cares about others. He'll understand in time."

"I think he already gets it, but like he said, it's still his dad." He felt Ethan press a kiss into his curls, sending a tingle up his spine. The touch of Ethan would never be commonplace or unremarkable to him. That a man such as Ethan was touching him would always astound and thrill him.

It only took another few minutes before they were on their way. In the end, Ben had changed his mind, and Zach had agreed to take Maya so Ben could hang back a little to ensure they weren't being followed. Ben took the pack from Zach, keeping his gaze fixed on his eyes just in case, but Zach kept his eyes averted.

It wasn't an easy hike; the slow gradient, the packs, the leftover ravages from last night's storm all conspired to make hard work of it. The twins drifted in and out of sleep, but the three fleeing members of the cult never once complained. Ethan and Ben stopped them frequently to drink and rest, but none of them muttered a word about being tired or griped about being sore from the trek.

They reached the clearing, where Cameron was to pick them up, just before lunch. While Ethan got everyone settled and began sorting out food, Ben tried again to reach Cameron.

"Any luck?" Ethan asked as he returned to their little group.

"Nothing. Must be the storm. I'm sure I'll get through soon." Ben smiled after answering, when he noticed Phia and Mary staring at him intently. Though neither had caused any kind of fuss since the two groups had encountered each other, Ben didn't want to risk a panic. He looked at Ethan and slightly tipped his head to the side. Ethan got his message and stood, walking a little way from the rest of the group. Ben quickly joined him.

"Listen, Ethan, the storm might have done more damage than we thought. I've got no idea how long it might take to get through to Cam. What do you think our next move should be?" Ben was used to working alone in situations like this but he valued Ethan's opinion and wanted them to be a team.

"We can't sit still, can't give them time to catch up. What if we do a zigzag trek north? Walk for a few hours and then find somewhere to hold up for the night. Then if—when—we get through to Cameron we can make our way back here."

"Agreed. But, Ethan, I think if we can't get on to Cam by morning, we walk out. Maybe keep trying Cam, but find a new extraction point. We should—" Ben fell silent as he noticed Zach cautiously approaching them.

"What's wrong?" Zach asked as soon as he was close enough.

"Nothing."

Zach turned an angry glare on Ben, and he knew instantly he'd underestimated this young man.

"I'm not stupid, Ben, and despite what my father believed, neither are the girls. We all know something's not right. So, why don't you be honest with us?" His stare was challenging, daring Ben and Ethan to keep treating them like...children.

"Okay. It's not bad yet, but we may not be able to get our ride out of here. That means, we may end up having to walk out."

Ben was surprised to see Zach smile. "Is that all? None of us are afraid of hard work. We're used to it. The women, even the female children, do all the work at the camp. And because I wasn't...quite a man, according to my father, I shared in the chores. Walking out of here won't be a hardship for us."

"Well, I'd say we've been schooled, Ethan." Ben laughed. "Let's enjoy our rest, okay? And then we can get back to the hard stuff."

Ben linked his fingers with Ethan's, enjoying touching him like this whenever the mood struck. He'd reached for Ethan's hand more times than he could count over the years, every time having to wrench his hand away because they hadn't been each other's then. Ethan brought their joined hands to his lips and kissed Ben's knuckle, causing the giddy feeling in his guts again that was becoming so commonplace.

Zach had been right about them being able to handle the rigorous walk. Ben could see all three of them fatiguing, but not one word of complaint was uttered as the day wore on. They stopped frequently to allow the twins a chance to toddle about, go to the toilet, refresh themselves, and allow Ben a chance to try to make contact with Cameron. Ethan watched them all like a hawk, especially his nieces, and observing Ethan being so protective of the little group was so damn sweet that Ben could have happily sat and watched for hours.

It was close to four in the afternoon when Ben called a halt at the base of a steeper climb than what they'd encountered so far. They all unloaded their burdens, and Mary, as usual, came over with some crackers for the twins, chatting away happily with them as they ate and drank.

"What're you thinking?" Ethan asked.

"I'm thinking I don't want to make that climb. It's four now and we've come a fair way, so I think the best option is to find somewhere to hunker down for the night." Ben observed intently as Ethan wiped the sweat from his brow with the buff he'd tied around his wrist. Ethan looked devastatingly handsome with his face flushed from their hike; sweat beading in the graying wisps of his hair, his muscles tightly bunched and visible under his close-fitting shirt.

Ethan nodded. "Agreed. Did you see anywhere we passed that might suit?"

"No, but I'm thinking there'll be some crevices around here we can use, given the incline. You stay, watch the kids, and I'll hunt around, see what I can find."

Ben could see the argument forming behind Ethan's features, but Ethan held his tongue and nodded. He knew he'd hate the idea of Ben being out of his sight as much as

Ben hated the idea of not being within view of Ethan. That's how it'd be now when danger was around. And Ben had no fucks to give about that.

"Gotta say, I didn't see this coming."

Ethan looked baffled as he replied, "See what coming?"

"This need to have you where I can see you—all the goddamn time. I've always been an independent kind of guy, but I need you. I need you around me, near me. I didn't think... I've never felt like that."

Ethan sidled up closer to Ben and tugged him so their bodies were flush together. "Is that a bad thing?"

"It's not a bad thing at all. It's an unexpected thing. I can relax when I can see you, see that you're safe. Simple." Ben shrugged and tipped his head back, asking for the kiss he so badly wanted.

Ethan obliged eagerly, pressing their lips together, but Ben could feel he was holding himself back. The fact they had a young audience not far away was probably putting a cold shower on Ethan's usual passion.

Ben moaned into the kiss and reluctantly pulled away, letting his fingers trail through Ethan's sweat-damp hair. He pressed his forehead against Ethan's and smiled at the soft sigh that escaped from Ethan's mouth.

"This is good," Ethan whispered. "This is exactly what I wanted."

Ben pulled back enough to be able to look into Ethan's eyes. "What is?"

"This closeness. I watched Ryan and Lucas for the last few weeks, watched how close they were—how intimate— and I wanted it. I was so damn jealous of what they have, but I think I can have it with you."

Ben couldn't stop himself from leaning in and stealing another kiss. "It's all I've wanted for the last two years." This honesty between them was what *Ben* had longed for.

"Um...excuse me, Ethan."

Both he and Ethan startled at Zach's voice. They took a small step away from each other but not too far, and Ethan immediately grabbed his hand, much to Ben's delight. He'd been with a few men over the years who, while not exactly in the closet, weren't happy to be caught too close to Ben either.

"What's up?" Ethan's voice rumbled in his ear sending another of those Ethan shivers up his spine.

"Phia just wanted to check if it was okay to quickly wash the twins in the stream? It's fairly warm, so there must be a hot spring around."

"Of course. Actually I'll come and help." Ethan turned to him, a wide smile on his handsome face. "Ben?"

"Oh, I wouldn't miss this. I'll have a look around for a campsite as soon as we're done."

Chapter Fifteen

ETHAN

"How did I get roped into this again?" Ethan asked no one in particular just as Maya sent another splash of the cool water his way. Riley was slung onto his back, clinging there for dear life, even though he'd assured her repeatedly he'd never let her go, and he kept one of his massive arms tucked back firmly around her. He understood her trust issues after what had happened to her, not to mention, she didn't know him at all.

"Ethan, you're losing three nothing to a two-year-old. You've got to be ashamed, buddy." Ben croaked a laugh as Ethan lost for the fourth time, once again enduring the splash to his face from his victor. "Oh, god, make that four nil."

"Hey, aren't adults supposed to let kids win?"

"Not me," Ben quickly replied. "Nope, that little pixie is going down when it's my turn."

Ethan loved hearing the laughter in Ben's voice. But despite the lightheartedness of the moment, Ethan could see Ben where he was sitting, his gaze constantly roaming, always vigilant, watching, just in case.

They didn't stay in the water much longer. Mary and Phia dried and dressed the twins while Ethan dried himself. The water hadn't been cold, but it hadn't exactly been warm either. He couldn't resist jumping in with Maya and Riley though. They were definitely livening up as whatever they'd been given worked its way out of their system.

Just as he pulled his pants over his ass and buckled up, Ethan felt the warmth of Ben's body behind him. Ben's arms circled around him, tightening, and pulling Ethan back against him. He felt Ben rest his head on his back and heard his muffled voice as he spoke. "Thought you might need some warming up."

Ben cinched his arms even tighter, and Ethan laid his hands over Ben's clasped ones. Even through their layers, he felt the contours of Ben's body fitting perfectly against his own as if they'd been statues hewn from the same rock and then magically brought to life. A perfect match.

"Say it, Ethan," Ben murmured.

"Say what?"

"I know you've got some horribly bad bit of dirty talk on the tip of your tongue. Just say it."

"I thought you wouldn't want to hear my dirty talk because it's so bad."

Ben released him and walked around so they were now face-to-face. "Are you kidding? I find it adorably endearing. Now, say it."

Ethan tried not to watch Ben as he said the words but found his gaze constantly wandering back to Ben, unable to look away for long. "I was going to say that...um, if you keep pressing that body of yours against me like that, I wouldn't warm up, I'd overheat and spontaneously combust." Ethan winced as he finished, cringing at the words as he heard them out loud.

"Oh, Jesus. Let me give you a tip: less is more, and maybe you're right and sometimes it might be better to keep it in here." Ben smiled and tapped Ethan's temple. Ethan laughed with him despite his embarrassment. Hell, he'd humiliate himself everyday if it put a smile like that on Ben's face. "Fuck, I love you, ya big doofus. Now, give me some sugar before I go off to find us a campsite."

Ethan put his hands on his hips and cocked an eyebrow at Ben. "'Give me some sugar.' Really?" Ethan scoffed.

"Thought I'd try it out." Ben shrugged. He leaned forward and threw his arms around Ethan's neck, tipping his head up. Ethan loved how he did this. He was asking for a kiss, waiting for Ethan to give it, and it was adorable.

"Be safe," Ethan murmured before pressing his lips to Ben's forehead and then trailing soft kisses over his nose and cheeks before finally allowing himself the pleasure of taking Ben's lips.

They were both flushed and breathing hard when they finally broke apart, and Ben slipped away into the tree line.

Ethan walked the short distance back to where the others were. Zach was pointing out something high in the treetops to one of the twins, while Mary was following the other around as she wandered about, occasionally bending over to touch something or pick up a leaf or stick. He walked to where Phia was sitting, drinking from one of the bottles and closely monitoring the others. Ethan sat beside her and grabbed for one of the other bottles to take a drink. They'd been lucky to find plenty of springs and streams where they'd been able to fill their water bottles, especially now that they'd added so many to their group.

"Why do you kiss him? Touch him?"

Phia's question startled him, coming out of nowhere as it had. From what Zach had told them, she'd obviously never seen a gay couple before. "I care about him," he answered simply.

"I cared about my friends, but I never kissed them. That was for my husband; he's not your husband."

"Maybe he will be one day." Ethan smiled at the thought. It was a long way off, but still...

Phia's head whipped around to face him, her eyes enormous. "But how could he be?"

"Look, Phia, I guess there's a lot about the world outside of your group that you don't know about. Some men love other men, and some women love other women is the most basic way I can explain it. And they can get married if they want."

"But how is that possible?"

"It just is." He shrugged, not really wanting to get into that whole conversation with her. He wondered what else might shock the hell out of her when she came face-to-face with the outside world. She didn't seem disgusted, only shocked by the idea.

"You can marry?" Zach asked. He had Riley in his arms as he came and stood closer to Ethan and Phia. Ethan's breath hitched when she held her little arms out toward him, and Zach leaned down to place her on Ethan's lap. Ethan took her willingly, her weight nothing, but her smell and the feel of her—everything.

"Sure," he finally managed to answer Zach's question.

"Wow," Zach breathed and sank to his knees. "Actually marry."

"Yeah. It's good. I mean, not everyone is happy about it, but you're never going to please everyone, and people should be able to live the life that makes them happy. They shouldn't be ashamed of who they are." Ethan flicked a glance to Zach and saw his cheeks color. Hopefully, one day the damage Arnold Piper had inflicted on his son would be repaired.

It didn't take long for Riley to start fussing on his lap, so Ethan stood and followed her about as she explored their surroundings. He was at a bit of a loss. They couldn't set up camp, and they couldn't go anywhere until Ben came back, though, Ethan suspected if they had to move on, Ben would be able to find them.

Phia and Mary dozed off after a while, so Ethan kept his eyes on both twins as they continued exploring together. They weren't talking much at all and what they did say was usually only a word or two, but they seemed to be having some kind of conversation with each other that clearly only they understood. Zach was still sitting beside Mary and Phia, a subdued and thoughtful expression on his features. He was a good-looking young man who would benefit from a few extra pounds once they got out of here.

A little hand tugged on his fingers, and he looked down to see Maya smiling up at him. He could easily tell them apart from the little dimple Maya had that Riley did not, if Mary had identified them correctly to start with. Maybe it was Riley who had the dimple.

He squatted and looked in the direction she was pointing. Riley quickly joined them, coming to stand at his other side, with her tiny hand resting on his thigh. Through the shrub, about six feet away from them, he spotted a small brown creature that was about ten inches long. It looked like an otter, though, Ethan knew that wasn't possible. Maybe a ferret or weasel. Whatever it was, the fuzzy little thing wasn't at all fazed by their presence as it continued foraging for whatever it was looking for.

Maya giggled in his ear as the small animal continued with its antics, sniffing through the undergrowth and kicking up leaves. Riley was silent, but when Ethan turned to her, he could see she was watching intently as the creature began digging at the ground.

As Ethan turned back to the animal, there was a flash of movement, too fast for him to really gauge what he was seeing. It wasn't until he heard the rattle that he fully understood. The rattlesnake hardly moved once it had made its bite and the poor animal was either dead or stunned immediately. As carefully as he could, without drawing the snake's attention, Ethan stood, grabbing both girls around their waists and lifting them away from danger.

Thankfully, they were both silent as he began backing away as fast as he dared. He'd been in dangerous situations before, but Ethan thought his heart was about to beat right out of his fucking chest, it was thumping so loudly.

"Nake," Maya said as he continued moving away.

"That's right, sweetie, a snake. A dangerous snake, so hold on tight while we get away from it."

His eyes never left the snake that was preparing to consume its prey. There was no way he wanted the twins to see that, but neither did he want to turn his back on the fucking thing as it was still only about twelve feet away. He wouldn't allow himself to think about the fact that he couldn't even see where he was placing his footsteps and how many other rattlesnakes might be around.

"Zach," he called.

"Yeah?"

"Get the girls up." He tried to keep his voice even, not allow panic to seep into it.

"What's wrong?"

"Get them up. I'll explain in a second." Ethan didn't think he was able to drag his eyes away from the circle of life going on that he'd had a prime seat to only moments ago.

He heard the others close at his back now as the girls slowly came awake at Zach's insistence. When a hand touched his back, it was all he could do not to jump out of his fucking skin. Bullets, knives, psychos he'd be able to manage, but slithery fucking snakes—no, just no.

"What happened?" Zach asked again.

"Rattlesnake. Let's move, okay?"

"They don't usually attack, you know. If we stay away from it, it'll stay away from us. And if it rattles, that's only a warning that it's scared."

"It just ate that weasel or whatever it was, and it didn't rattle until after it had bit it."

Zach gave him a 'well, duh' kind of look. "That's because it was its prey, so it didn't want to warn it off."

Phia already had a pack on her back, and Mary had both carriers in her arms. Zach smiled before shouldering the second pack. Ethan didn't even consider putting the twins down; he wasn't sure he ever would again.

"Our best bet is that clearing we passed a little way back," Zach said as he started walking, thankfully in the opposite direction to the snake. "No logs, boulders, things like that. They like to hide under those kinds of things."

"How do you know so much?" Ethan asked as he trailed after the group.

"I grew up in campsites. My dad may have been crazy, but he didn't want to die of a snakebite, so he learned how to survive in the wild. He taught me—until he realized I was...not good enough."

"You seem plenty good to me, Zach. I'd have headed to the boulders near the stream."

"Classic hiding spot, Ethan. Under rocks, overhangs. Come on, didn't you learn this kind of thing?"

"Nope. No real need to when you've always lived in big cities, I guess," Ethan answered, enjoying the distraction from the thought of the monster he'd just escaped from.

"I bet Ben would know."

"I don't think we need to mention this to Ben."

"Mention what to Ben?" the man himself asked from behind. Ethan just about jumped out of his fucking skin again.

"Ethan saw a snake," Zach casually replied.

"He did, huh?"

"It was a fucking rattlesnake that is right now consuming some weasely-otter thing."

"Weasely-otter thing? Oh, that's my great outdoorsman."

Ethan rolled his eyes and kept walking, doing his best to ignore the snickering he heard from...well, from everyone except the twins.

"Nake," Maya called out, pointing back over his shoulder.

"Yeah, pixie, Uncle Ethan saw a snake," Ben cooed.

"Me saw."

"You saw it too? Wow, not many little pixies get to see snakes. But we can't ever touch them, can we? Because if we touch them we could hurt them or they could hurt us, so we only look with our eyes, never our hands."

Maya nodded earnestly and then turned again to watch where she was being taken.

"There's a good spot not far from here. There's a...it's not a cave but almost like a fake wall. We can get the tent behind it, and it's easily defensible if needed." Ben spoke softly as they continued walking.

"What about..." Ethan hesitated and then pressed on; preparing himself for the ribbing he was sure would come. "What about snakes?"

"I'll clear it out; make sure there's none around. No snake is going to get the girls, Ethan, or get you either."

"Well, maybe your snake can get me..."

"Oh, god. I take it back; it's not adorable or endearing. You need some serious lessons. I wonder if there's a *How to Talk Dirty for Dummies* book."

"Ha. Ha. Let's get to this campsite, okay?"

"You good with the girls?" Ben asked.

"Yeah. Yeah I'm good."

It only took them half an hour to get to Ben's campsite and it was perfect. They'd have a rock wall to their backs and to one side, making it hard for anyone to sneak up on them. They didn't have the storm to keep Piper's men away tonight, but Ethan hoped they'd put enough distance between them and that the zigzagging they'd done would make them just a little harder to follow.

Chapter Sixteen

BEN

They were making good time, considering the load they were carrying, but still, Ben suspected they weren't going fast enough. A group of men or women traveling without the burdens of packs or babies would make better time than them—especially if revenge was pushing at their backs. He had no way of knowing if people from Piper's camp were actually out there, coming after them, but the prickle at the back of his neck told him they were.

They'd had no trouble overnight, all of the youngsters quickly falling asleep after the long walk during the day. Ethan had been jumpy, the encounter with the rattlesnake clearly playing on his mind. For a while, Ben had thought he was going to stand all night with the twins in his arms. He'd only put them down after he, Zach, and finally Ethan himself had done a thorough check of the campsite. Of course, then he'd spent the rest of the night stalking every move Maya and Riley made. Not even relaxing once they'd drifted off to sleep.

Fortunately, Ben had been able to contact Cameron in the early hours of this morning, so they were making their way back to the extraction point.

Zach and Phia carried both packs, which they'd lightened considerably. Ben was still wary of leaving too much behind in case something went wrong and they missed the rendezvous with Cameron. "Hope for the best, but plan for the worst" had long been drilled into him. Keeping that thought in mind had seen him through some near disasters over the years.

Maya was strapped to his front; at least, Mary said it was Maya. She'd had some interactions with the girls back in the camp and seemed confident in telling them apart in the light of day. They'd made the assumption that Maya had been called Miriam and Riley Rebecca by Piper and his people. Maya had nodded off a few times, but every now and then Ben looked down into the biggest and clearest eyes he'd ever seen. The girls were all Maggie; he could see little of anyone else in them, but sometimes he caught a quick flash of their uncle in Maya's eyes.

A few times, the little girl had looked as though she were about to burst into tears, but Ben would press a kiss to her hair, talk softly to her and then burst into a very quiet version of whatever song would pop into his mind. Maya had giggled her little head off when he'd sung "Rumpshaker" to her—much to her uncle's horror.

Ben had also glanced across to Ethan more than once and each time caught him staring down at Riley, who'd mostly been happy and content snuggled up to her uncle. Ethan had worn a thoroughly besotted expression each and every time Ben had looked at him. These girls were going to have their big old uncle wrapped around their teeny tiny fingers in no time.

If his estimates were correct, they'd be at the pickup point in maybe twenty minutes. Rather than his nervousness easing, though, it was ratcheting up. It was his experience that shit usually went to hell right at the last minute.

"Twenty minutes out, Ethan. Let's take a moment."

The little group came to a grateful stop, and Phia, Mary, and Zach immediately went for the water bottles. They were young and seemed healthy, but it was no easy walk to the elevated spot they'd chosen for Cameron to land his chopper, especially after the long hike the day before.

Ben offered both girls one of the crackers Maggie had suggested they bring along for the girls to eat. They were easy to manage, and the twins apparently loved them. He motioned for Ethan to step a little away from the others, though they kept the twins fastened to them in their rigs. They were too young to understand what Ben was about to say anyway.

"Ethan, I'm going to hand Maya off to Zach. We're close, so I'd prefer to be unrestricted...just in case."

"Have you heard something?" Ethan immediately asked.

"No, nothing at all. But, experience tells me that the last minute of a mission is usually when it goes balls up. I want to be ready."

Jesus, Ethan was fucking perfect. Exhausted, frightened, dripping sweat, and smelling every one of those hours that he hadn't showered, Ethan still turned Ben's shit on. "So beautiful." The words slipped from between Ben's lips as though they were drawn to Ethan every bit as much as Ben was. The smile that split Ethan's lips was enough to make up for the embarrassment of allowing the unguarded words out. Ben reached up and gently swiped his thumb along Ethan's lower lip.

"I don't think I've ever known someone who can wield words with the same devastation as you do, Ben. Every fucking time you get me—right here." Ethan pointed to where his heart would be if not for the toddler strapped against his chest.

"And that's a...good thing?"

Ethan leaned over him, careful of the two children pressed between them and pressed a kiss to Ben's forehead. "It's a wonderful thing."

Ben smiled, and for once, words failed him as he began unstrapping Maya from his body.

"Zach," Ethan called and the young man was beside them in seconds. "We need you to take Maya. Ben needs to...he needs to be free to move so he can help us all into the chopper," Ethan finished, clearly unwilling to alarm Zach.

Ben helped Zach get Maya situated on his chest, while aware of the young man's eyes steadfastly upon him. He took the pack Zach had been carrying and slipped it on his back, careful of his rifle already slung across it. He and Ethan had discussed the rifle when they'd geared up and had both concluded that Ben carrying it was the safest option despite him also carrying Maya. Bundled in her carrier she couldn't reach it, and Ben was a weapons expert—there was no way that gun was going off unless he wanted it to.

Once he was loaded up, Zach walked back over to Phia and Mary. It took only seconds for Ethan to say what Ben had been waiting for. "He's got such a crush on you. Tread carefully with him."

Ben smiled and nodded in reply. He knew what Ethan meant about being careful. Zach had only just figured out that men could like other men, and a first crush was always tricky. He'd have to let him down easy at some point, but fuck, he was dreading it.

From what Ben could see, Phia and Mary still seemed to be holding up well, considering the situation they found themselves in. Young people were resilient and Ben hoped that with time these three would be okay. He knew Maya and Riley were going to be okay because he knew that Ethan would do whatever he had to do to make sure of it.

They walked in silence, the only sound coming from the occasional cries or giggles of one of the twins. Mary walked beside Zach, cooing to Maya at the first hint of any distress from the toddler. Phia walked beside Ethan but kept considerable distance between them, only glancing every now and then at Riley who was happily babbling in her uncle's arms.

As they continued on, Ben dropped a little farther back; if there was trouble, he wanted as much distance between it and Ethan and the others as possible. Not too much farther and they should be able to hear Cameron's chopper. It was a beautiful, clear morning after the storm that had raged two nights before, so the landing and flight should be smooth. With any luck, in a few more hours, they'd all be safely home at Cameron's.

"I see it," Zach called out. Ben turned to face in the direction Zach was looking and could make out his brother's helicopter flying low and directly toward them. The landing spot should be only about half a mile away. Their timing was perfect.

Ben opened his mouth to call back when he heard noise coming from behind him. He froze where he was, listening, concentrating hard to stretch his hearing, so he could try to make out what he was listening to.

Something was moving behind them—and moving quickly.

What should he do? In front of him, the others kept walking, and he suspected Cameron was only seconds away from touching down. Behind him something—or someone— was approaching. He had no clear understanding of what Piper's group was capable of, or how far they might be willing to go to stop them.

Ben dropped his bag, keeping only his rifle strapped to his back. He had several other weapons concealed on his body, and he knew he'd be able to slow down up to three men with his fists alone given the right circumstances. He had to drop back to see what was coming at them and stop whatever it was, if needed. He had to give the others time to get on the chopper and safely away from here.

The foliage was dense all around, and it was easy enough to slip in and backtrack toward the noises that were still audible. If it was Piper's men, he needed to slow them down or stop them.

When he felt he'd put enough space between them, Ben crouched and waited. He couldn't hear any voices, but he could hear labored breathing. Piper's men would have had to be moving fast to catch up, or they'd left the camp while the storm had still been going strong.

There was no way for him to know how many were coming, and if they had fanned out, it would be hard for Ben to get to them all. He closed his eyes and breathed deeply, doing his best to slow his rapidly beating heart. As the *thump thump* from his chest became softer, he made out the soft crunch of feet on undergrowth. He clearly heard two sets of footsteps, though that was no guarantee that there weren't more of Piper's people out there.

One man was to his left and the other to his right. He needed to stop both. Ben moved, silent as a ghost, farther behind the men and came around to deal with the one on his left first.

The man was about Ben's height but definitely heavier. Ben stalked him, not making a sound as he wrapped one arm around his head, covering his mouth and nose to stop him from calling out, and to bring on unconsciousness. He held the man's waist with his other arm and swept his legs out from under him with one leg. Ben held him all the way down, not giving him an inch even as he struggled. By the time the pair of them hit the ground, the other man was out. Ben wasted no time zip-tying his hands and feet before moving on to his next target.

The second man was bigger, so Ben would need to use more force to put him down. It was unlikely he'd be able to do it as soundlessly as he'd taken care of the first man.

Ben approached quietly, while sizing up his options. He'd use the Japanese stranglehold on this guy, as much as he didn't want to. It could be deadly and Ben didn't want to kill—he would and could, but he didn't *want* to.

Moving quickly, he threw his left arm around the taller man's throat. The man began to struggle immediately. His windpipe was in the crook of Ben's elbow as he placed his left hand into his right elbow, and his right hand on the back of the man's head. Ben pushed the head forward, squeezing the side of his opponent's neck. By now the man's blood pressure would be dropping, unconsciousness seconds away.

When it happened, the man collapsed to the ground, taking Ben with him. They landed with an audible thud, and Ben froze, listening for any indication that he'd been overheard.

The forest remained quiet.

Ben checked his quarry and found he, too, was still breathing. He zip-tied him quickly and ran to catch up to Ethan and the others, hoping there were no more men to deal with.

As he reached the clearing where Cameron had landed, he saw Zach passing Maya into Ryan's waiting arms. Mary and Phia were already in, Ethan was unclipping Riley, looking around desperately at the same time. Ryan handed

Maya to Phia and Zach jumped in next. Ryan stretched his arms out to take Riley from Ethan, when suddenly there was a muffled bang, and Ethan dropped to the ground, Riley still half strapped to him in her rig.

Over the sound of the idling chopper, Ben couldn't make out the direction the shot had come from, but he dragged his eyes from Ethan's prone form and scanned the area. He looked frantically around and finally spotted a man sheltering behind some trees at the edge of the clearing, to his left. He had a rifle pointed toward the chopper but was holding fire. Ben guessed his first shot was meant as a warning. He'd get no such warning from Ben.

The rifle dropped easily into his arms from its strapping, just as intended. Ben took a moment to line up his shot. The wind coming from the rotors would make it difficult, but it wasn't the first time Ben would be firing under conditions like this. Many times he'd been dropped from a helo, firing before he'd even cleared the gusts from the rotors.

Ben took a breath, lined up his target, and took the shot. The shooter fell backward, hitting the tree behind him. Predictably, he dropped his weapon to clutch at the wound in his shoulder.

"Ethan! Go! It's clear," he shouted, trying to ensure he'd be heard over the roar of the rotors. Simultaneously, he stood from the crouch he'd been in and turned to head toward the helicopter.

"Not another step," the cold voice hissed in his ear, at the same time he felt cool metal press to his temple. A hand wrenched the rifle from his grip, while another grabbed his arm and pushed him forward. *At least two of them, then.*

Ben could see Ethan, still with Riley in his arms, turn toward him. If Ben fought, he knew Ethan wouldn't get in that helo. He knew Ethan would come after him—and he couldn't allow that. He flicked his gaze to the cockpit, catching his brother's horrified look. Unsure of how jittery these men were, he didn't risk calling out and instead mouthed "go" to Cameron. It'd kill Cameron to leave him behind, but he also knew his brother would never risk the lives of children.

"Shoot it," someone yelled in his ear.

"Where? We don't wanna hit the kids," came a reply. Ben did his best to tune the knuckleheads out as he watched Ethan being practically dragged into the chopper. He could see Cameron screaming at him while Ryan and Zach were each pulling at his arms. Ethan was still desperately trying to unclip Riley, presumably so he could pass her off and come back for him.

Ben caught Cameron's pleading glance again and knew what he was asking. Ben shook his head. Cameron had to take off the second Ethan was in the cabin; Cameron couldn't let him get away.

A shot rang out, too close, and then all Ben could hear was a loud and painful ringing in his ears. He watched as Ryan leaned forward and practically scooped Ethan's legs up into the cabin of the helicopter, which immediately pitched forward and up, the body of it turning so the occupants were out of the firing line.

"Stop shooting, you idiot," a voice called from beyond the tree line. Their hand guns would do little damage at this point, but if they used Ben's rifle... Fortunately, his captors listened to the commanding voice and lowered their weapons.

BEN STOOD STIFFLY between his imprisoners, his eyes never leaving the escaping helicopter. He was already preparing his counterattack now that Ethan was safely away. He knew he'd missed his chance, though, once three more men stepped into his field of vision. The middle man was the nastiest looking piece of work Ben had seen in years, and he was no stranger to nasty men—and women.

The man who approached him stood a little taller than Ben and had a salt-and-pepper stubble covering his square jaw. He was almost completely bald and possessed the dullest, grayest eyes Ben had ever seen. His thin lips crooked up into a smirk as he pulled his arm back and unleashed an uppercut to Ben's vulnerable midsection. With two men holding him up, preventing him from fighting back, it didn't take long for Ben to lose consciousness when the man pistol-whipped him.

Chapter Seventeen

ETHAN

"Put us down! Cameron! God damn it, put us down," Ethan roared, but Cameron steadfastly ignored him. The rescue chopper continued on its path, leaving Ben, and Ethan's fucking heart, behind.

"Cameron!" he tried again but still received the same silent response. "That's your fucking brother down there."

Still, Cameron remained silent, concentrating on flying them out. In the cabin, he could see Mary and Phia huddling together with a crying Maya between them. Zach sat opposite with a hand on their knees doing his best to soothe them. Ryan sat beside Zach with Riley in his arms, bouncing her a little as her lower lip trembled in preparation for the tears that were close to the surface.

"Ethan, please, try to calm down. You're scaring the kids, and I'm sure they're already frightened enough," Ryan spoke calmly and quietly, though, Ethan could plainly see fear in his eyes.

Ethan reached up and scrubbed at his face with his hands. He needed to cool down or he'd be no help to Ben at all.

Where the hell had those men come from?

Ethan had been at the chopper, blissfully unaware of the approaching trouble. He'd just realized Ben still hadn't caught up to them when the first shot had come and sent him to the ground. Ben had taken care of the shooter. Ben had covered all of their backs the whole time, and Ethan had left him there—left him behind.

"Ethan?"

"I'm okay, Ryan. I'm...okay." He shook his head. No, he really wasn't okay. "We've gotta go back. We've got to go back for Ben."

"We have to get these kids out first and then we'll go back. We can't risk the kids...you know that." Ryan flicked his gaze between him and Riley, who was sitting quietly in his lap with her gaze fixed on Ethan. He gave her a little smile and received a tentative grin in return.

Ryan was right. He'd get the kids to safety, and then he'd go back for Ben, and he wouldn't fucking stop until he had him back safely in his arms.

It took an agonizing forty minutes for them to reach the helipad back in Cody. Ethan could see quite a crowd assembled, including Maggie, who was sitting on a camping chair with Lucas beside her. She looked so fucking tiny and weary. The others standing around looked like law enforcement, though, not just your average cop. Ethan suspected FBI or one of the other letter agencies.

As soon as the rotors powered down, Ethan was moving. He took both toddlers in his huge arms, their weight negligible, and carried them to their mother. Maya and Riley both started squirming in his arms the moment they spotted their mom but Ethan held fast. He wasn't letting them down to risk getting hurt at the last moment.

Maggie didn't seem to have the energy to move from her chair, so she stayed seated and merely pulled the girls to her as soon as Ethan set them at her feet. Ethan watched, with tears pooling in his eyes, as his sister crushed her daughters to her. Whether it was intuition or the girls had gotten used to the fragility of their mother, Ethan could see how gentle and careful their returning hugs were.

Unable to wrangle his emotions, Ethan dropped to his knees and swept his three girls into a hug. He couldn't quite determine if Maggie was crying or laughing. His own emotions were sweeping through him like a tornado. How was it possible to feel so happy while fear and sadness were both pressing upon him like dual heavy boulders?

Ethan held tight to the girls for as long as he could. But he knew he couldn't sit around and enjoy the reunion. He had work to do and he suspected the first thing would be to face Cameron. He'd promised him he'd bring Ben back safely, but he'd utterly failed. Fuck, he was dreading letting go to face Cameron, but the sooner that was done, the sooner they could go after Ben.

As he stood, he pressed a kiss to the tops of Maggie's and the twins' heads. His sister tilted her chin and watched him, her eyes wide and red rimmed from crying. Neither spoke, but Ethan knew they both understood he had to go. He did his best to send a promise to her through his gaze alone that he'd be back.

Cameron was waiting for him only a few yards away. Ethan could see the tension in his body, which was coiled as though to strike, and he wondered if he'd be the unhappy recipient of that attack. He deserved it; he knew that much.

Ethan took a steadying breath and cautiously approached the bigger man. From the corner of his eye, he spotted Zach, Phia, and Mary, with Ryan, talking to some of the suits. As soon as he and Cameron settled their business, that was where he was heading; he planned to enlist their help to get his Ben back.

"Cameron, I'm so sorry—"

"Save it. Do you plan to get him back?"

"Yes."

"Do you care about him at all?"

"I love him." And there it was. Such a simple statement, three tiny little words, and yet one of the hardest sentences for people to say. Though it had slipped easily enough from his lips just then. Perhaps it was easy to say when it was true—when you couldn't hold it in anymore.

Ethan watched Cameron's face soften, but the tightness in his body never eased. "Good. Let's get him the fuck back, then." Cameron turned and strode toward the group of officials still engaged in conversation with Zach and Phia. Mary had wandered over to Maggie and the twins. Lucas stood over them, looking for all the world like the sentinel that Ethan was supposed to be.

"Agent Banner," Cameron called as they got closer. Ethan watched a tall ginger-haired man in the middle of the crowd straighten and turn toward them. Ethan could have picked him as the leader of this group from his bearing alone. Some people wore leadership well, and Agent Banner was definitely a leader. He was a handsome man, and though his face remained stoic and impassive, Ethan could see genuine care burning from behind his hazel eyes.

"Cameron, come on over. We've just been getting some intel from young Zach and Sophia here." Agent Banner's gaze flicked to Ethan, and Ethan knew immediately he was being sized up—judged. "You must be Ethan. I'm Agent Banner, FBI. Not sure how much you know, but short story is we've been watching Piper's camp for a while, but we've had nothing to act on until now. Zach tells me Ben's still there." It was both a statement and a question with the agent clearly wanting more information.

Ethan flicked his head, indicating for the agent to follow him away from the others. He didn't want Zach and Phia overhearing. Cameron and another agent joined them as Ethan relayed all the information he had on both the camp and what had happened, doing his best to sidestep around how the cult leader had been shot.

"Jesus, I should have known Ben would go off half-cocked like this and get his ass in trouble—man has a damn knack for it." Banner half grinned as he spoke.

"You know Ben?" Ethan asked.

"We met years ago, back in the military. He saved my ass a few times, and I've returned the favor a couple of times since then. I still owe him, though, so I'm gonna do whatever I can to get him the hell out of there. You in?" He turned his questioning hazel eyes to Ethan.

"Whatever I have to do, Agent Banner, I'm in."

"Excellent. Call me Alec. Even though I'm here officially, I suspect, because Ben's involved, we're gonna need to go off script a bit on this one." Agent Banner, Alec, clapped Ethan's shoulder and strode away, back toward the large group of agents who were currently in the process of what Ethan could only describe as gearing up. He watched as suit jackets were removed and replaced with bulletproof vests with the large, gold FBI lettering. Other agents were checking weapons and various other pieces of equipment. There were maybe twenty agents in all, and Ethan wondered if that would be enough.

"So, what's the plan?" Ethan asked as he followed Alec.

"Well, now I know Piper's wounded and potentially out of the picture it kind of changes things. Ben bought us some time. Hopefully, we can get the negotiators in, and they'll be able to talk our way into the campsite. Zach says an older man called Watson is—was—second-in-charge, so he'll be running the show now. Zach seems to think he's more moderate than Piper, so hopefully, we can get this sorted, no muss no fuss. The sticking point is Ben."

Just the sound of his name had the bile rising in Ethan's throat. He had to get him back, had to save him. The thought of losing him without ever having told him how much he loved him was like a bucket of icy-cold water dousing him, the shards of frost tearing into him, a thousand little needle pricks covering him in agony.

"Hey, Ethan...that's why you and I are going in first. We'll get him out, with any luck before the negotiation starts; that way, he can't be used as a hostage, or god forbid, slaughtered with the rest of the cult." Alec flinched at his own words, and he flicked an apologetic glance to Ethan and Cameron who had also quietly followed along. "Sorry. Sometimes I've got no tact."

"I can take you in...drop you close," Cameron offered, apparently blowing right past Alec's insensitive words.

"Actually, that's what I had planned. They've got to know that we'll be coming—as in, *the authorities* will be coming—so I figure if we get our choppers flying in over here—" he pointed to a spot on the large map that had been laid out in the back of one of their SUV's "—we can land here. So, hopefully, the focus in the camp will be on what the guys in the other helos are doing."

"There's nowhere to land there, but we can rappel down, which will work even better. If Cameron can get in low, the trees should offer coverage, and they may not see us rappel down." Ethan added.

"I'll get you low enough. There's plenty of slopes in this area, so we can use that as a kind of camouflage if you like. They won't see you going in."

Ethan nodded, agreeing with the logic. "As long as they think no one's on the ground, we should still have time to get in and get Ben."

Alec nodded along, agreeing to the plan, much to Ethan's relief. He glanced up at Ethan and gave him a quick wink. "Technically, you'll be going in as a guide, given that you've been in the camp before. As a civilian, though, you can't come in with me to get Ben out."

Ethan straightened to his full height, preparing to do battle with Agent Alec Banner if he had to. He was going in to get Ben, and not even the entire FBI was going to stop him. Just as he opened his mouth to speak, he noticed the small grin and yet another wink coming from Alec. He guessed this was what he meant about going off script to get Ben back. He nodded his understanding, and the three of them, along with the other agents, spent the twenty minutes they had to wait for the FBI helicopters and more agents to arrive, going over the plan and hashing out responses to various scenarios that may arise.

Finally, after everyone had arrived, Alec gave them all a ten-minute warning while he and his team made final preparations. Ethan and Cameron wandered over to where Maggie was still sitting. Maya and Riley were playing with some toys she'd obviously brought with her, and Mary was playing with them. Ryan and Lucas were talking a little way off with Zach and Phia. Ethan headed toward them.

"Zach, Phia. This is Cameron, Ben's brother, the pilot who flew us out." Ethan watched as Phia dropped a little curtsey and wondered again what kind of misogynist bullshit the women of the cult had been exposed to. Cameron offered her his hand, which she took after several moment's hesitation. When Cameron turned and offered his hand to Zach, he too hesitated to take it, and Ethan couldn't quite figure out why. Zach hadn't been like this with him and Ben, but he eventually took it.

"Good to meet you. Ethan tells me you were both a great help getting the little girls out."

Phia nodded, her eyes downcast while Zach jumped and finally released Cameron's hand. Zach coughed a little before managing to choke out a simple, "Yes." It was an unusual reaction from the young man who'd been, not exactly confident, but certainly calm and collected—and able to string a sentence together—in his and Ben's presence.

"We're going back to get Ben and do what we can to make sure everybody is safe at the camp," Ethan offered.

"I...um, heard that agent talk about my father... You told him that Ben..." Zach shifted uncomfortably while trying to find the words. Cameron reached over and put one of his enormous hands on Zach's narrow shoulder. The difference in size was so obvious that it looked to Ethan as though Cameron could crush Zach with one hand.

"I'm sorry, Zach. I'm sorry your father was wounded, but I know Ben, and he would have only done it to save others...if there was no other choice," Cameron spoke quietly, perhaps afraid of spooking Zach, given his obvious discomfort around him.

"My father is not a good man, and he would have killed every person there—men, women and children. I don't blame Ben. I'm glad he did what he did. That wasn't my concern." Zach raised defiant eyes to Cameron, and as Ethan watched, he thought, for the first time, that maybe Zach would get through this shit storm he'd been raised in and come out okay on the other side. "I don't want Ben to be in trouble for what he did though. Maybe if I had—"

"No. None of this is your fault, Zach. You did your best," Cameron reassured.

"We'll take everyone back to Cam's place," Lucas said, "and get them all settled and comfortable."

"I'd like to go with you," Zach murmured to him, so quiet that Ethan almost missed it. He turned to deny him, but realized he was actually looking at Cameron. "I liked the helicopter, and if it's okay, I'd like to fly back with you. I'm not sure if I can be any help, but maybe I..." His words drifted off as he seemed to run out of the bit of confidence he'd mustered to voice his request.

Cameron shifted nervously and scratched at the back of his neck, sending a pleading glance to Ethan. "Um...I don't know about that. It could still be dangerous. It might be best if you stayed here."

Zach flushed red to the tips of his ears, and Ethan did his best to contain the small bubble of laughter threatening to burst from him. Seemed the Cronin brothers had both cast a spell over Zach Piper.

Zach scuffed at the ground with the toes of his boots and straightened his spine. He glanced at Ethan before turning his glare to Cameron. "I know how dangerous it might be. That's my family back there...the people in the commune. They're not all bad."

Ethan could see a standoff brewing and chose to excuse himself to say goodbye to Maggie before they left. She sat huddled in her chair with her eyes closed, but Ethan could tell from the small smiles that played across her lips whenever one of her daughters spoke or laughed that she wasn't asleep.

"Maggie," he said as he kneeled down beside her. "I've got to go. We're going back to get Ben and try to help the others in the camp."

Maggie opened her eyes that shone with nothing but happiness for the first time since he'd come back into her life. She reached out with a frail hand and took hold of one of his. "Come back safe, Ethan, and with Ben. You deserve him, you deserve to be happy."

Ethan pressed a kiss to her cheek and gently fluffed Maya's and Riley's hair as he stood and walked away. No big goodbyes because he knew he'd be back—he had to be; Maggie and her kids depended on him now and he wasn't going to let them down either.

As he approached Cameron's chopper, he noticed Agent Alec Banner was already seated inside and ready to go. The rotors were turning, working their way up to full speed, and Zach was sitting in the cockpit next to Cameron. Ethan smiled to see the young man had won that battle.

Chapter Eighteen

BEN

As he took yet another fist to the stomach, Ben could at least be thankful he was dealing with amateurs. Just a little higher and slightly upward and they'd get his solar plexus—and that would sting. The blows to his guts he could manage, even after the broken nose. Sure, he was hurting, and he definitely wanted them to leave him the fuck alone, but they hadn't yet hit one of his sweet spots. No kidney shots, no blows to his neck, jaw, or behind his ear. Either they didn't want to do too much real damage, or they didn't know how.

"I'm gonna ask you again...who the fuck are you? And where are our children?" the man growled in his ear.

Ben spit out blood that pooled in his mouth from the broken nose and glanced up at the man who was taking such delight at using him as a punching bag. He couldn't have been much younger than Ben, and if it wasn't for the snarl that twisted his features, he would have been an attractive man. His knuckles were bloody from his assault, but he wasn't a fighter. Given half a chance, Ben knew he could take him easily.

"Who are any of us, really? It's the great conundrum of our time—who are we? What are we doing here and wh—" The man did his best to beat the smartass out of Ben, but better men than him had tried—and failed. A beating he could take.

"Any luck, Peter?" asked an older man as he swept into the tent where Ben was being held.

"Not yet. He's got a big mouth, though, so once he starts singing, he's not gonna shut up," Peter replied.

The older man squatted in front of Ben, and he knew immediately from his snarl and cruel eyes he was related to Peter, the fucktard who'd been failing to break him for the last half hour or so. He was also the nasty-looking fucker from earlier.

"My name's Justin Watson, son, and I suspect, thanks to you, I'm going to be the next leader of our family now. I'm very curious to know who you are, why you tried to kill Arnold, and most importantly, why you stole my granddaughters." There was a sharpness in this man's eyes that was missing from his younger version—and there was also a creepiness that was making Ben's skin crawl.

"First off...I'm not your son, but I'm guessing 'fists of fury' over there is. Second, I don't know anything about shooting poor old Arnold, but if I'd wanted to kill him he'd be well and truly dead. And lastly—and I'm going to say this real slow and clear so I'm not misunderstood—those little girls belong with their mother, not in some freak-show tent city."

"Is it a freak show to live as our lord commands, to spend our time in worship of god?"

"It is if you're marrying little girls off to grown men, and it goes way beyond freaky if you plan to have everyone either kill themselves or each other," Ben snapped back, feeling the fury of what had been going on here ripping through him once more. Bad enough when adults hurt each other, but when there were children involved...little else infuriated Ben more.

Ben expected some sort of defense or excuse or explanations of a misunderstanding to be forthcoming from Justin Watson, but instead, the man blew right past the accusations. "Rebecca and Miriam are my granddaughters, and I want them back."

"Their names are Maya and Riley, and by now, they'll be safely with their mother, and you will never get your hands on them again," Ben replied through gritted teeth. The old guy made his skin crawl with his eerily calm demeanor, and Ben would have much preferred for Peter to continue his beating rather than being creeped out by this guy.

"I'm fairly certain we don't have a lot of time here. Peter tells me Zach was also taken away in that helicopter, and if you are the type of people I think you are, then Zach will no doubt be speaking to the authorities right now about Arnold Piper and his plans. Piper always did underestimate that boy." Watson shook his head as though he couldn't quite believe anyone having a problem with the mass suicide of hundreds. "I wish you people would understand that we follow god's law only—not the law of man. So, I'll make this simple...you'll get on the phone to whoever you need to speak to in order to bring my granddaughters back, or I will kill one child for every hour you delay. And we have enough children here to make it a very distressing couple of days for you."

Ben's stomach tossed and turned a thousand fucking times as he considered Watson's threat. A cold sweat prickled all over his skin, and he seriously thought for a moment that he may be sick. He'd been threatened with bluffs before, but this time he didn't doubt for a second that this lunatic would do exactly as he'd just promised.

Watson leered down at him with the coldest, nastiest look Ben had ever seen. "I'll give you thirty minutes to think it over."

Thirty minutes. There was nothing to think over. There was no way Ben was bringing those little girls back to this maniac, and there was no way he was letting any other child come to harm. Watson had given him a gift—thirty minutes to work out exactly how he was going to get out of this mess—and as the men had all foolishly followed Watson from the tent, they'd left him alone to plan.

First thing was to get these fucking zip ties off, which is surprisingly easy if you know how. Ben brought his tied hands to his mouth and pulled on the zip tie with his teeth, tightening it as much as possible. He put his hands in front of him and pulled them back as hard as he could onto his stomach, snapping the ties easily.

The next step was getting the hell out of there—if they didn't have him to blackmail, then the kids would be safe. As much as he'd love to stick around and give Peter and his dad a bit of payback, the best option in this case was to run.

There'd be a guard at the tent flap, he knew that much. These people may be amateurs, but they weren't bumbling idiots. Ben cast his glance around, looking for anything he might be able to use to cut the heavy tent canvas. He'd been stripped of everything he had on him, when they first brought him back to the camp, and it had all been taken away to god knows where. In fact, the tent he was in was mostly empty apart from what looked like a pile of bedding—pillows, blankets, a few sleeping bags.

Ben only spent a few minutes searching through the items for some kind of knife before deciding not to waste any more time. He'd just have to go out the front door and hope that there were only one or two guards around. The fact that it was broad daylight wasn't going to make the job of getting away from there unnoticed any easier.

As silently as he could, Ben sidled up to the door flap of the tent. He kneeled and listened, trying to make out how many people may be outside the door. For the first few minutes, there was little noise to hear. A few footsteps as people passed by, the shuffle of feet on the other side of the canvas indicating at least one guard and some mumbled conversations he couldn't make out. In the distance, he could hear a sound that was getting louder and louder, and if he wasn't mistaken, it was the noise of several helicopters getting closer and closer.

It wasn't long after the sound was first audible that movement in the camp picked up. It was likely that this was the cavalry coming in to save the day, which meant that either Watson would be back for him any second to use as a hostage, or far more likely—and terrifying—he'd implement the suicide protocol. One thing Ben did know was that there was no way Watson would be going out with the rest of his *family*. Only a few moments with him and Ben could see him for what he was. He was a narcissist. The man was too arrogant, too in love with himself to ever want to die. Would he take everyone else out though? Ben suspected the answer was yes, so the question now was what the fuck he was going to do about it.

Ben could hear heavy footsteps coming closer to the tent. He quickly inched back to the position he'd been left in and did his best to hide his unbound hands. He strained to hear whatever might be going on outside.

All he could make out was a muffled conversation, but he was able to catch a few words that allowed him to understand the gist of it. FBI helicopters were flying near the camp, and Watson had urged everyone to lay low. A disembodied head popped through the flap and gave him a quick once-over. Ben did his best to appear beaten and broken. Obviously satisfied that the prisoner was still there, the guard backed out, leaving Ben alone to once again consider his options.

There was really only one course of action to take. He had to protect the children. He knew roughly where they were, thanks to Zach explaining the layout of the camp. But would they all be there now? Watson would probably send everyone to an area where they would be conveniently all together if he needed to implement the Jonestown protocol. The school tent would be ideal to keep the children in one place.

The guard was simple enough to take care of. Once Ben had him inside the tent, he used torn-up pillowcases to bind and gag him. He shouldered the weapon he'd stripped from the hapless guard and edged his way to the entry of the tent. When he poked his head through the flap he could see that there was absolutely no one around.

Despite the emptiness of the camp, Ben moved cautiously. There were innocent people here, and he had no interest in hurting any of them who may get in his way. It looked as though he'd been right and Watson had sent most people to cover. He knew roughly where he was in the camp from watching as he'd been led in earlier. Zach's map of the camp was still fresh in his mind, and he used it now to make his way toward the school tent.

In the distance, he heard the sound of the helicopters that had so spooked Watson. It was hard to make out exactly how many, but it sounded as though there were at least three on the eastern side of the camp. The acoustics in the gully-like area where the cult's campsite had been established wreaked havoc with his hearing, however, and he really couldn't be terribly accurate about the sound or the direction it was coming from. For a brief moment it sounded as though other choppers were coming in from the west and Ben wondered if they were planning on surrounding the camp.

All he could be certain of was that the situation was escalating quickly, and he needed to do whatever it took for the children who would be caught in the middle of this shit show to be safe. He sidled along the back of one of the tents that lay opposite the school and carefully poked his head around. He'd learned fast during his deployments with the military that if you stuck your head out too long when trying to survey your surroundings you'd likely get the bloody thing shot off. Ben had become an expert of a quick look to take in every detail possible.

There was a man and a woman at the door of the tent. Both were armed and both looked physically imposing. When he'd pulled back from the corner and retreated to cover, he recalled the images of the two guards, assessing which posed the greater threat. People tended to naturally assume the man would be the bigger problem to deal with, but Ben had seen plenty of women in battle so there was no way he was making that assumption. Women could be every bit as hardcore as men, and if their children were involved, things could get brutal. Though there was no guarantee, if they'd been brainwashed by Piper and his cronies, that these people's instincts would be to save the children.

The man was taller than the woman he stood guard with, but her bearing was definitely more confident and aggressive. She looked as though she knew how to handle herself, so Ben believed she'd be the bigger danger. He firmed up a plan hoping that those inside the tent had been instructed to stay there, regardless of what they heard, because it was extremely unlikely he could do this without making noise.

"Ben," a voice from behind him hissed. It didn't frighten him at all—he'd told no one here his name. The only other option was that Ethan had come back for him, and that was a thought that both thrilled him and terrified him at the same time. Ben suspected the shit was about to go down here, and he didn't want Ethan in the middle of it.

He turned in the direction of the voice and caught a glimpse of Ethan and another man furtively rounding the back of the tent he was huddled against. Ben watched as they sidled toward him and allowed the hint of a grin when he recognized the man with Ethan. Fucking Alec Banner; he should have known he'd be in the thick of things. The man never could stay away from a fight and always, always protected the innocent.

"Jesus, Ben, thank god you're okay," Ethan whispered, reaching out a hand to gently stroke his fingers down Ben's swollen cheek, carefully avoiding his broken, bloody nose. Ben closed his eyes and leaned into the touch, relishing it despite the predicament they were in.

"The girls? Zach?"

"All safe. Cam got us out. What the hell were you thinking?"

Ben picked up on both the fear and anger in Ethan's words and reached over with his own hand to lay it gently on Ethan's cheek. It wasn't really the time or the place, but if he knew one thing about this life it was that it could all be over in the blink of an eye, and Ben didn't believe in missed opportunities.

"I was thinking that I love you, and I couldn't stand to watch you get hurt." Ben shrugged as though it was the simplest notion in the world, and to him it was.

"You stupid fuck. Do you think it was any easier for me? Fuck," Ethan quietly gritted out, obviously conscious of their surroundings. "I fucking love you, too, and do you know how hard that was for me to fly away from you like that? To leave you behind. Jesus"—Ethan dragged his fingers through his hair, pulling at it hard enough that it must have hurt—"this is so not how I wanted to say this to you."

Ethan loved him. He'd said the words, and Ethan was definitely not the kind of man who said something he didn't mean. Ben had the sudden urge to shout for fucking joy but instead favored Ethan with a smile so big he wondered if he might actually split his face.

"You love me?" he whispered.

"How could I not?"

"This is very touching and all, but do ya think we could put your romance on hold for just a moment and deal with the bad guys?" Alec finally spoke, and Ben marveled that it had taken him so long.

"What the hell are you doing here, Banner?"

"That's Agent-in-Charge Banner to you, asshat. And I'm here to save your freaking life, Cronin."

"Well, that'll bring it down to five you still owe me. Good to see you, man." Ben smiled before leaning toward Ethan and pressing their lips together. His entire face throbbed, but he needed this kiss. When he'd taken enough to tide him over until they were alone and somewhere safe, he pulled back and winked at Ethan. "I heard what you said, Ethan, and when this is done, we're gonna have an epically long talk about this." He gestured between them.

"Let's get the hell out of here, okay? My men will hold for another ten minutes to let us get out before they set down and try to negotiate with these clowns."

"Not leaving, Alec. There's a tent full of kids over there, and I'm not leaving in case the guy in charge decides to go ahead with Piper's plan." Ben's tone left no room for argument, though he expected to get none from either man—he knew the kind of men they both were and neither would leave children alone and unprotected. "I've met Watson," Ben continued, assuming Ethan had already told him about Piper and that Alec would know who Watson was from Zach. "He's a mean son of a bitch, and I don't doubt for a second that he won't take out those kids—and there's nothing spiritual at all about his motives. He's just your garden-variety psycho."

"All right. What's your plan?" Alec replied.

Chapter Nineteen

ETHAN

Ethan's heart was still thumping in his chest as he stood watch, and it had nothing to do with what was going on around him. He'd told Ben he loved him, and it had been so fucking easy to do. He hadn't even thought about it. The words had just come out of their own volition, and they were the most truthful words he'd spoken.

He hadn't at all liked being left here as lookout while Ben and Alec had gone to deal with the guards at the school tent, but Alec had been adamant that it was his ass on the line if something went wrong. He'd watched Alec hand over a silenced weapon to Ben and felt a little pissed that he hadn't been offered one. Ethan begrudgingly agreed to stay behind after a short squabble about Ben also being a civilian—to which Alec glanced at Ben and fucking laughed. He wasn't sure what the hell that meant, but he was damn well going to find out when this was over.

From his vantage point, he watched as Ben and Alec approached from either side of the school tent and easily subdued their targets. At least Ben managed it with ease. Alec seemed to have a minor struggle with the woman he was trying to quietly overcome. The woman was putting up one hell of a fight, but it still only took a few minutes for both guards to be bound gagged and hauled to where Ethan waited.

"Let's get them secured in an empty tent," Ben whispered. "If you think you can manage that, Agent-in-Charge Banner." He smirked. "Seems like you've lost your touch, man."

"Fuck you, Cronin. Lioness protecting her cubs, and you knew that, you fucker," Alec quipped.

Ethan would have to add finding out more about Alec Banner and his relationship with Ben to the long list of things he wanted to talk to Ben about when this was over. But for right now, he'd just have to shove down that spark of jealousy that flared while watching them banter together.

For whatever reason, there were plenty of empty tents, and in no time, they had the guards inside one and the flap secured so that it couldn't be opened by them. They'd only have to crawl with their bound hands and feet to the sides of the tent and push on them to draw attention to themselves, but luckily there was no one around to see them. It was damn eerie.

Ethan could hear soft murmurings from the school tent, but the noise was minimal and he suspected the children were as doped as Maya and Riley had appeared to be when he and Ben had first pulled them out of this nightmare. He thought of his two little nieces now safely back with their mother, getting checked out by a local doctor. They were so tiny, so helpless. Their mother had tried her best to keep them safe, and fortunately when she couldn't, he and Ben had been able to step in. How many kids out there had no one to protect them? The familiar anger at the thought of kids in harm's way, especially at the hands of adults, threatened to emerge, but Ethan pushed it down. Not the time or place.

"Ethan, we're going to watch the tent to make sure no one goes in. Alec's going to put on the guard's hat and take his position. He's a similar build, and hopefully, with his hat pulled down, he'll be able to pass for him on a cursory glance. We'll be watching so we can back him up," Ben explained.

"What about your people, Alec? Did you get through to them?" Ethan asked.

"I gave them the go-ahead. Briefly explained what we were doing and our suspicions." Alec spoke quietly, with an economy of words. "Don't worry. We've learned a lot since Waco and Jonestown and others. I'm confident we can end this peacefully," he added after Ethan threw him a concerned glance.

Alec turned and walked toward the school tent as casually as if he had always belonged there in the cult's campsite. Ethan had to admire his bravado.

"There never has been and never will be anything between Alec and me, Ethan," Ben whispered as soon as Alec was out of earshot.

Ethan turned startled eyes to him. "What? Why...I mean, I know. I never thought..."

"Yeah, ya did. And I gotta tell you, it's adorable that you were jealous," Ben smugly replied.

Damn, this man was going to be the fucking death of him. Ethan could feel the flush burning its way across his cheeks and up his throat. He heard Ben actually giggle and couldn't stave off the smile that bloomed on his pinked face.

Ethan turned from Ben in an effort to keep his mind on the job. He heard helicopters powering down in the distance and braced himself for whatever may come their way in the next few moments. He'd learned a long time ago that people were more than capable of doing the most shocking things. He never underestimated anybody's propensity for evil.

Alec was positioned outside the tent, his body hunched a little in an effort to disguise his identity. A quick-passing glance would more than likely satisfy; his body shape and size was close enough to the tied-up guard and their dark clothing was similar. Ethan hoped it would be enough, because he had no desire to get into any kind of fight with children so close. He also hoped that if a skirmish did come their way it wouldn't end up in a firefight. Those canvas tents would offer no protection at all to the kids inside, and if Ben was correct, the camp leaders weren't especially interested in preserving the lives of their young.

It was still remarkably quiet with only the dwindling noise of the helicopters powering down breaking the silence. Ethan strained to hear anything that may indicate trouble coming their way, but so far there was nothing.

"You all right?" he asked Ben, who had preternaturally stilled beside him.

"Feels off," came his clipped reply.

Ethan scanned their surroundings again looking for anything out of place when the silence was shattered by the report of gunfire. As one, he and Ben ran from their position and made their way to Alec's side. Ethan could see Alec was listening intently through his earpiece and whatever he heard he didn't like, if the fury that came over his features was any indication.

"Fuck, it's gone to hell. Watson didn't wait for them all to get out of the helos before opening fire. We've got to get these kids out. Miller said they can hold their own, but Watson's probably gonna send someone for the kids. We need to move."

Ben was half inside the tent before Alec had even finished speaking, with Ethan hot on his tail. He wasn't letting Ben out of his fucking sight.

The scene he encountered once he'd cleared the flap of the tent was like something from a nightmare. There had to be at least twenty kids spread out on the floor of the tent. The youngest, a newborn, being cradled in the arms of a boy of maybe fifteen, who appeared to be the oldest in the group. The boy was staring at them fiercely as if daring them to try to hurt the children.

Two men, each with rifles in their arms, stood at either end of the group. The rifles were being held loosely, the men holding them clearly not expecting any kind of interruption to their plans.

Ethan could feel the presence of Alec close to his back and felt rather than saw him raise his arm. In front of him, he watched as Ben similarly raised his.

"Put your weapons down," Alec demanded. His voice was calm, his voice icily soft. It was a command, and if the men had any sense they'd obey it immediately.

Unfortunately, one of the men didn't seem to have any sense at all as he began to raise his weapon directly toward some of the children. Ethan braced himself for what he knew would come.

The twin-muted retorts of Alec and Ben's silenced weapons still managed to echo in the cramped confines of the tent. Ethan's focus went immediately to the children. He didn't much care how injured the men who'd no doubt been prepared to murder every innocent child present were—or even if they were still breathing. He did know, without checking, that they were out of action. He trusted Ben, knew what he was capable of, and Ben trusted Alec. That was good enough for Ethan.

Most of the children looked blankly around, many of them gasping, and even a few had stifled screams when Ben and Alec opened fire, but the whole scene was disturbingly subdued. As he observed the little faces staring back at him, he saw mostly resigned, almost glazed-over expressions—particularly the older ones. A few of the younger children were crying, but even their cries were quiet and contained.

Alec and Ben were occupied with the men they'd shot as the tent flap was pulled back, and another man entered. Ethan didn't hesitate. He lashed out with his right fist, sending it into his opponent's nose with a satisfying crunch of broken cartilage. He didn't allow the man a second to recover before jamming his left fist into his exposed and vulnerable stomach. To finish off and ensure his victim was finished, he brought his knee up to slam into the already broken nose as the other man bent over, gasping for air from the blow to his stomach.

It was over in a matter of seconds, and it was only then that Ethan stopped to think that maybe this man meant no harm at all—maybe he was one of Alec's men. As difficult as that guilt would be to bear, it'd be easier than if he'd done nothing and innocent children were hurt.

Ethan crouched beside the man where he'd fallen, curled in on himself as his body tried to acclimate to the pain that must have been coursing through it. There was no struggle or attempt to resist as Ethan bound his hands and feet with zip ties.

When he stood, job done, he came face-to-face with Ben, who asked quietly, "You okay?"

Ethan nodded because he was. Ben was alive; he was alive, and all the children were okay—so far. "Yeah. Yeah, I'm okay. What's the plan?"

"Alec's trying to get through to his people again to find out what's going on. If things look good from his end, then we stay here...make sure nobody comes in to hurt these kids. If things are going ass up, then we get the kids out." Ben was all business, and it was fucking attractive to see to say the least. It had always been hot to watch Ben when he was on the job, but this was an entirely new level. He was strong, competent and dangerous—and it was a fucking turn-on. He didn't know what that said about him but he didn't really give a crap. Ben was his—every single bit of him, including this deadliness.

"How're they?" Ethan asked, nodding toward the men Ben and Alec had shot.

"Flesh wounds. They'll live. We've patched them up, and the FBI medics will get them on the way through."

The children were huddled together, seemingly having suffered no further shock at Ethan's violent display. He saw the oldest boy, still with the newborn nestled in his arms, exchange glances with one of the older girls. He wondered if they were going to have a problem with them. Would they fight back? After all he, Ben, and Alec were just strangers to them—strangers who'd shot and incapacitated men these kids would have known all their lives.

What the hell would he do if they did fight? He had zero interest in getting into it with a couple of kids.

"Okay." Alec's brusque tone interrupted his thoughts of what-ifs. "Miller said they're making progress, but it's slow going. We've got agents sweeping through the campsite trying to prevent any mass suicides or murders, but Watson is hindering their progress. Miller can't guarantee he'll get here before Watson and his people. We need to move these kids to at least buy Miller and the team some time."

"What about one of those tents we passed on the edge of the campsite? They all seemed empty and big enough to hold us all," Ethan suggested.

"Perfect. At minimum, it'll take them some time to find us as long as we can keep the kids relatively quiet," Alec replied, looking around at the wide-eyed children.

"Don't think that's gonna be a problem. Not sure what the hell is going on here, but these kids seem drugged too." Ethan glanced again at the older boy and girl who, though oddly quiet, still seemed to be more animated than the rest of the group.

"Alec, you take the lead, I'll bring up the rear...and Ethan you stay in the middle."

For whatever reason, maybe the overall stress of his situation or maybe that spark of jealousy was bigger than Ethan originally thought, but Ben's order pissed him the hell off. "I'm not the weak link, Ben," he snapped back, immediately regretting his words especially when he turned to catch Ben's hurt gaze.

"I've never thought that, Ethan. Not for a second."

Ethan reached out and let the tips of his fingers gently trace over the apple of Ben's cheek. "Of course you haven't. I'm sorry... I didn't mean... Let's just get this done."

All three men turned to the group of children, and Ethan figured this was likely going to be their biggest problem—convincing them to follow three strangers who'd just hurt people they knew and likely cared about.

What the hell could they say to these kids? How could they possibly convince them to trust them? Ethan suspected that if they could get the older ones on their side the others would easily follow along.

"Son," Ben's voice held no gruffness as he spoke to the oldest boy. "What's your name?"

"Isaac," came his clipped reply.

"Isaac, we need to get these children out of here."

"No, sir. Mr. Watson told us to stay here until he came for us." Isaac's voice was timid yet still contained the hint of a backbone. Ethan thought he would have been a naturally confident young man under different circumstances. It was a perfect example of the whole nature versus nurture debate boiled down into one frightened young boy.

Ethan crouched down so he was eye to eye with the boy. His size could be intimidating to grown men, let alone a small-statured teenager.

"Isaac, Mr. Watson is uh…very busy right now. You've probably heard all the noise going on. All we want to do is to help you get all of these children to safety." Ethan watched as Isaac digested his words, his gaze flickering to the three bound men in various states of consciousness, sizing up the situation as best he could.

When his gaze eventually returned to Ethan, there was accusation in his pale gray eyes. "You hurt them."

"We didn't want to," Ethan hurried to reassure. "We knew the children were in here, and we were scared they were going to be hurt, so we had to stop these men from getting in our way. I promise you… I promise you that the only thing we want to do is keep the children safe."

Ethan was banking on Isaac wanting to do the same thing. He could hear Alec shifting behind him and suspected the FBI agent was getting seriously antsy to get out of there. To do that, they needed to win over Isaac, who was now sharing another look with the older girl.

"Okay. We all stay together, though, and nobody…*nobody* else gets hurt."

"I swear. Thank you, Isaac." Ethan turned to Ben. "I think most of them can walk. I can carry the two little kids there, leaving you and Alec free to watch our fronts and backs."

Just the barest hint of a smile tugged at Ben's lips before he clapped Ethan on the shoulder. "Let's do this."

Chapter Twenty

BEN

From his place at the back of the group, Ben could see Alec moving efficiently, yet carefully, through the campsite. Alec's head darted from side to side as he appeared to be vigilantly watching for danger, while at the same time searching for a safe place to stash the children.

A few years older than Ben, Alec had been an excellent soldier when he'd known him way back in the past. He'd been the ideal man to have at one's back, front, or side in any situation. It blew him away that he'd somehow found his way to be here today, fighting at Ben's side again.

Ben let his gaze drift to the children following behind Alec, who were unnaturally quiet and docile, as the twins had been, and he wondered again what the hell had been done to them, or given to them, to make them that way. At least they'd been able to talk Isaac around so he was helping rather than fighting against them.

Well, really, it had been Ethan who'd talked him around. His Ethan, who walked taller than any of them in the middle of the group. Ethan, who stole his breath away with just a look.

Ben could tell from the stiffness of his movements that Ethan was fully alert and aware of every single thing going on around him. He had seen this version of Ethan plenty of times when they worked together. His broad shoulders were hunched a little from the burden of the two young children he carried in his strong arms. Despite this, everything about his bearing screamed that Ethan was ready to spring into action at a moment's notice if needed—and Ben couldn't deny Ethan in sentinel mode was a fucking turn-on.

It may have been luck or maybe just the skill of the team he worked with at Krispin Security, but in the two years Ben had been working with Ethan, the only time there'd been trouble more dramatic than an overenthusiastic fan or badly behaved paparazzi had been when Lucas's brother had tried to kill him and Ryan. Ethan and Ben had been collateral damage that day, but Ben remembered how it had all played out. He remembered how Ethan had run into a burning room with no thought to his own safety. He also remembered how he'd collapsed to the ground, Lucas flung over his back, as they'd reached the bottom of the stairs. Ben had never been so terrified in his life—and he'd been in plenty of sticky spots, including that same day when he'd been shot moments before Ethan had run into the fire.

The silver lining to that horrible day had been the absolute certainty that he needed to tell Ethan how he felt. He'd watched Ethan collapse to the ground, unconscious from smoke inhalation, and known in that second that he couldn't keep his feelings to himself anymore. Ethan deserved to know someone loved him. Of course, the big fucker had taken off before he got the chance to tell him anything.

Well, I've been given another chance, and I'm taking it. There's no way in hell I'm going to let Ethan run from me again.

Ahead of him, he glimpsed Alec raise his arm and come to a stop. After quickly checking around him, Ben ran forward, halting at Alec's side.

"I'm pretty sure this tent is empty, and big enough for us all to get in. It's either this or we take them into the woods. Your call, Cronin," Alec whispered.

Ben nodded toward the tent. "Let's do it." He didn't wait for Alec to reply before he edged closer and gently tugged on the zip. As quickly and quietly as he could manage, he yanked the zip up and pried open a gap big enough for him to squeeze his head in to take a look around.

As Alec had suspected, the tent was empty of people. There were some inflatable mattresses scattered around and piles of folded clothes in one corner. In another corner were baskets of what he assumed to be dirty clothes waiting to be washed. Ben unzipped it all the way, pulled the flap wider and gestured for Alec to start leading the children inside.

Like little robots, the children followed Alec one after another into the tent, none offering any protest to the situation. Only Isaac and an older girl looked even remotely as though they were truly aware of what was going on. His blood was fucking boiling at the state these kids were in, and he itched to make someone pay—even though he'd already made a start with Piper, he now wished he'd finished the job properly.

Once they were all in, Ben stayed outside, standing guard again over the helpless children within the tent. It took less time than he expected for Ethan to poke his head outside, his big body quickly following after.

"How much did it cost you to be out here with me instead of babysitting inside?" he asked Ethan.

"I owe Banner a box of Cubans," Ethan gritted out.

Ben threw his head back and only just managed to stifle the laughter that threatened to burst out of him. "I've got a box of Montecristo No.2's that I won from Alec years ago. Give those back to him and he may just forgive you for leaving him alone in a tent with twenty-odd kids."

"He's a good friend of yours?"

"We went through a hell of a lot together. I haven't seen him for years... I lost contact with people after I was recruited. He's a good man...and a good friend," Ben replied. He had lost a lot of friends over the years, to death or just life pulling them in opposite directions. It would be nice to get one back.

He turned and looked up at Ethan, who was standing stock-still beside him, his gaze tracing over every bit of ground that surrounded them, watching. "You were good back there...with Isaac, I mean."

Ethan glanced at him. "He's a scared kid, but I could see he cared about the others. I was just hoping he cared enough not to start anything with us."

"Ethan...in all this mess, I don't think I've even told you how very sorry I am about Maggie. I'd give anything if I could do more for her...for you."

Ethan turned his entire body so they were facing each other, keeping his eyes fixed on Ben's. "You've done more than I could've asked for already. I don't think... I don't think anyone can help Maggie now, but getting her girls back was the best thing we could have done for her. And I couldn't have done it without you." A sad smile caught at Ethan's lips as he finished speaking, and in that moment, Ben could almost feel the grief that awaited Ethan when he lost his sister. All that time wasted because of their parents and their utter refusal to face the reality that one of their sons was a monster.

"I know you'd prefer it never happens, and I hope more than anything it doesn't happen for a long, long time, but one day you're going to be a wonderful father figure for those girls." If there was one thing Ben had learned through the loss of his own parents, it was not to stick his head in the sand about it. He'd always hated when people tried to tell him that maybe his mom would be okay even when there was nothing surer than her imminent death.

Ben was relieved when a happier grin tugged at Ethan's perfect lips. "Jesus"—he shook his head—"can you imagine when they're teenagers? I've always wanted to scare the shit out of some punk kid coming to date my little girl, even though I never thought I'd actually have kids, and I'd give up the idea in a heartbeat to keep Maggie—" Ethan faltered, the words seeming to catch in his throat.

"I know you would. I know," Ben soothed. "I'm gonna be there for you—however you need me. I'll be there, Ethan."

Ethan's eyes shone with unshed tears when he looked at Ben. "Fuck, listen to us sappy old goats...Jesus." He shook his head, seeming to shake away the gloominess of the conversation at the same time. Ethan laid his palm on Ben's cheek, his thumb brushing gently against his skin. "Thank you, Ben."

Ben answered with a wink and then turned his head to look back out at their surroundings when he heard footsteps drawing nearer. Ethan stiffened beside him. Ben pulled the Glock from his waistband, ready to deal with whatever eventuality was approaching. He wished Ethan also had a weapon, but like so many other combat situations he'd found himself in, they'd just have to make do.

A tall figure came toward them. In spite of the darkness, Ben could immediately tell two things about the person who was approaching them. First, it was a woman, and second, she knew exactly what she was doing. Ben hoped that meant she was on their side. She was no lioness protecting her cubs like the last woman they'd encountered. Besides, he couldn't imagine the misogynists running this show would have allowed too many women to even handle a gun, much less wield it with the confidence and professionalism that this woman displayed.

She suddenly turned in their direction, her gun held steady and extended from her body. Her face was mostly in shadow, but she was looking directly at them. "FBI," she called, her voice calm and confident. "Put your weapon down, hands locked behind your head. Now."

Ben moved slowly, cautiously. He suspected this agent wouldn't spook easily, but he didn't want to give her any reason to flinch. He lay the gun down and away from his feet and slowly stood and laced his fingers behind his head. Ethan had already assumed the position.

"My name is Ben Cronin. This is Ethan Stone. We're here with Agent Alec Banner. He's inside the tent with the children." Ben spoke with the same calm confidence the woman had used.

"Agent Banner?" she called out.

"Agent Morrison," Alec replied. "I'm coming out...hands first." Ben knew people got jumpy under high stress, and Alec would not want to be shot by a nervous colleague, so he was moving as cautiously as Ben had moments ago.

Slowly, Alec emerged from the tent, hands out in front and clearly visible to Agent Morrison. "Libby. It's all good here. We've got the children safe. What's the status with Watson and the rest of the commune?"

"Only a few stragglers left. Benoit and Peters are chasing them down. We've got the uninjured rounded up and under guard. Backup is incoming and most of the hostiles have been neutralized." Libby Morrison had lowered her gun when Alec had confirmed his identity, but she remained vigilant, poised for further action.

"How about our guys? Any injuries?"

Agent Morrison scoffed and offered her boss a lopsided grin. "Williams has got a scratch—again. I'm surprised you can't hear him screaming from here."

"Oh, Jesus. I can't go through that again." Ben could almost hear Alec rolling his eyes as he replied. Alec had always been a tough son of a bitch, and if you weren't bleeding out of your eyes or you didn't have at least one limb hanging off, then as far as Alec Banner was concerned, there was nothing wrong with you.

"Okay. I'll get Miller to send some guys over, and we'll start bringing the kids out. Are the adults all pretty calm under guard?" Alec questioned Libby.

"Yes, sir. Most are fairly docile. A few of the men are still agitating a little, but most have settled right down, especially without Watson around to fire them up."

Alec nodded and walked a little away, talking into his comm, presumably to Agent Miller. Libby still stood stiffly, her eyes shifting to glance between him and Ethan. If Ben read her right, she was sizing them up.

"So...you're bare-ass Cronin?" She smirked.

"Ah, for fuck's sake. It happened once. I'm gonna kill Banner," Ben groaned. "You lose your clothes and have to walk naked through a black-tie event one time, *one time,* and you never live that shit down."

"Bare ass? Really? Tell me more." Ethan's smart-ass tone had him rolling his eyes.

"Nothing more to tell," he answered as Libby Morrison chuckled to herself.

"Okay. Let's get these kids out of here." Alec's authority was stamped clearly in his manner. He was the agent in charge again. Two other agents were approaching, and Ben could feel himself start to relax—just a little.

Ethan headed back into the tent, Ben following closely behind.

"Isaac, we're going to take you guys to be with the rest of your…group. Everything has settled down now, and there's no danger." Ethan spoke quietly to the teenage boy who watched him with intelligent, wary eyes.

Isaac nodded, and the girl he'd been sitting with stood with him, and together they got the rest of the children back on their feet. Some of the younger ones had drifted off to sleep, so Ben and Ethan helped to rouse them. They let a few of them sleep while the older ones began moving out of the tent, led by the girl. Isaac remained behind with the still-sleeping ones, unwilling to leave them alone. Libby and a few more agents came in to carry the remaining children.

Ben looked around to ensure the tent was clear before following Ethan and Isaac out. When he stepped through the flap, it took a split-second for him to register what he was seeing.

Alec and the other agents were walking away from them, loaded down with their sleeping cargo. Ethan stood side-on to Ben, his arms raised in the air, palms forward. Isaac stood close to Ethan, facing him, and behind him was Justin Watson, a pistol held tightly in his grip, the barrel resting against Isaac's temple.

"I'm not interested in getting into another fight here. But I'm taking Isaac with me. He's my insurance that I won't be followed. I haven't finished my work yet, and I can start another family." Watson shrugged and turned his smirking face to Ben.

Ben wanted nothing more than to rip that fucking grin right off his face. Isaac seemed completely unfazed that this man had a gun to his head, and the thought of the brainwashing that must have been done here for him to so calmly accept his predicament had Ben's anger flaring all over again.

Neither Ethan nor Ben moved, and he daren't shout for help. Watson was a loose cannon, and Ben didn't want the guilt of Isaac's death on his shoulders—that would be one death he couldn't shake off or justify.

Ben watched as Watson slowly backed up, dragging the compliant Isaac with him. The boy kept his eyes down, his bearing resigned, though apparently not afraid.

Once they were out of sight, Ben turned to Ethan. "Let's get Alec."

"Fuck that," Ethan replied. "No time. We can get him."

Ben watched, stunned, as Ethan stormed off into the trees after Watson and Isaac. Maybe he wasn't the only impulsive, somewhat wild one in this couple. He couldn't help his small smile at the thought of that.

Chapter Twenty-One

ETHAN

It was fully dark now, and spotting Watson and Isaac in the blackness wasn't easy. Ethan didn't want to follow too closely behind and risk spooking Watson, nor did he want to leave too big a gap and risk potentially losing their trail. He knew Ben was following right at his heels, and the thought comforted him. Watson had turned out to be a wild card in this nightmare, but Ethan needed to remain confident that he and Ben could handle him.

He felt Ben grab at his elbow and bring him to a stop. He lowered his head, making it easier for Ben to whisper into his ear.

"Hold up. Their pace is slowing," Ben whispered.

Ethan had no fucking clue how he'd known that, but trusted Ben implicitly, even more so after the last couple of days. Ben encouraged Ethan to continue walking, Ben bringing up the rear. This had been his call to go blindly after Watson, so if anyone was going to pay for that choice, it would be him and not Ben.

As they moved farther away from the noise of the campsite, Ethan finally started to make out the sound of Watson and Isaac, breathing hard while tromping through the trees. He could hear sporadic grunts, suggesting Isaac was enduring the trip rather than willingly following along. Ethan had seen how he'd fretted for the young children he'd taken responsibility for, and he suspected Isaac was, even now, more concerned about them than the trouble he'd found himself in.

They must have traveled at this slower pace for at least fifteen minutes before Ben once again halted him with a firm grip on his elbow. The touch reminded Ethan they should have been back at Cameron's by now, safe among their family and friends and free to hold each other.

Once again, he leaned down and felt Ben's breath against his cheek before he felt his soft lips brush over his ear. "They've stopped. This is our chance, Ethan."

Ethan nodded, preparing to reply to Ben when Justin Watson's voice floated clearly through the shrubs to them. "Don't waste your time praying, Isaac; there is no god to help you. Surely, you know that." Watson's voice dripped with contempt as he spoke to the boy.

"Sir?" Isaac's reply was hesitant and confused.

"Master Piper was crazy. Believing in all that god nonsense. He wanted to sacrifice us all to his god, Isaac. I've never wanted that. I've never wanted to kill any of you."

From their vantage point, Ethan could see neither Watson nor Isaac, so he had no idea how Isaac was reacting to what Watson was telling him. He was an obviously intelligent boy, but he'd been raised under Arnold Piper's doctrines, and it wasn't easy to break from those, especially when he was still so young. Watson, on the other hand, was a grown man, so if he didn't believe in Piper and his message, then why had he hung around?

"The only good thing Piper did was give us all plenty of women to cater to our every need. The brats I could have done without, but all the women and being waited on by them, being master to them...that's the life, Isaac. And that's the life I'm going to rebuild once we get safely away from here. I watched Piper for years, and I learned how he turned people, how he manipulated them until there was nothing left of the person they were. It's not hard at all. People want to belong...want to feel loved. I can give them that, and they'll give me whatever I ask in return."

"But—" Isaac sounded utterly confused.

"You can either come with me as my first follower, or I'll drop you off somewhere once I'm safely away."

"You don't believe?"

Watson chuckled, a gleeful sound. He was clearly amused by Isaac's incomprehension of what he was being told. "No, I don't. The lifestyle suited me, but come on, Isaac, there is no god, and if there was, I don't think he'd want us all to die for him."

Ethan had heard enough. He wasn't a believer himself, but Watson was cruelly hosing down everything Isaac had been raised to believe. More importantly, he didn't want Watson to walk away from this and start his own nightmare somewhere else. He looked at Ben, whose wide eyes found his, his head shaking in disgust.

"I'm going in from behind. Distract him?" Ben asked.

"You got it." Ethan quickly pressed his lips to Ben's, unwilling to ever leave his man's side again without giving him what could be a goodbye kiss. Life was fleeting and could be brutal and unexpected in its ending, so Ethan never wanted to regret not having one last kiss with Ben.

They didn't linger over the kiss, but Ethan could feel Ben's passion in each slide and press of his lips. When Ben pulled away, he gave Ethan a wink before turning and heading into the trees. Before he was out of sight, Ethan rose to his full height, waited a few minutes for Ben to get in place, and sauntered toward the voice of Justin Watson, who was still talking to Isaac about his future plans.

Situations like this were as much about a good bluff as a show of strength, and Ethan had to approach his quarry with as much confidence, real or otherwise, as he could muster. As he rounded the tree line, he spotted Isaac, who was standing with his back to him, but facing Watson who was only a few feet away. Watson moved quickly once he spotted Ethan, reaching out and grabbing Isaac's arm, pulling him closer to his body, while at the same time turning him so Ethan could see the shock in the boy's face as he became aware of his presence. The gun was once again pressed to Isaac's temple.

"I'll kill him if you take a step closer."

Ethan took two steps closer, praying the bluff would work.

"Stop!" Watson roared.

Ethan moved a little closer. He was still not close enough to touch either man, but he was getting there. "I'm not interested in you, Watson. Leave the boy and go. I won't stop you," he lied. Watson was dangerous. He'd opened fire on the fucking FBI; he'd threatened to kill people, so there was no way Ethan would let a reckless man like that slip through his fingers.

Watson's eyes narrowed to slits, but he never glanced away from Ethan. As far as he could tell, that meant he had no idea Ben was somewhere behind him, getting closer and closer.

Ethan shifted his gaze to Isaac, and his stomach dropped. The teenager didn't look good at all. If Ethan was seeing right in the dim light, Isaac looked close to tears, and his slight body was definitely trembling. It seemed the boy's stoic veneer was finally starting to crack.

"Look, Watson, if you don't trust me, then how about a swap? Let Isaac go; he's harmless and frightened, and you can take me instead. I can help you get away," Ethan tried, knowing that, wherever he was, Ben would be cursing up a storm and giving him a death stare right now for offering himself up like this.

Watson didn't answer or move, but Ethan was sure he would be mulling things over. Calmly, Watson shifted the gun from Isaac's temple and pointed it directly at Ethan. For an awful moment, he wondered if Watson would pull the trigger. Instead, he beckoned Ethan over, while at the same time, pushing Isaac away.

Ethan was close to Watson now, close enough he could almost feel the cold metal of the gun barrel pushing against his sternum. "Thing is, big man, I don't want anyone coming with me." Watson smirked.

The man's words registered instantly, and Ethan braced himself for the shot that would take him away from Ben for good.

He heard the shot but never felt it. Watson's aim had moved, and he'd fired beside Ethan's body. By the time Ethan turned, he saw Isaac falling to the ground behind him, screaming in pain; turning back to Watson, who was out of his reach, he noted the gun was now pointed back at him. He didn't know whether Watson meant to shoot both of them or if he hoped Ethan would forget about him as he got Isaac the help he needed. He didn't really give a fuck what the man's plan was. He was going to fucking stop him.

Ethan lunged forward, his long reach working in his favor, as he took two steps and landed a vicious blow to Watson's smug face. With his other hand, he gripped his wrist and flicked it, the pain of the maneuver causing Watson to drop the weapon he'd been holding. Ethan yanked him forward, not allowing him a moment to recover. Watson tried to struggle but Ethan's hold was too tight, and in seconds, he had him spun around, planted face-first in the dirt with Ethan's knee lodged firmly on his back.

"Big mistake, you stupid fuck," Ethan hissed in Watson's ear as he bent forward and pressed him harder into the ground.

Watson struggled a little under him, but the effort was negligible. Ethan considerably outweighed him. He turned his head and wasn't surprised to see Ben kneeling beside Isaac's prone form. "Leg wound. Not bad," Ben panted out. "I'll get this tied up, and I'll go back for help." He flicked a glance to Ethan and winked. "Gotta say, that was fucking hot. But we'll have a serious talk later about getting too close to guns."

Ethan rolled his eyes but couldn't help the smile that sprang to his lips. He'd never had what could be called a boring life, and with Ben around it certainly didn't seem as if it would quiet down anytime soon. He struggled with Watson, getting the zip ties on him before removing his knee from the other man's back.

"Best fucking invention ever." He smiled as he pulled at the last zip tie around Watson's ankles. Once Watson was trussed up, Ethan picked up the gun, tucking it into the waistband of his pants, and moved over to where Ben was still working on the gunshot wound in Isaac's leg.

A strip of material that looked to have been torn from Ben's undershirt was tightly wrapped around Isaac's calf; a small red patch of blood had already soaked through. It wasn't a bad wound to have if you had to get shot, but it would still hurt like a bitch; yet Isaac sat quietly and let Ben tend to him without a fuss, after his initial scream of pain.

"You got him?" Ben asked.

"He's not going anywhere. You want me to go back for Alec?"

"Nah. I'm done here, and besides, we all know I'm faster." Ben stood and glanced around Ethan to where Watson would be struggling on the ground. "Keep an eye on him, okay?"

Ethan leaned forward, grabbed Ben's head, and brought their faces together, their foreheads resting against each other's. "Be careful," he whispered, kissing Ben gently first on the tip of his nose and then less gently on his lips, before Ben turned and ran.

But as Ben cleared the tree line, Ethan called out to him, "And hurry back, Cronin, we've got some...things to do." He winked, though it was unlikely Ben would see that in the dark.

"Oh, you've got no idea the *things* we've got to do, Ethan." Ben's voice was low and gravelly, and the sound of it, even more than the words he spoke, shot a spear of lust straight through Ethan's body. He shivered, watching until Ben was completely out of sight, and then focused his attention on Isaac.

"How're you doing?"

Isaac turned wet eyes to him, and Ethan couldn't help admiring the grit of the young man. "Hurts," he panted out.

"It's a clean wound. You'll be okay once we get you to the hospital."

"Never been to one before." Isaac was breathing hard through the pain, but Ethan wanted to keep him talking. Distraction was a powerful tool in these types of situations.

"You'll love it. They'll fix you up and then give you all the ice cream and Jell-O you can eat."

"Don't know what that is...ice cream and Jell-O."

The boy's words were a reminder of the sheltered life he'd lived until now. It'd be a long road for him and the others. It was hard to convince people they were living in a shared delusion when they were still essentially living in it. With time, he hoped the people Piper had had under his spell would realize what had truly been going on. Keep their faith in god, by all means, but hopefully, they'd put their trust and love in better people, ones who deserved it and didn't want to use them.

"Well you're gonna love it."

Isaac's gaze shifted to Watson, who was still writhing around in an effort to escape and not paying any attention to either the boy he'd just shot or Ethan.

"Why did he do that?" Isaac stuttered out, the shock of the events evident in his voice.

"The guy wanted to escape, and he figured if he shot you I'd let him go so that I could tend to you. And he was right—I would have. But he's a dangerous man, so he had to be stopped. There was no way I could let him get away"

"I thought he cared about us."

Ethan could hear the betrayal in Isaac's voice, the sadness that he'd been hurt by an adult he should have been able to trust with everything.

Ethan was no kind of therapist and didn't want to offer trite words to appease Isaac. He offered him the truth instead, and maybe it was the first time in his life that someone had actually given Isaac that. "A lot of people only care about themselves, Isaac. It wasn't personal. You were just a means to an end for him, a way for him to escape, and he took it. Many people will say and do anything to get what they want without a thought for the hurt they cause others."

"But we...we're all supposed to love each other. Master Piper said we must love each other...but some of us didn't. Some of us didn't love at all." Isaac finished, his glare still on Watson, and Ethan watched as Isaac's reality blew apart under his scrutiny of today's events. It wasn't often he witnessed someone's entire world explode right in front of his face.

"Why did you and the other man help us...help me?"

"Not all people are selfish. Most people are trying to do the best they can, and that includes helping people who need it."

Isaac watched him, a frown on his face and questions burning his eyes, but he simply nodded and stared back over at Watson. Ethan hoped to god the cavalry would get here soon... He was no good at this kind of thing, and he suspected Isaac had about a million questions that he would need answered before he could start to move on with his life.

Chapter Twenty-Two

BEN

"You go take your shower while I finish up with Ethan," Alec ordered, and Ben turned and flipped him a disgusted look. "And don't bother looking at me like that, Cronin. I know you were hoping for a shower for two, but your libido will just have to be patient. The sooner I get this report done, the sooner I can leave you two alone to do...whatever fucking dirty things you've probably got planned."

Ben laughed, as first the color drained from Ethan's face, and then a flare of red flushed his skin from his throat to the tips of his ears. Beside him, Cameron was similarly flushed, but he at least managed an eye roll. Just to add to Ethan's discomfort, Ben walked forward, plastering his body to Ethan's, kissing him hard and dirty on the mouth, before sauntering toward the door. "Jealous, Banner?" Ben smirked.

"Because you get to do that to him?" Alec tipped his head toward Ethan. "Hell yeah, I'm jealous." He laughed, and Ben thought Ethan was about to burst into flames he'd turned so fucking adorably red.

"Asshole," Ben muttered as he walked out the door and headed for the bathroom.

It had been hours since he'd caught up to Alec's men, who'd been sent out to track them down once Alec realized that he, Ethan, and Isaac were missing. Hours that he'd spent answering questions, helping to clear the camp, and finally having Cameron fly them back home. Alec had come with them after being relieved by his superiors and being tasked with getting the statements from him and Ethan and writing up full reports.

The story of the Piper Cult had exploded in the national media, possibly even going international by now, and Alec's bosses wanted no faces captured by the news media that had descended on the site. Hence, Alec had been sent away. A celebrity FBI agent was no fucking good to anyone.

They'd made it back to Cameron's to find that Maggie and the girls were on their way to San Francisco with Ryan and Lucas. Ethan had spoken to Maggie on the phone and said she'd sounded happy but tired. Lucas and Ryan had arranged everything with the Krispins and were traveling with a group of bodyguards who wouldn't let anyone or anything near any of them. The entire story would blow up soon enough, once the two big stars' side involvement in the crazy fucking cult takedown was found out—and it would be found out—Ben had no doubt of that.

Ben let the hot water rain all over his aching body. He'd reluctantly allowed the paramedics to check him over after losing an epic stare down with Ethan. Nothing was broken except his nose, and he had no other serious injuries from the beating he'd taken, but he still ached all over. The hot water soaked into his skin, easing the aches, and Ben just couldn't be fucked to move.

He tried to close his eyes, but every time he did, all he saw was Ethan charging at Watson, who had a fucking gun pointed at his chest. He'd been too far away to get there, and in the dark, with no clear shot, he'd been unable to fire at Watson without risking Ethan. With his fucking heart in his mouth, all he'd been able to do was try to get to them as quickly as possible. He didn't know of any greater terror than someone watching the one they love in danger.

"Hey," Ethan's voice growled in his ear. He hadn't even heard him come in the room, much less get undressed before joining him in the shower.

"Hey, yourself. You finished already?" Ben turned to face Ethan. He let his gaze lazily trail down the length of his big body, admiring the hard planes and thick muscles before pulling himself into Ethan's waiting arms.

"Yeah. My statement was pretty much one word...ditto. Not sure Alec was overly impressed with that, but he laughed and told me, 'Get the fuck outta my sight; you two assholes deserve each other.' So, here I am...and here you are all wet and warm and—"

Ben didn't let him say more, part afraid of what awful dirty talk might come from Ethan's gorgeous lips and part completely unable to resist taking those fucking lips with his own for one more second. So, he pulled him down and did just that, plastering his mouth to Ethan's in the kind of desperate and lewd kiss he'd needed since watching Ethan fly away from him in Cameron's helicopter.

It was fucking delicious, not only the taste of Ethan, but the way their wet bodies slid in concert, at times catching together and other times slipping easily against the other. And if Ethan didn't stop the obscene little moans that were falling from his mouth, this whole thing was going to be over in seconds. Maybe that would be a good thing because Ben wanted the first time he took Ethan into his body to be in a fucking bed, and he wanted it to last. The secret romantic in him demanded nothing less.

"Ben," Ethan groaned and slipped his big hand between their bodies. He easily caught both of their hard cocks, wrapping his palm around them and squeezing just a little.

Ben didn't ease up; he chased Ethan's lips and flicked his tongue along the seam until Ethan opened and he could taste him again. Both bodies were moving sensuously, and it only took moments of Ethan's hard stroking before he felt Ethan's cock stiffen even more against his own and jerk as he came. It was enough to finish Ben off, and he stifled a roar only by sinking his teeth into Ethan's shoulder as he rode out his own orgasm.

"Fuck," he panted and looked up into Ethan's face. "Fucking hell, I love you."

"I love you too. Have for a long time... I just... I didn't know. I'm not used to that, and I didn't know what it meant, the way I feel around you."

"What do you mean?" Ben asked. Ethan looked lost, a little startled even as he leaned against the tiled wall at his back.

"I've never been in love before, and um...whenever I was around you my feelings went crazy, and it almost kind of hurt... I'm not making sense, but it was hard to be around you, because I felt so much when you were near me, but I didn't understand what I was feeling. It used to scare me." Ethan cupped his face and pressed a gentle kiss to his lips, and Ben drank in the tenderness. He liked things a little hard and rough between the sheets, but he also loved the tenderness that Ethan bestowed on him. "I'm not scared now," Ethan whispered.

"You're just a big old sap, aren't you?" Ben brushed his lips against Ethan's collarbone. "I love kissing you here. Your scent is so strong...right here." Ben punctuated his words with a kiss to that very spot.

"Who's the big old sap now?"

"Yeah, yeah. Let's clean up, okay? There's a big, soft king bed with our name on it, waiting for us." Ben turned and picked up the soap, lathering his body as quickly, yet efficiently, as he could.

Ethan stood behind him, his long arms coming over his shoulders, his hands reaching for the soap before he began washing Ben's body. It was fucking wonderful—the intimacy of being washed by Ethan was overwhelming.

When Ethan was done with him, Ben returned the favor. He took his time, ensuring that he washed every inch of Ethan's large, hard body. *Fucking perfect.*

"Sorry?" Ethan murmured over his shoulder.

Had he spoken his thought out loud again? Probably. Ethan made him forget everything around him; he had the power to scramble his brain. "I said you're fucking perfect. I think you were made just for me, Ethan Stone."

Ethan laughed, and it was such a sweet sound, especially after the last few days. "Just get a move on. I'm pretty sure Alec and Cameron are gonna be waiting for us when we get out of here. They were cracking a bottle of Jack when I left them."

"Oh, Jesus. That's not a good idea."

"Angry drunks?" Ethan asked.

"No worse...sappy drunks. If Cameron doesn't give you some kind of 'welcome to the family' speech, I'll be shocked. And don't fucking let your head be turned by Alec; he's a bit of a sweet talker with a few in him."

"Oh?" Ethan raised an eyebrow at him.

Ben kissed away the water dripping on Ethan's lips. "I've told you... Alec and me, strictly friends; besides, he'd be more interested in you. He likes his men a bit older." He smiled as he finished washing Ethan.

By the time they came out of the bathroom, it was clear Alec and Cameron had already managed to down a few drinks. They were both laughing uproariously when Ben followed Ethan into the living room.

"Didn't think we'd see you again tonight, boys," Alec drawled.

"Somebody's gotta supervise you two with the liquor."

"And I suppose you think you're the proper person to do that, baby brother?" Cameron spoke clearly, but the effect of the drinks was already noticeable in the brightness of his eyes and the looseness in his usually rigid shoulders.

"Hell no. Ethan's the responsible one in this duo. In fact"—Ben turned to Ethan—"I don't think I've ever seen Ethan hammered."

"And you're not going to now. Sit, and I'll get us some drinks." Ethan walked over to the small bar Cameron had in the room. It was well stocked, and Ben knew Ethan would find whatever he was looking for there.

"So, Alec was just telling me a few stories from back in the military..." Cameron grinned, and Ben knew they weren't the *good* stories.

"What happened to the code, Banner? What happens in the army, stays in the army...ya know?"

"I don't think that's an actual thing, Ben. Besides, I think Cameron should know all about his brother—and what's more, Ethan should definitely know what he's getting into."

Ethan chose that moment to return with Ben's drink in hand and a wicked smile on his face. "Oh, I think I should definitely know what I'm getting into. Let's talk."

"Well, I'm sure you already know about the hay bales, two firemen, spooked horse, and the military police?"

"No. No...just nah-ah." Ben jumped up, undecided whether tipping his drink over Alec would be enough to shut him up or if he needed to take more drastic, physical action.

Alec threw his head back, laughing like the villain he was, before regaining control. "All right, all right. I'll save that one till you've got a ring on his finger, and he can't get away from you so easily." Alec took a sip of his drink as Ben took his seat. "How did you two meet?"

More than happy with the more sedate tack this conversation was taking, Ben answered, "We both worked for the same personal security firm. Pretty normal meeting, really."

"I'd enjoy that normal if I were you, Ethan. You won't get much more with Cronin around."

"Jesus, Alec, I'm not that bad," Ben said.

Alec raised an eyebrow in reply. "Aha. Honestly, though, you look good, Ben. Happy. I guess the big guy is to thank for that."

Before Ben could reply about how happy he was, a soft voice called Cameron's name from the doorway. Ben turned to find Zach standing there, shifting on his feet and looking awfully nervous. Cameron jumped up from where he'd been sitting and strode over to the young man.

"You okay, Zach?"

"Just a nightmare," he replied, nodding.

"Do you want to sit with us for a while?" Cameron asked, and Zach looked over his shoulder at them, shifting his gaze to each man.

"No, that's okay. I just... I just needed to know you were here."

Ben watched as Cameron's hand moved toward Zach before he pulled it back to his side. "I'm right here, Zach. I'm not going anywhere... You're not alone anymore."

Zach nodded again and offered a slight smile before turning and heading back to his room. Ben flicked a glance at Ethan who boggled his eyes, raised his brows, and mouthed "wow" to him.

When Cameron sat back down all three men were staring at him.

"What?" Cameron asked, shrugging.

"I thought Zach would've gone to be with the rest of the commune members," Ben answered.

"He didn't want to go. He's pretty mixed up, doesn't want anything to do with them right now. I, uh...I told him he could stay here for a while." Cameron lowered his gaze from Ben and Ben noticed the indecision in the set of his brother's body. He wasn't at all sure he'd done the right thing.

"Well, I think you've got yourself a fan there, Cam. Be careful with him, okay?"

"You know I will," Cameron mumbled his reply.

"So, back to the firemen and the horse..." Ethan said, relieving the tension in Cameron's shoulders. Ben loved him just a little bit more for coming to his brother's aid like that—even if it was going to be at the expense of whatever dignity Ethan may have thought Ben possessed.

Chapter Twenty-Three

ETHAN

"Ya know, I'm just drunk enough that I'll let you do any dirty little thing you want to me." Ben giggled, wriggling in the hold Ethan had around his waist as they made their way down the hall to their bedroom.

"You've had two drinks, and I'm pretty sure you're up for the dirty little things stone-cold sober," Ethan whispered in his ear, ridiculously pleased when he felt a shiver work its way through Ben's body.

"You know me so well."

"I'm about to know you a whole hell of a lot better, if you'd move your ass just a little quicker." Ben's ear was right at Ethan's mouth as he spoke, so he couldn't help nibbling on the tender flesh of his lobe. Ben's answering groan had Ethan's cock even harder than it had been, and he knew Ben could feel it pressed against his ass as they kept walking toward their room.

Jesus, if Ben didn't stop moving so fucking seductively, they'd be lucky to make it to the bedroom. Ethan picked up his pace, practically shoving Ben down the hallway.

For a brief moment, the memory of the knowing look Cameron had given them when they'd excused themselves moments ago almost put a damper on his mood, but the smell of Ben, the taste and feel of him, was more than enough to block out the idea that Cameron knew he was about to get naked with his brother.

"Come back, Ethan," Ben whispered. His plea was enough to slam the door on any thoughts that didn't involve worshipping the man who now stood facing him with such loving and longing all over his beautiful face.

Ethan smashed their lips together, his hands on Ben's shoulders, propelling them the short distance to their door. They leaned against it, their kiss remaining heated and unbroken as Ethan struggled with the doorknob. Ben's hands were everywhere, as though he was trying to touch every inch of Ethan, maybe to assure himself this was all real. To Ethan it felt like every fucking fantasy he'd ever had.

The door finally cooperated, and he flung it open, making sure to hold onto Ben so he wouldn't go anywhere when the support at his back disappeared. They stumbled through the threshold, giggling and pulling at each other's clothes. Ethan barely had the wherewithal to close the door as Ben tugged at the hem of his shirt.

The two struggled with each other's shirts and pants; thankfully, they'd had the foresight to stay barefoot after their shower, or Ethan was fairly sure they'd have fallen in a muddled heap on the floor about now.

Ethan continued his forward motion, trying to get them to the bed. Their hard cocks brushed against each other as they moved, every touch a fucking spark jolting its way through Ethan's body.

"Oh, fuck, Ben," he moaned.

"Bed...bed...get me to the fucking bed," Ben grunted out around his continued onslaught of Ethan's lips. Christ, the things he did with his tongue. Ethan had never been with anyone so...enthusiastic about sex before. It was fucking awesome.

They hit the bed, both of them tumbling to the mattress, Ethan doing his best not to land too heavily on Ben. He either succeeded, or Ben didn't mind bearing his weight at all as he began tracing Ethan's skin with his magic tongue.

Together they shuffled up the bed, unwilling to allow any distance between their bodies. Once he had Ben where he wanted him, Ethan wasted no time nipping down his throat and across his collarbone. His tongue circled first one and then his other nipple. Ben's hands clutched at his hair, pulling and tugging as his body writhed under Ethan's touch.

"Ethan..." His name was an almost-pained sigh falling from Ben's lips as he asked for more. "I've wanted you in my bed for so long. I'm so fucking crazy about you."

In answer, Ethan flicked his tongue at Ben's belly button before trailing down to lick at the join between his torso and thigh. He lapped at the skin there, pulling back for a moment to whisper, "Right here, Ben. This is where I smell *you*: the cinnamon and...you. Drives me fucking insane."

Ben moaned and Ethan dragged his tongue to that same spot on the other side of Ben's body.

Ethan felt heat radiating from Ben, felt the tremors of desire raking through his body, and smelled his arousal. He lifted his head, winking at Ben before licking a path up his shaft. He felt Ben's cock twitch under his tongue, and he heard the almost-constant moans slipping from Ben's lips. Every one of his senses heightened, all of them assaulted with the pleasures of Ben's hard, firm body.

It was all so much and so fucking good that he was quickly running out of patience to be inside the tight body under him. Ethan circled his hand around the base of Ben's cock, drawing it into his willing mouth. The primal taste of Ben exploded on Ethan's tongue, and he damn near came then and there. Ethan hollowed his cheeks and sucked; drawing Ben as far into his throat as he could manage, all while Ben writhed and pumped his hips.

"Jesus, Ethan, suck me. Hard. Oh, fuck, yeah, all the way," Ben babbled as Ethan's need grew painfully.

He pulled off Ben's dick with a pop and urged him over onto his stomach. Ben rummaged for something at the head of the bed, and Ethan realized what he was doing when a condom and bottle of lube landed near his hand.

The only light in the room came from a dim lamp in the far corner, but it was enough to cast a warm glow over Ben's smooth skin, little shadows falling only where that skin was puckered with scars exposing the brutality of Ben's past. Ethan allowed his eyes to roam over the glorious expanse of his back, his strong arms, and perfect ass. He reached down to stroke his own cock as his gaze drifted farther to Ben's muscled legs. Ben was absolute perfection.

"Fuck, I just wanna eat you alive, Ben," he crooned.

"Later. How 'bout, for now, you just fuck me through the mattress?"

"I can do that." Ethan reached for the lube, flicking the cap open with his thumb. He knelt between Ben's thighs, using his knees to force Ben's legs farther apart. Once his fingers were wet with lube, he traced them around Ben's hole, feeling that delightful fucking shiver race through him again. He gently eased a finger in, slowly moving it around, loosening and stretching Ben until he was ready for another finger and then a third. He crooked them, searching for his prostate, then tormented Ben mercilessly once he found it. As Ben's body humped and quaked, Ethan knew neither of them would last much longer.

Their combined panting and the crinkle of the condom packet were the only noises in the room as Ethan ripped it open and rolled the condom down his steely length. He lay his body on top of Ben, cautious of his heavier weight but wanting the full-body contact. One hand held some of that weight off Ben while the other stroked reverently down Ben's side, coming to rest on his hip. Using all his strength, he pulled to his knees, dragging Ben with him so he was also on hands and knees.

"Now, Ethan...please, now," Ben whimpered.

How the fuck could he resist? He gently pulled Ben's ass cheeks apart and lined up the tip of his cock. He pushed slowly, doing his best to ease inside Ben's body. Ben let out a long moan and then pushed back, fully seating Ethan.

Both men let out a simultaneous moan of *oh, god* when Ethan bottomed out. Ethan fought against his body's instinct to move and stayed still, allowing Ben time to adjust. Ben snaked his hand around to grip Ethan's ass, holding him snug against his body, and it didn't take long for him to start wriggling his ass where it was pressed against Ethan's groin.

It was all the permission he needed.

Ethan gripped Ben's hips and pulled out almost to the tip of his cock before he slammed back into Ben's willing body. He remembered what Ben had said about liking it a little rough, and he was more than up for the challenge. He tightened his grip on his hips and pounded into Ben, every thrust pushing Ben's body, testing his strength.

With each thrust, Ben let out a grunt or a moan, his breath panting, but he never faltered, his body never buckling under Ethan's pounding.

"Ethan, fuck, Ethan. That's it. More."

More. If he gave him any more, Ethan was pretty sure he'd break the fucking bed. He pulled out and manhandled Ben off the mattress until he had him face-first against the wall. He wasted no time pressing back in and resuming his movements.

Ben was up on his toes, his face turned to the side, one cheek pressed against the wall, a constant chant of yes coming from his lips. Ethan leaned down, nuzzling into the crook of Ben's neck, nipping and licking at the skin there.

"Ah, fuck, maybe I was wrong before. You smell so fucking good here, too, Ben."

Ethan licked a line up Ben's throat and used his hands to tip Ben's hips out and up, changing the angle of his thrusts so his cock would hit that perfect spot in Ben every few thrusts. If the growls and desperate breaths coming from Ben were any indication, it was working.

He could feel the tingle starting in the base of his spine, signifying his imminent release. Ethan moved one hand around Ben's body, gripping his hard cock, stroking him in time with his thrusts. Ethan didn't know which way to turn; he desperately needed to come, the thought of it consuming him. It only took a few more thrusts before the pleasure exploded and he was coming inside Ben's tight body. Ben gave a low, long growl, and Ethan felt his dick jerk and his come trailing down over his hand.

Ethan stayed where he was, pinning Ben to the wall until his breathing eased and his legs stopped feeling like jelly. He'd never come so fucking hard in his life—it took everything out of him.

When the storm passed, he guided Ben to the bed, pulled the top sheet back, and ushered him under the covers. As Ben moved to get comfortable, Ethan walked to the bathroom, dealt with the condom, and grabbed a wet washcloth. He cleaned himself, rinsed out the cloth, and returned to Ben. He had him cleaned up and settled under the covers in minutes, and he tossed the cloth before sliding into the bed next to him.

They shuffled around until they were comfortable, with Ethan as the big spoon, and Ben let out a contented sigh. "Ethan, that was...that was amazing."

"God, Ben, yeah, it was." He'd never, *never* had sex like that before, but if he had his way, he'd be doing it again and again and again for the rest of his life. Even now, after being so thoroughly satisfied, Ethan felt his dick twitching at the feel of Ben's tight ass pushing up against him, and he knew he wanted nothing more than to sink back inside as soon as he could.

"Ethan, I've... I've been with a lot of men, but I've never had it like that." He turned in Ethan's arms to face him, and Ethan thrilled at the feel of Ben's hands on his cheeks and the look of adoration in his eyes. "Tell me what I have to do to keep you," Ben whispered.

Ethan dipped his head and pressed his lips to Ben's. He moved gently, tenderly brushing his lips against Ben's soft ones. "Just keep being you—Ben—there's nothing you can do to get rid of me. I love you, and I am all-in with you."

"Sweet talker," Ben replied, pulling Ethan to him again. Ben's fingers threaded through his hair, tugging a little at the strands. "I love you too."

Ben suddenly barked out a laugh, surprising Ethan. "Sorry," Ben spluttered. "I was just thinking about when I met you. The first thing I thought was 'oh fuck, I want to climb that like a fucking tree.' And the second thing, when I looked into your eyes and I saw... this sadness there, I thought 'oh, god, I want to make sure nothing hurts him ever again.' That's how I knew I'd fall in love with you. I've never thought that about anyone before. Never wanted to...I don't know...fix...someone so bad before."

"I need fixing?" Ethan asked, making sure to keep his tone light.

Ben laughed and shook his head. "Fix wasn't the right word. I wanted to help make you feel better...make you happy."

"I knew what you meant."

"Asshole." Ben yawned. It had been a long couple of days, and he had to be as exhausted as Ethan felt.

Ethan pressed a kiss to the top of his head. "Go to sleep, Ben. Go to sleep now because some time during the night I am going to want you again, and you're going to wake up with my hard cock already inside you. So get your rest while you can."

"Oh, you are really starting to get this dirty talk. Tell me more..."

Ethan whispered all the filthy things he could think of into his ear as Ben drifted off to sleep, cocooned in his arms. And he was a little proud that Ben only laughed a handful of times at his dirty talk.

Chapter Twenty-Four

BEN

"You gonna be okay, baby brother?"

Ben huffed and crossed his arms. "I am not a baby, Cam, and, yes, I am gonna be okay." Ben looked into his brother's face, catching his gaze with his own. Of all the people in his life who had come and gone, Cameron had been the one constant. They'd always be there for each other, would always have each other's backs. Ben could imagine a wrinkly, hunched, ninety-year-old Cameron still asking if his baby brother was going to be okay, and the thought of that was all anyone really needed—to know that at least one person had them. Ben could hardly believe his luck that he had two such people, because he did now. He had Ethan too.

Ethan was a guard, a protector, a sentinel, and Ben would be the same for him—and it felt good.

"You kick his ass if he tries any more bullshit with you, all right? Or I will."

"Cam, he's solid. I promise you. He was scared of his feelings, of what I meant to him. But he's not afraid now. He's not going to hurt me."

Cameron held his gaze for a long time, searching for the truth in Ben's words. His smile told Ben that he'd obviously found it. "I'm happy for you. He's a good man—yes, I can admit it. It's just hard for me to trust, ya know?"

"I know." Ben patted his brother's arm as the ghosts of his past glided over his face, haunting his normally soft-blue eyes. Cameron had been hurt, and all Ben could hope for at this stage was that maybe one day he'd be able to look past that nightmare and reach for some happiness with someone again. "You'll come visit us soon?"

"Oh, I wouldn't miss it. Watching you deal with Maggie's little girls should be quite entertaining." Cameron's smile slipped from his lips. "It's going to be hard, Ben. He's going to need you."

Ben turned to look at Ethan, who stood at the tail of the helicopter quietly talking to Zach. "Yeah, it will be, but I've done hard before. I can help him...I will help him." Ben jumped at his brother then, and Cameron caught him as he always did. They held tight to each other, well-schooled in making sure all goodbyes were good ones—just in case.

"Love you, Cam, and thank you...for everything."

"Love you too. And any time...you know that."

They walked toward Ethan and Zach, and Ben watched with affection as his brother and his lover said their goodbyes. It was as warm as he could hope for. He knew that Cameron liked Ethan, despite the hiccup in their relationship. Ben shook Zach's hand and wished him luck. He kind of felt bad that he'd been dumped on Cameron, but the two seemed to get on well, and as long as Zach's puppy-dog eyes every time he looked at Cameron didn't cause a problem, he thought things would be okay there.

Ben threaded his fingers with Ethan's as they left the hangar and made their way toward the commercial terminal in Casper. It'd be a five-hour trip back to San Francisco with their stop in Salt Lake City, but as much as Ben wanted to get Ethan back to his sister, the selfish side of him was quite happy to take just a few more hours to have Ethan all to himself.

Ethan's hand was warm in his, his skin smooth in places, but rough in others, to show his man wasn't afraid of some hard work. Ben couldn't allow himself to think too much about how those fingers had felt roaming all over his body last night because it just wouldn't do for his dick to get hard in public with so many strangers about.

As the images and sensations rushed him, though, Ben needed to get his mind off all the naked fun he'd had with Ethan. "So, Maggie's settled, then?"

"Yeah. Lucas has got her into some fancy place. He's organizing all that, and apparently Ryan is interviewing nannies." Ethan flicked him a glance and a small smile twisted his lips.

"I'm sorry I'm missing that."

"Well, he's just thinning out the list. Maggie and I will have final say. Maybe you can sit in on that," Ethan suggested.

"Only if there's a couple of hot mannies on the short list." Ben winked.

Ethan rolled his eyes, but still managed to favor him with an adoring look. "I'm gonna have my hands full with you, aren't I?"

Ben leaned closer, tugging on Ethan a little so he'd dip his head toward Ben's lips. "And your mouth, and your ass, and—"

Ethan laughed and spluttered, "Okay, okay, I get it. Did you go to a class to learn this dirty-talk business or does it just come naturally?"

"It's a gift." Ben shrugged.

Any further talk was inhibited by the sudden influx of the other passengers who'd made their way to the gate.

It was a full flight, both of them flying coach, which made it terribly uncomfortable for Ethan, who had to squeeze his big body into the tight-fit seats. It was times like this that Ben was glad he hadn't quite managed to grow as large as his twin brother.

BY THE TIME they pulled up to Ethan's apartment, Ben was exhausted. Traveling on a flight with at least nine crying babies had not been fun, and Ben wondered if he looked as shell-shocked as Ethan did.

"I didn't think a kid could scream that loudly for that long." Ethan turned his boggled eyes to Ben's.

"It had to have been a fucking record, right? Like we'll see it on the news tomorrow about the kid who broke the Guinness World Record for longest and loudest cry, and we can say we were there."

"It wasn't worth it," Ethan mumbled.

A bedraggled-looking Lucas opened the door to Ethan's apartment for them. It had been decided that it would be best to bring the twins here so they could get used to their new home immediately. "Oh, thank god."

His words and his disheveled appearance didn't bode well for how well Lucas had handled two little girls over the past thirty-six hours.

"Ryan, they're here. We're free... I mean, we can go," Lucas bellowed back over his shoulder at a not-visible Ryan. Lucas's shout was met by one loud cry and an even louder giggle before Ryan came into view, a giant grin on his face that illuminated the contented expression set on his features.

"We're not going yet, Lucas. Now, get back in here. They can smell your fear, ya know."

Ben struggled to contain a burst of laughter at the mortified look on Lucas's face.

"They're plotting something, Ryan," Lucas adamantly replied.

"They're two. They can hardly string a sentence together, let alone plot your downfall. Now, suck it up, and finish helping Riley get dressed."

"She doesn't want to put it on."

"She's not going to visit her mother naked, so I don't care what you have to do, get that dress on her."

Lucas grumbled and huffed away, stamping his feet much like the two-year-old he was trying to dress. When Ben turned to Ryan, his face was lit up with a mischievous grin, making Ben sorry he'd missed all the fun Ryan had obviously been having at Lucas's expense.

Ryan hugged both Ethan and him once Lucas had left the entryway to return to the battle of the dress. "So glad you're here. How are you both?"

"We're good, Ryan. It's done and sorted. We'll probably have to testify down the track, but hopefully the people from Piper's cult will get whatever help they need to move on. How're things here?" Ethan asked.

Ryan turned and glanced over his shoulder before he spoke. "Well, the girls are great. They found a high amount of Phenergan in their system that would account for their listlessness, but they seem to be bouncing back just fine. Lucas, it seems, isn't quite ready for fatherhood. He thinks the girls have been plotting his destruction…which, I've gotta say, has been very entertaining."

"They're settling in okay?"

"Yes. They are very resilient. They met some of the nannies from the agency, but they really want to see their mom. We've waited for you so you can take them to Maggie. We thought we should also let Maggie get settled before the girls go to see her."

"Thank you, Ryan. I can't ever thank you and Lucas enough." Ethan pulled Ryan into a hug as he spoke, and Ben could hear the slight catch of emotion in his voice. Ethan went to walk past Ryan and into the living room.

"Ethan, I'm dying for a coffee. Can I get you one before we go see Maggie?" Ben asked.

"Please. I'd love one."

Ben walked toward the kitchen with Ryan following behind.

"How's he doing with all of this?" Ryan asked.

Ben shuffled around the kitchen making coffees as he replied. "He's a tough son of a bitch but when Maggie... He's going to be a wreck, but he'll get through it."

Ryan scratched at the countertop and shifted on his feet. Ben could tell there was something on his mind, but he continued making the coffee, allowing Ryan the time to formulate what he needed to say.

"Ben, I've been thinking..."

"Yes..."

"I've never... I've never seen anything like Maggie's suffering while her kids were gone. She didn't know if they were safe, or what was happening to them. The pain in her face was unbearable to even look at. I can't imagine what it must have felt like for her." Ryan faltered and took a breath. Ben stayed silent, waiting for Ryan to get to his point.

"I realized that thousands of parents go through this. Missing kids, kidnappings, murders. It's...it's just awful. Then I thought about you and Ethan and me." Warm brown eyes flicked up to meet his own, but Ben had no idea where Ryan was going with this, and his fidgeting had increased, his nerves getting the better of him.

"What about us, Ryan?"

"Well, I was thinking that… I need a new career and you and Ethan have the skills, so I could be the money man, the paper pusher while you and Ethan could do…well, you could do what you do."

Ben still wasn't sure what Ryan was talking about, but the hint of an idea was beginning to take form, and he wondered if he was in the same ballpark as Ryan.

"I want to start a foundation or agency or whatever it's called, where we track down and go after missing kids. I want to help other parents like Maggie, and I want you and Ethan to go in on it with me." Ryan straightened his posture and rested his stare on Ben's, almost daring him to disagree with his idea.

The truth was, in that quick flash of hearing Ryan's idea, Ben liked it. A lot. Ben knew the police did the best they could and the FBI was great. But they had multiple cases to focus on and were often hampered by the constraints and protocols of official investigations. Ben wasn't interested in running around breaking the law like some sort of vigilante superhero, but he didn't mind sidestepping it when needed. And the rush of retrieving Maya and Riley for their mother, he had to admit, had been fucking awesome.

"You're interested," Ryan stated with a huge grin on his face.

"I'm…intrigued," Ben replied. "There's a lot to it, though, Ryan. I'm not sure what Ethan will think, and I can't imagine Lucas is going to be thrilled with you getting involved with something that could potentially be dangerous."

"I know, Ben. I know. I've thought about it. I have, and it may not work, but I'd really like to at least sit down and talk about it with you guys. Would you… Do you think we can at least do that?"

Ben nodded his head and offered Ryan a smile. "Yeah. Yes, I think we can do that. Maybe we can talk to them tonight after we've seen Maggie and the girls are asleep. Right now, though, I think we should probably get in there and rescue Lucas." As if to punctuate his words, a scream rent the air, quickly followed by a crash, and then the tinkle of Ethan's laughter.

That sound alone was enough to allay Ben's fear that something dreadful had happened to cause the scream. When he and Ryan walked into the room, Ben had to bite his lip to hold in the laughter that threatened to burst from him. The consternation on Lucas's face as he stood there surrounded by the dregs left from what had to have been an indoor tornado—or the two-year-old girl still dancing around him—told him that any laughter would not have been welcome.

Chapter Twenty-Five

ETHAN

It had been a little over twenty-four hours since Lucas had brought Maggie into this palliative care facility, and Ethan could already see a noticeable difference. Maggie had vetoed the idea of having care in Ethan's home—she hadn't wanted her daughters to witness her decline up close every day.

Perhaps it was more the fact that her daughters were now safe rather than the care facility that had added color to her cheeks and a sparkle to her eyes. Ethan didn't much care what it was; he was just delighted to see his sister looking relatively well, all things considered.

"You look good, Mags. How're you feeling?"

"Great...well... better anyway. Doctors ran some tests when they admitted me. We're going to have a consult about treatment options tomorrow. I'm tired, but good. Are the girls with you?"

Ethan swallowed past the lump in his throat. Every now and then the reality of his sister's condition snuck up on him and threatened tears. Maggie didn't need him to cry for her though; she needed him to be there for her, to offer her his strength when hers waned. "Of course. They're outside with Ben, Lucas, and Ryan. I just wanted a few moments alone first, then we'll bring them in to say goodnight."

"Ethan." Maggie reached for his hand, her grip negligible, but Ethan felt it deeply. "I can never, *never* repay you for what you and your friends have done for me."

"No...no, I should have been there. I should have been here for you all this time. I should have checked on you. I... It hurt so much thinking you all hated me and I was just protecting myself by trying to forget about you, but I should—"

"This is not your fault," Maggie interrupted. "None of this is your fault, and you're here now when I really need you."

Ethan straightened and looked into his sister's eyes, allowing his sincerity to bleed into his own so that Maggie would truly understand what he was about to say. "I'm not going anywhere, Maggie. I'll do whatever you need. I'll be here for your girls forever, and I'll be right here beside you until..."

"You can say it, Ethan. The end, you'll be here until the end, and I am so grateful for that. I'm also glad that you'll have Ben to lean on." She smirked, and just like that, the heavy mood lightened. "He's hot, Ethan. You're so lucky. Tell me...are his abs as tight as they seem beneath his shirts?" Maggie giggled.

Ethan threw his head back and laughed. "God, Mags, don't let him know how hot you think he is. His ego is big enough already."

"All right, I'll keep it to myself. But seriously...you and him, I couldn't ask for better fathers for Maya and Riley when...well, when the time comes."

That shard of pain ripped into him again, but it danced with the incredible pride he felt in the face of his sister's bravery. "I'll never let them forget you. I promise you'll be the biggest and best part of their lives."

A tear rolled down his sister's cheek but true to the courage she'd displayed since their reunion, Maggie smiled and patted his hand. "Okay. Enough of this. Bring those angels in here and let's spend some time as a family, yeah? And drag Heckle and Jeckle in here too. We'll make a party of it."

"Heckle and Jeckle?" he asked as he headed toward the door to Maggie's private room.

"Yeah. Have you seen them try to manage Maya and Riley? I shouldn't laugh, but, oh, I'd give anything to be around to see them have kids of their own."

They stayed an hour with Maggie, and she'd been asleep before they'd even left the room. Maya and Riley had come out of the fog of being drugged and Ethan delighted in every word, giggle, and cry that came from their little mouths. He could see the love between mother and children, and like everything about the situation with his sister, his delight in witnessing it was tempered by the thought of the devastation to come with Maggie's loss.

Watching them now as they drifted off to sleep, Ethan couldn't keep the smile from his face as he remembered watching Maggie in much the same way when she'd been the twin's age. They looked so much like their mother had that Ethan realized how lucky he was to have them in his life.

His parents could have, and very nearly did, ruin his life by cutting him off. He allowed himself to think about them for a moment—the bitterness that had been etched into every line on their faces the last time he'd seen them. He'd always known they'd blamed him, not for what his brother had done, but for exposing him—for making them face the truth about their oldest child. To his parents, Ethan's sin had been unforgivable, causing them to lose so much.

Ethan stood from the chair he'd been sitting in, confident the girls were finally asleep. He tiptoed from the room, fearful of waking them, and found Ben in his living room sharing a drink with Ryan and Lucas. In truth, he'd expected those two to be long gone already but was oddly pleased to find them still there, despite wanting to have Ben all to himself again.

"They're asleep?" Ben asked as he stepped into the room.

"Out like lights," Ethan replied.

"After how many Creedence songs?" Lucas laughed.

Oh, god, they heard. Ethan could feel the flush burn its way to the tips of his ears. He'd sung three songs for the girls, not kidding himself for a second that his voice was anything but horrible, and yet the girls had seemed to enjoy it, finally nodding off during a rather terrifyingly bad rendition of "Born on the Bayou." "Shut up, Evers," he countered.

Ethan grabbed the beer Ben offered and clinked the neck of the bottle against Ben's. "So...I thought you two would have run screaming by now."

Lucas huffed and side-eyed his boyfriend. "Oh, believe me, I was ready to run hours ago, but apparently our boyfriends have cooked something up between them that they'd like to share with us," he replied.

Ethan couldn't help the little stutter in his heart at the casual mention of Ben being his boyfriend. He loved the sound of it. He turned to catch Ben's gaze and raised his eyebrows at the furtive glance Ben shot at him. "Really? Well they best start talking I guess, then maybe you and I, Lucas, can figure out what it's going to cost them to get their way."

Ben and Ryan shot a look at each other before they both stood, and Ryan began speaking.

"Let me get this straight," Lucas asked a good ten minutes later. "You want to open some kind of agency to find missing or kidnapped children. Ben wants to do the grunt work along with Ethan, and you are going to kind of run it and fund it? Did I miss anything?"

"No. That um...that about sums it up," Ryan replied with a defiant expression on his face. He was clearly gearing up for the backlash he suspected was coming his way.

Lucas stood, his arms flailing about as though he didn't know quite what to do with himself. "You're crazy... They're crazy, right. Ethan? I mean this is not your line of work, Ryan. This is dangerous, and you don't know what... Do either of you know what you're doing? I don't... I can't—"

Ryan reached out and rubbed his hands up and down Lucas's arms. In moments, he'd calmed his bewildered boyfriend. Perhaps Ethan should remember that trick for his own man, who had rather uncharacteristically remained quiet for much of the discussion.

"And you?" Ben's soft voice drifted across to Ethan, and he turned to look into serious pale-blue eyes.

"I'd, um... I think it might be something worth investigating."

"What?" Lucas almost screamed.

"I'd really like to look into it. I mean think about how we helped Maggie. There's plenty more families out there whose children are just...gone one day. We can help them, and we should." Ethan watched as the corner of Ben's lips curled into a smile.

"But there's police and...and FBI and... Ryan, please, it's dangerous," he finished on a whisper.

"Ryan would never be in danger," Ben answered. "I swear, he'd never be in danger, and he'd be working with us. We'd never let anything happen to him."

"You're set on this?" Ethan asked, addressing his question to both Ben and Ryan. Both men nodded in response. "Okay. Well, I think it's at least worth considering, Lucas. I mean Ben's right about Ryan—we'd never let anything happen to him."

"I'd stay out of trouble, Luke. And I've been offered that contract with Hugo Boss. It's worth a fortune, so most of that money could fund us. We could intersperse some private investigator work to bring in an income so we don't have to charge families for finding their kids..."

"You've really thought this through, haven't you?"

"I have."

Lucas nodded, his gaze never shifting away from Ryan. "Okay. Let's look into it."

Ryan and Ben's faces both lit up in huge smiles and though the work would be difficult and devastating at times, Ethan believed this moment right here was going to change their lives forever. Ryan was practically vibrating, his enthusiasm spilling over and fueling Ben's own.

Ethan and Lucas sat back and listened while the two of them bounced ideas off each other. It was like watching a couple of schoolboys talking excitedly about a football game. Everything about Ben drew him in—turned him on. His company was at once calming and thrilling, the duality of those emotions leaving him pleasantly exhausted.

Another hour later and it was enough. He'd heard enough for one night, and now he just wanted Ben all to himself. He cleared his throat and stood. "Okay, okay, no more...not tonight. This all sounds good but I think we all need to get some sleep. All I know about kids is that until they're teenagers they usually wake you at the ass crack of dawn. So...Ryan, Lucas, thank you again for what you've done. I'll never be able to repay you but good night. We'll talk tomorrow, okay?" He moved toward his front door to usher them out when something occurred to him. "Ah, shit. You've got no one watching you. I'm so sorry, in all the chaos, I forgot."

"It's fine. Harry's at our place, waiting. And I texted my driver twenty minutes ago, so he'll be downstairs, waiting. We're fine, Ethan," Lucas answered. He was standing now, too, pulling at Ryan's hand to lead him toward the open front door. They both shook his and Ben's hands as they left and promised to be back in the morning to start making some concrete plans for the future.

After they walked out, Ethan closed the door and leaned against it, his gaze trailing up and down Ben's perfect body as he stood before him similarly checking Ethan out.

"Are we really gonna do this, Ethan?"

Ethan took a few steps forward until his body was almost flush with Ben's. He slid one of his big hands around the back of Ben's neck, the tips of his fingers playing with Ben's curls. "I think we are. I think you, Ben Cronin, can do anything you put your mind to, and I think there is no one more deserving of having you on their side than children, especially vulnerable ones. So, yes, we are going to do this." He pressed his lips to Ben's, enjoying the slight taste of beer he found there.

"Thank you," Ben whispered. "You're such a good man."

The room seemed hotter than it had just a few minutes ago, though Ethan knew it was more the heat coming from the body he held tightly against him. Ben's lips parted easily beneath his when he licked along the seam before pressing their lips firmly together, moving, tasting, sliding, in a kiss that made his knees weak. He'd never been an overenthusiastic kisser, but with Ben, there was just nothing better.

One of Ben's hands dipped into the waistband of his pants, his long fingers flirting with his ass, while his other hand held him by the back of his head, not allowing him to pull away from the kiss. Ethan had one arm around Ben's waist, bringing him tighter and tighter against him, maybe in the hopes of making them become one. Who the hell knew at this point? Ethan sure as hell didn't. The overwhelming sensation of being with Ben like this short-circuited his thought processes until he was nothing but sensation.

"Take me to bed, Ethan," Ben whispered against his lips, nipping at them when he was done.

For a second, Ethan thought he might lose control of himself and go all caveman on Ben, grabbing him and tossing him over his shoulder to take him to his bedroom. Such was the spell Ben and his gorgeous fucking body had cast on him. Instead, he linked hands and pulled Ben in the direction of his bedroom, his breathing harsh and his cock rock-hard.

Chapter Twenty-Six

BEN

"Ethan..." Ben groaned. "Ethan stop a minute."

From where Ethan's head was currently nuzzled into his groin, he looked up at him; his warm navy eyes lit up in passion and with such intensity behind them that Ben couldn't hold back a gasp.

"Come back up here," Ben whispered.

"You don't want me to..."

"No, I mean, yes... I do want you to blow me, but I want to tell you something, and I can't concentrate when your tongue is lapping at my dick, so get up here."

For such a big man, Ethan was quick, and Ben soon found himself almost nose to nose with him before Ethan pressed a gentle kiss to his lips. "What is it, baby?" he murmured.

Ben sat taller in the bed, leaning his back against the headboard. Ethan moved around until he was lying with his head in Ben's lap. Ben wasted no time tangling his fingers in the soft strands of Ethan's dark chestnut hair. It was longer than Ethan typically kept it, and the gray at the sides was more prominent than usual. It was fucking gorgeous.

"Ethan, I, um...I love you, and I'll be honest...sometimes I find that a little overwhelming." Ethan's head began to rise from his lap, and Ben could tell he was about to freak out. He wasn't getting his words out like he'd hoped. "No, it's okay," he said, gently pushing Ethan back onto his lap. "I don't mean that in a bad way. Ugh…I'm not making sense. What I mean is that sometimes I just don't know what to do with what I feel for you—the strength of it. Like just now…it was like I wanted you to suck my dick, but at the same time, I wanted to look into your eyes for hours and tell you over and over how much I love you until I knew you got it. Sometimes I just don't know which way to go. Does that make any sense at all?"

Ethan propped himself up on one elbow and turned to face Ben. "It makes perfect sense. Sometimes I wanna turn you over and pound into you, but at the same time I want to hold you against me so tight that there's no room for either of us to move an inch. I want it dirty and romantic, and I want lazy days and crazy days, and I want to take my time with you, but then I can't get at you quick enough. It's like a fucking whirlwind but, Ben. I love every fucking minute I get to be yours."

"Jesus, I'm going to make you come so fucking hard. Saying shit like that to me. Get those perfect fucking lips back around my cock, Ethan."

Ben's hips bucked off the mattress as soon as he felt his shaft being pulled into the warmth of Ethan's mouth. He grunted and writhed under the assault of Ethan's sinful lips, desperately trying not to choke Ethan in his enthusiasm. It just felt so good.

"Oh, god," he moaned, his mouth suddenly watering for the taste of Ethan on his tongue. "Lie down, on your side."

Ethan did just that, and Ben shuffled around so his head was at Ethan's knees. He flicked the bedding out of the way and set to work on Ethan's hard shaft. The heft of it on his tongue, the taste of the drops of precome seeping from his slit, and the musky smell flooding his nostrils all combined to whip Ben into a frenzy of desire. When Ethan cottoned on and got back to work on his dick, Ben thought things might get no further than this, and he'd come any damn second—and happily so.

With both their mouths full, there was no dirty talk between them, but the salacious grunts and groans that slipped between both of their lips were more than enough to satisfy the more lewd side of Ben's nature.

Ethan pulled off with a pop, his ragged breaths loud in the quiet. "Ben, can I...? I need you."

"You can have my ass anytime," he answered after giving Ethan's perfect cock one last lick. He wormed around again, lying on his side, waiting while Ethan rifled through his bedside table, hopefully for lube and a condom. "How do you want me?"

"Get on your back. I want to look into your eyes when I slide inside you."

"With fucking pleasure," Ben replied breathlessly. Ethan's dirty talk had come on in leaps and bounds and Ben fucking loved it. He made himself comfortable, spreading his legs wide in invitation—one he knew Ethan would accept readily.

He rested his hands behind his head and lay back watching intently while Ethan rolled a condom down his perfect length, giving himself a few tugs for good measure. Ethan was teasing him and Ben couldn't get enough. He pulled his feet toward his ass, allowing Ethan a better view, before reaching one hand down to stroke his own cock and smiling at the mesmerized look in Ethan's eyes.

Ethan squirted some lube on his fingers and wasted no time breaching Ben's body with them. Ben let out a groan at the intrusion and relaxed into it. Ethan's fingers felt so good, but they were simply the appetizer, and Ben needed the main course.

"I'm ready, Ethan," he panted.

"Not yet," was all the reply he got before Ethan crooked his fingers running them over his gland and sending Ben's thoughts into oblivion. Ben writhed and groaned and humped and whimpered as Ethan continued torturing him with those fingers. He thought he'd called out "no more or I'll come" but couldn't be sure. He was lost to his passion. The hunger for Ethan was consuming him and for a moment Ben worried that his need for Ethan was too much, and it would devour him.

But then Ethan was there whispering in his ear, "I've got you. I'll take care of you. Relax, and let me in."

Ben felt the tip of Ethan's cock at his hole, pushing, straining to get inside. He relaxed—Ethan had him, Ethan was going to give him what he needed. He moaned, long and low, as Ethan worked his cock inside him, every inch adding to the burn, the fullness, the fucking pleasure.

All the while Ethan's eyes remained focused on his, never looking away, never flinching. Ben had never felt so loved, so valued and accepted as he did when Ethan was fully inside of him and looking at him with absolute adoration in his eyes.

"Ben, I love you," Ethan ground out before pulling out and slamming back inside. Oh, Jesus, fuck, Ethan knew just how to give it to him.

Ben curled his legs around Ethan's body, doing whatever he could to pull him even tighter against him, even though there *was* no space left between them. Ethan was chanting in his ear over and over how much he loved him and something about how perfect he was, though, Ben was so lost in his desire he wasn't even sure what was real anymore.

Big hands suddenly reached under his back and lifted him off the bed so that he was sitting in Ethan's lap, still impaled on his cock. Ethan's warm lips were ravaging his own, their tongues dancing as Ethan continued jerky little thrusts up into his body. Ben arranged his knees on either side of Ethan's body and took over, raising himself over Ethan before slamming down. He dragged his lips away from Ethan's and leaned back to change the angle, pegging his prostate with Ethan's cock every few thrusts.

Ben watched as sweat dripped down Ethan's firm, broad chest, and he leaned in to lick a trail from nipple to throat, savoring the salty flavor. Ethan let out a curse and pulled Ben tighter against him, both working hard to find their release. It was a quandary: never wanting *this* to end, but at the same time, knowing when the end came it was going to be so, *so* fucking unbearably good.

Ethan's grip on him was tight, and Ben threw his arms around his neck, pulling Ethan's head into the juncture of his head and neck. He could feel it coming. Ethan's body was quivering, his breath ragged and harsh. He felt him grow impossibly larger inside of him before his movements stuttered and faltered as he came. Ethan's teeth nipped into his neck as he muffled his cry. It was...god, it was so fucking good.

Ben joined him in his release, his cock untouched, and it was unlike any orgasm he'd ever experienced. He was shocked to feel a tear slip from his eye as he circled his hips to wring out every last bit of his pleasure.

Neither of them moved for what seemed like hours. They clung to each other until their breaths eventually calmed and their heart rates eased. Ethan was the first to pull back, staring deep into Ben's eyes while his fingers caressed the features of Ben's face. He reverently traced his cheek, behind his ear, across his forehead and up into his hairline, then gently over his lips. Ben felt worshipped.

"That was..."

"I know."

"Ethan, I've never come like that before. You didn't even touch my dick. I didn't touch it. Nothing was touching it. That's unheard of."

"That's love, baby."

"Oh, Jesus." Ben laughed.

When they disentangled from each other, Ethan sauntered into the bathroom. Ben laughed at how ludicrously pleased with himself Ethan seemed as he swayed his hips while leaving the room. He was back in moments with a wet facecloth but wouldn't allow Ben near it. Instead, he laid him out on the bed and washed his body clean with the same care and reverence he'd shown moments ago.

Ethan tossed the cloth and wiggled his way under the covers with Ben. He laid his head on Ben's chest. Ben loved that he did that. He was often the smaller man, and to some men, that meant that he did the cuddling in to the bigger body, but not with Ethan. Ethan seemed to love cuddling in to him just as much as the other way around. Ben carded his fingers through Ethan's hair, which was damp with sweat.

"We probably need a shower," he suggested.

"Later. I just want you to hold me for a while," Ethan murmured against his chest.

"You all right?"

"Mm-hmm." Ethan began circling his fingers over Ben's abs, occasionally tracing the lines he found there. "We're going to do this, aren't we?"

"Do what?"

"All of it. Us, the agency, Maggie and the girls."

"Yes, we are."

Ben felt Ethan nod against his chest. "It's a lot."

"It's worth it," Ben replied and pressed a kiss into Ethan's hair.

Ethan sat up and put a hand to either side of Ben. He stared into his eyes for a long time before speaking again. "You're worth it, but I...I'm scared."

"Of what?"

"I'm scared it might be too much. I'm scared you might end up hating me. I can't bear that, I can't. So, promise me, if it's getting too much you'll walk away before you hate me."

Ben had known, or rather suspected, what Ethan's parents' treatment of him had done, the damage it had caused. To be hated by your parents was bad enough, but to be hated in favor of a son who'd killed women was intolerable. Ethan had always come across as a confident man. This was the first time Ben had really seen the vulnerability that lurked beneath the veneer.

Ben cupped Ethan's cheeks and brought their faces closer together. "I love you, Ethan, and, yes, there's a lot coming our way. But I could never, never hate you. Besides, I love a challenge, and keeping me busy with all of this is a good thing. You never want to see a bored Ben." He smiled, hoping to ease some of Ethan's doubts.

"Oh? What does a bored Ben look like?"

"It's not pretty. I don't want to scare you off, but in the past, it involved some toenail polishing, some extreme sports, and there was one rather unfortunate hair-crimping incident."

Ethan let out a throaty laugh and then looked at Ben, all serious again. "Well, I can think of other ways I can entertain you, should you ever get bored." He winked.

"I'm so in love with you, Ethan. And I don't scare easy, and I want to do this with you—all of it. I can't fucking wait to share my life with you."

Ethan kissed him then, softly and sweetly, and Ben felt everything in that kiss—all the love, desire, fear, excitement—everything.

Epilogue

ONE YEAR LATER

"It's Momma's birthday today, Uncle Ben Ben?"

"Yeah, Maya, it is."

"And we bringed her flowers?"

"Yep, some beautiful flowers."

"But we bringed her flowers every Sunday."

"We do, but your momma doesn't need anything else now, pixie, and she loves flowers." Ben glanced across the gravesite at Ethan, who held Riley in his strong arms.

For eight months, they'd visited Maggie's grave every Sunday, and every time, they'd brought fresh flowers and Ethan had shared a story about their mom with the girls. Ben figured Maya and Riley would grow up knowing their mom better than a lot of kids whose moms were still with them.

It had been a fucking hard eight months since they'd lost Maggie. For a time, Ben had been terrified that he was losing Ethan to his grief, but he should have known better. Ethan was an amazingly strong man who'd had so much heartbreak in his life, but he'd eventually fought his way back from the edge.

"Uncle Efan, tell me about Woody and Buzz again." Maya smiled. It was one of her favorite stories about her mother, and it was a happy one.

"Well, your momma was about the same age as you are now, and I took her shopping one day to buy her a present for Christmas. I'd taken her to see *Toy Story* just a few days before, and she just loved it. When we got to the store, they had lots and lots of *Toy Story* toys, and I told your momma she could pick one. She stood there for a long, long time trying to pick something out. She had a Woody doll and a Buzz doll in her hands, and I asked her which one she wanted. She looked up at me with big sad eyes, but I still said she could only have one—"

"Like you tell Uncle Ben Ben with cakes? He can only have one 'acause two is piggy?"

"Yes, just like that, Maya." Ethan smiled at Maya and lifted his gaze to Ben. Damn, it was good to see the constant sadness finally starting to disappear from Ethan's eyes.

"And then she stoled the dolls?"

"Well, she just couldn't decide because she loved Woody and Buzz the same. So, when I turned my back on her, she put Woody under one arm and Buzz under the other and she ran. And she was fast, your momma. By the time I realized she was gone, she and Woody and Buzz were out the door."

"Did you call the police, Uncle Fan, 'cause she stoled?" Riley asked. Neither child could manage Ethan. Maya went with Efan but Riley was lazier and stuck with just Fan.

"No. I chased after her, and I made her take the dolls back and apologize to the lady in the store. She had a big talk to your momma about stealing, and your momma never did it again. I went back to the store a few days later and bought her Woody and...somebody else bought her Buzz."

"Momma was nice."

"She was very nice."

"We sit and talk to her now?"

"Sure, baby." Ethan lowered Riley to the ground, and she sat near her mother's headstone, fussing with the flowers there. Maya wandered over and sat beside her sister. Ben smiled as they babbled away, neither caring that they were talking at the same time. Ben could pick out words here and there and knew they were telling their mom about their week, just as they did almost every week.

"They're doing good, aren't they?" Ethan spoke quietly to him, but Ben could hear the doubt in his voice. His man needed some reassurance.

"They're doing great, Ethan. They're happy and healthy; they love us and each other. I don't think they could be doing any better than what they are."

Ethan kept his gaze fixed on his nieces. "Maybe I should start thinking about taking on more work, then. What do you think?"

Ryan had been like a tenacious pit bull with the idea of an agency that went after missing children. He'd shot down or overcome every objection that anyone had come up with or obstacle that had stood in their way, and Ben knew without him it never would have gotten off the ground. In the end, they'd gone into a partnership of sorts with the Krispins. Ryan ran the business with their guidance and backing. In the six months since they'd opened, they'd managed to find and bring seven children home safely, each from a parent who had been trying to keep them away from the other parent. In addition, there'd been two cases that had ended tragically and three were ongoing.

Ben loved the work and had even talked Alec Banner into leaving the FBI and coming on board. Ethan hadn't exactly been thrilled with that, especially because he was only working sporadically while both he and the twins tried to adjust to Maggie's death. That left Ben and Alec doing a fair bit of work together.

"The girls love KinderCare on the days they go, so if Shelly can't work the extra days, we can see about getting them in there. Or maybe we can look at a live-in nanny. We can make it work, Ethan."

Ethan turned and pulled Ben closer to his side and pressed a gentle kiss to his lips. None of the desire and lust he'd felt for Ethan had waned in the year they'd been together, and Ben was certain it never would. Ethan was his—perfectly, wonderfully his.

At Maggie's insistence, they were completely honest with the girls about their relationship, and they hadn't had a moment's trouble with them. All in all, life was good for them now after the darkness of Maggie's loss.

"We can, can't we." It was a statement not a question, now; Ethan once again full of his usual confidence.

They stayed for only a few minutes longer until the twins looked as though they were about to drift off to nap in the warmth of the day. The shade that was cast over their mother's gravesite by the giant oak tree nearby was perfect to lull them both to sleep. Ethan and Ben each took one girl in hand, and they walked toward their car.

They'd only made it a short distance when Ben noticed a large figure approaching them from the opposite direction. He recognized Cameron immediately. That his brother was in town unannounced was cause enough for Ben to frown, but the fact that he'd chased them down at the cemetery raised the hairs on Ben's arms. Something was definitely wrong, and after what Cameron had told him over the last few months, he suspected it had something to do with Zach.

"That Cam?" Ethan asked.

"Yeah."

"Jesus, every time we have plans for the girls to stay over with Ryan and Lucas so we can have some alone time, he turns up. Is he fucking psychic?" Ethan laughed.

"Cam," Ben called when he was close enough not to have to raise his voice. "Everything okay?"

"No. I need your help. I need everyone's help."

"What's happened?" Ethan asked, all serious now.

"I need you to find Zach."

About the Author

Karrie lives in Australia's sunshine state with her husband and two sons, though she hates the sun with a passion. She dreams of one day living in the wettest and coldest habitable place she can find. She's been writing stories in her head for years but has finally managed to pull the words out of her head and share them with others. She spends her days trying to type her stories on the computer without disturbing her beloved cat, Lu—Lucifer when he's in trouble—curled up on the keyboard. She probably reads far too much.

Email: author@karrieroman.com

Twitter: @karrie_roman

Website: www.karrieroman.com

Other books by this author

Saved
Advent Adventure (coming November 2018)
New Year's Shippin' Eve (coming November 2018)

Until You Series
Shipped
Trusted (coming October 2018)

Coming Soon from Karrie Roman

Trusted

Until You, Book Three

PROLOGUE

"Zach, stay there, honey."

"But, Momma—"

"It's okay. Momma's, okay."

Momma said she was okay and Momma didn't lie to him, but there was so much yelling and he was scared. How could she be okay with all that yelling? He wanted to scream, but Momma told him to stay real quiet. He wanted to go see what was happening, but Momma told him to stay in the stream and finish washing. It sounded like Momma needed help. But he was just a little boy and Father always told him he was no good at anything, so what could he do to help anyway?

But she was his momma and she was the only one who loved him.

That shouting was getting louder but he couldn't hear Momma yelling back now; she was crying and making a funny noise. He was going to go help; he didn't care if Father said he was a useless little shit. She was his momma. He looked down so he'd put his hand on the right rock to hoist himself out of the water, but something was wrong.

The clear water of the stream was all red—the brightest red he'd ever seen.

Zach screamed.

Zach wasn't sure if the scream in his nightmare carried over into the real world—he hoped not. He sat quietly for a moment, listening. He couldn't hear anyone coming toward his room. Sweat danced trails down his back and plastered his hair to his head. His body was working through the last of the tremors as his breathing slowly calmed back to normal.

This wasn't the first time he'd had this nightmare, and it wouldn't be the last. But it seemed worse this time, and Zach couldn't quite work out why. Perhaps it was the turmoil of the last few days.

Three days ago, Zach had fled his father's religious cult with two young girls, one a maybe fourteen-year-old who'd been about to be forced into marriage with his father. The three of them had almost literally crashed into two men, Ben and Ethan, who had been searching for Ethan's infant nieces. The little girls had been kidnapped by their father and taken to the cult. It had all been such a mess, made even worse by his father's plans for the mass suicide of the cult members.

But he was safe; the girls were safe; everyone was safe. Ben and Ethan and the FBI—they'd saved everybody.

Right now he was sleeping in the house of Ben's brother, Cameron. Cameron had also helped in their eventual rescue. Just thinking about Cameron woke up the butterflies in his belly, causing them to flutter around like crazy.

When he'd first encountered Ben out there in the wild, he'd thought him beautiful—and then he'd seen him kissing Ethan. Raised as he had been, secluded from the world in his father's cult, Zach had no idea that men could actually be together in the same way that the men had been with the women of the cult. He hadn't known that such a thing was possible. Suddenly, the way Zach had always watched the men of the cult with such fascination and yearning had made sense. *He* finally made sense.

But all of that was nothing compared to how his body had reacted when he had seen Cameron for the first time. Beautiful hadn't seemed like a good enough word to describe Cameron. Zach didn't even know of a word that could define the perfection he saw in Cameron Cronin. All he could think about was how he wanted to press his lips to Cameron's just like he'd seen Ben do to Ethan.

For now, the remnants of the nightmare clung to him, refusing to leave him in peace, so he knew he'd never get back to sleep. In the past, there'd never been anyone to comfort him, no one for him to go to for a few whispered words or a gentle touch to ease him through the lingering terror, but tonight Cameron's face flashed in his mind, so he pushed the covers back to go in search of him. Everyone had been kind to him since his escape, but there was something about Cameron, something he didn't understand but knew it made him feel good—safe—anyway.

As soon as he left his room, he could see lights down the long hallway and soft voices coming from the same direction. Zach walked quietly, unsure of his welcome.

Four men sat in the room at the end of the hall: Cameron, Ben, Ethan and the FBI agent who'd been in charge of the raid on his father's cult, Alec Banner. They were talking, and none of them seemed to notice his arrival.

"Cameron," he called softly. His voice was so quiet he wasn't even sure if Cameron would hear him from across the room but he must have because he jumped up from his seat, immediately striding forward.

Zach's tummy churned in that good way as he watched Cameron coming toward him. Everything about him was so perfect. He was tall and broad, thick muscles cording his arms and legs. He was so handsome. His face looked hard like it had been chiseled from stone, all angles, but it was stunning to look at. He had just a bit of stubble covering his jaw, and Zach yearned to scrub his fingers over it just to see if it scratched his skin like he thought it would. Cameron's pale-blue eyes never wavered as he watched Zach with concern.

"You okay, Zach?"

"Just a nightmare," he replied, nodding his head.

"Do you want to sit with us for a while?" Cameron asked and Zach looked over his shoulder at the other men, shifting his gaze to each of them.

"No, that's okay. I just...I just needed to know you were here." His words sounded pathetic to his own ear, but he saw only concern in Cameron's gaze.

Cameron reached out an arm as though he was going to touch him and then just as quickly pulled it back. "I'm right here, Zach. I'm not going anywhere...you're not alone anymore."

Zach nodded, suddenly embarrassed that a dream had chased him out here to these men like a frightened child. He nodded and turned to walk back to his room.

When he got there, he pulled his blankets down onto the floor, hoping the familiar hardness of the ground would help him sleep. Comfort wasn't something he was used to.

Cameron had told him he wasn't going anywhere. He'd also offered for Zach to stay here with him until he got himself sorted out. The rest of the cult members were staying together. They'd setup a campsite just outside of town until the FBI had interviewed them all, but Zach didn't want to go with them. He'd always been invisible to most members of the cult—an outcast even among outcasts.

Zach had accepted Cameron's offer, because he'd need help learning how to live in this strange new world he'd been dumped in. He'd lived on the periphery growing up, knowing there was another world there but not really understanding it. Hushed and whispered conversations of the decadence and sinfulness of the world had often reached his ears. Awed stories about televisions and phones and other such evil inventions of mankind had often enthralled him. Regardless of the threads of knowledge he had, though, he really knew so little of this world he'd suddenly been thrust into since his escape. And with his father arrested and the cult disbanded, there was no going back behind the closed walls of their commune. He'd have to find his way in this world, and he'd have to find it alone—or maybe not as alone as he'd thought, if Cameron was being truthful with him.

Also Available from NineStar Press

Connect with NineStar Press

Website: NineStarPress.com

Facebook: NineStarPress

Facebook Reader Group: NineStarNiche

Twitter: @ninestarpress

Tumblr: NineStarPress